Copyright © 2024 Sophie E. Mills

All rights reserved. No portion of this book may be reproduced in any form or used in any manner without permission without prior written permission of the copyright owner, except for the use of brief quotations in a book review.

This novel's story and characters are a work of fiction. Unless otherwise indicated, all the names, characters, businesses, places, events and incidents in this book are either the product of the author's imagination or used in a fictitious manner.

For permissions
www.sophie-mills.com

ISBN: 978-1-7384612-1-9

LOVE IN THE FAST LANE

Sophie E. Mills

To Jamie.

Who I met in a Kimi Raikkonen online forum in 2005 and has been a great friend ever since.

One

Wilson Racing HQ – Silverstone – Northamptonshire – England
February 8th

The Wilson Racing factory loomed ahead, the purple and black logo a stark contrast to the grey of the warehouse. The car park was full, every team member putting in the hours to ensure they had the most competitive car.

Luke's rental looked out of place amongst the management's fleet, but they all glistened in the winter sun.

The clear blue sky brought a bitterly cold wind with it and Luke pulled his coat up around his ears as he walked to the front door.

Although the factory looked exactly like it had for the last three years, from the reserved parking spots by the front door to the giant *W* hanging from the side of the glass and aluminium walls, there was something different about it. What awaited Luke within those walls was vastly different than what he had left behind before the winter break. The team he'd known, the team he'd won with, had been reshuffled, changed, and moved about. It wasn't a welcome thought and a hint of uncertainty raced up his spine as he reached the entrance.

The mechanism buzzed as the receptionist let him in through the glass doors.

'Morning Lucy,' he said as he walked over to her desk.

'Hi Luke,' she replied, standing. She grabbed the signing-in book from below the ledge and slid it over to him. 'Did you have a good break?' Her voice wavered; her eyes wider than normal like she'd forgotten what it was like to have him around.

'It was fine,' he said, glancing up at her. She tucked a strand of hair behind her ear and averted her gaze. 'But I'm glad to be back. Did you have a nice Christmas?'

'I did, thanks. My boyfriend proposed.' She held out her hand to show him the ring.

'Congratulations,' he said, his mind elsewhere.

'Did you go anywhere nice?'

'I came home for Christmas but mostly I've been training.' If it was up to him, there would be no winter break. No forced holidays, or downtime. He never knew what to do with himself when he wasn't working. He had things to prove, and he wouldn't be able to do that sat around the table at his parents' house, listening to his sister drone on about the merits of having a hobby or a life outside of work. He was itching to get back into the car and prove to the world he wasn't a one-hit wonder. He scrawled his name across the page.

'I bet you can't wait to get started.'

'You know me.' He slid the book back towards her. 'New

year, new season…'

'Records to beat, trophies to win.'

'Exactly,' he said as his phone buzzed in his back pocket.

'I've let Mr Clark know you've arrived, and he'll be down shortly.'

'Thanks.' Luke nodded, and she blushed under his gaze. 'Tell me, how's it been since he started?' He leant forwards and Lucy shrugged.

'It's been fine. He's not as relaxed as David was, it's like he's got something to prove.' She glanced around the room, then closed the gap between them even further and lowered her voice. 'Albert Wilson's been in a lot more than usual though. Rumour is, he's not happy about the press attention. Jessie has had a rough few months.'

Luke nodded slowly. He didn't like the sound of that.

'Has the other guy been in yet?'

'No, but he's due in today. He has a meeting with Martin straight after you.'

'That's good to know,' he said, tapping the top of the desk with his palm. 'Thanks.' He gave her a smile then turned away, casting his eyes around the reception.

The walls were covered in photos, showing three decades of racing history, trophies lined up behind the glass, most with his name on. His eyes were drawn to the biggest one in the cabinet, the World Championship trophy that he had picked up at the end of the previous year. He smiled to himself as his phone vibrated again.

Luke drew it out of his pocket and scrolled to his messages.

> It was nice to meet you last night. Next time you're in
> the area maybe we could grab dinner? D.

Luke didn't recognise the number, but he assumed it was the guy his sister had tried to set him up with the night before. An ambush and a poor attempt at matchmaking. She knew he had no time for dating. There was no room for that in his life if he wanted to be two-time world champion. He had records to beat.

He kept a small smile to himself at the thought of lifting that trophy again.

The door on the other side of the room opened with a click and Martin Clark appeared.

'Luke, morning. Martin, it's nice to meet you properly,' he said, extending his hand.

He wasn't a tall man, a foot or so shorter than Luke with wide rugby player shoulders and a beer belly that showed his age. His skin was tanned to a golden brown from all the expensive holidays he went on and his grey hair was pushed to one side, a little long in style for him. Luke followed him through the door into a white corridor with purple and black carpet and canvases of the Wilson cars covering the walls.

'I won't give you the factory tour,' Martin said with a chuckle.

'How are you settling in?'

Martin was relaxed, no sign of nerves for his new responsibilities.

'It's definitely been a learning curve,' he said. 'Lots of new faces, things to learn. I've been chucked in at the deep end. Nothing I can't handle though.'

'You've got big shoes to fill,' Luke said with a fleeting thought to Martin's predecessor.

'I do. And the added pressure of being the championship-winning team to boot. I've got my work cut out for me, that's for sure.' He chuckled again, his chest puffing out like he'd personally won that championship all by himself. 'But I love a good challenge, it fires me up, gets my blood pumping, you know.'

'Is it much different from your last place?'

'Chalk and cheese,' Martin said. 'I ran a global marketing

company, I'm not sure you could get much different. But I'm glad I can finally chip my tooth in the racing world. It's been a lifelong dream of mine. You'll have to give me some pointers.'

Luke nodded.

'There's no better place than Wilson Racing,' he said, his blood pulsing through his veins as uncertainty clouded his mind. 'It's a family business, we've been working together for years to get where we are. We're a tight-knit group, and the whole team deserved that championship. None of us are shy of a little hard work. I hope we can replicate it this year.'

They reached the end of the corridor and the composite plaque on the door read "Martin Clark, Team Principal". Luke tried to imagine what this new era would look like.

'That's the plan,' Martin said as let Luke go in first. 'That's why we've got a new technical director and some fresh blood in the racing team.'

Luke frowned, biting down the words he wanted to say. Change wasn't always good, and, in this case, it made him nervous.

'Have a seat,' Martin said, pointing to the new leather armchairs that had replaced the battered fabric sofa David used to have opposite his desk. Luke took a seat and sunk low to the ground, barely seeing above the sleek black desk behind which Martin sat.

'Surely you don't change a recipe that works though?' Luke said unable to stop himself.

'It's never a bad idea to add more cheese to a pizza. And we've got the best cheese around,' Martin said, spreading his arms out wide and chuckling. Luke might not agree with Martin's methods but if he wanted to win again, he needed to keep the peace as best he could. They had to work together, against the rest of the field, through twenty-one races, in twenty-one different countries to win.

'So,' Martin started, pinning Luke with his dark eyes, and interlacing his fingers in front of him. 'How are we feeling about this season?'

'Give me a good car and I'll give you great results,' Luke said, staring back at him. It took a beat and then Martin's face broke into a smile as he laughed, sitting back in his chair as his stomach shook.

'I want that second championship as much as you do,' Martin said once he'd calmed down. 'I think the changes made so far will help us achieve that.'

'I hope so,' Luke said, and he wished he felt as confident as Martin did.

'We'll give you a good car and then we can let the racing do the talking.'

Luke nodded again, his mind whirring, already thinking about that first race; of the rush when he squeezed the accelerator. Martin cleared his throat.

'I'm not sure if you've seen,' he continued, 'but the team has taken quite a slating in the press over the winter.' Luke had seen but he'd argue it wasn't the team that had taken a slating but Martin himself and some of his questionable decisions. 'It's nothing we can't overcome of course but I wanted to touch base and make sure that we're on the same page for this season.' He cleared his throat again as if willing Luke to agree before he had to explain what he meant but Luke didn't, he let the silence stretch out between them.

'Formula One's an elite sport, it attracts a lot of attention, a lot of press. We have a number of stakeholders we need to think about in whatever we do, whether it be the FIA, Formula One Management, the sponsors or the fans, there are a lot of people who expect us to present ourselves in a certain way.'

Luke wondered where he was going with this, none of it was new information to him. He'd been in the sport much longer than Martin had. He knew how it worked.

'I know rumours happen, if you're in the public eye like we are, we can't escape it but some of the team's decisions have been questioned, namely who we've chosen as the second driver. It's unconventional to sign a rookie to a top team…'

'A risk some would say,' Luke interrupted but Martin wasn't put off.

'Maybe, but it certainly doesn't make me incompetent or reckless as some might have you believe. Anyway…' Martin tugged at his shirt collar, colour fanning over his cheeks. 'I guess what I'm saying is the team has been the centre of a lot of controversies these last few months, but I would like to leave that behind us now. I'm counting on you to lead by example and to keep the drama off track to a minimum.'

Luke stared at the man across the table and wondered if he'd watched a single race from last year because if he had, he'd know that Luke wasn't one for getting embroiled in spats or disagreements. He was racing, inside and out. His heart was made of rubber, fuel ran through his veins and his muscles were lean and aerodynamic like the curves of his favourite car.

'The team can't keep dealing with the scandals, I want everyone on their best behaviour for the whole season. We need to present a united front and support each other.' What Martin meant was he wanted the team to fall in line behind him and show unwavering faith in everything that he did. 'We need to keep it clean this year. Let our talking happen out on track and shush all the chatter outside. Do we understand each other?'

Luke thought for a minute. He didn't see it being a problem if they all wanted the same thing, he was sure they could work together.

'Sure, nothing matters more than winning.'

'Exactly. Not that I think it'll be too difficult for you with your clean-cut image. In fact, I'm relying on you to keep that up, our brands are intrinsically linked and that's only going to help us clear all this mess up.' Martin ran a hand through his thinning hair as Luke scrutinised him. 'In fact, I'd go as far as to say, you're a little too shiny. It wouldn't kill you to bring a girl or two to the paddock. We don't want the world thinking you're unrelatable.' Martin laughed again, fully relaxed and reclined in his chair.

'I'm assuming the whole team will be briefed on this?' Luke asked, thinking of his new teammate.

'Absolutely, the whole team.' Martin nodded and Luke was satisfied that they were all on the same page. His focus shifted then to the one thing he wanted to see. He didn't care for the politics, appearances, and the press, he cared about racing.

'Was there anything else?' Luke asked, leaning forward in the sunken armchair getting ready to leave.

'No, that was all.'

'It was great meeting you,' he said, shaking Martin's hand over the desk. 'And I'm looking forward to working together so we can secure both championships again this year.' He walked to the door and filed the conversation away in his subconscious.

'I'm counting on you Luke,' Martin shouted before the door slammed shut behind him.

In the corridor, Luke shook his head to clear his mind before he made his way down to the workshop. He didn't have time for Martin's dramatics, let alone lectures that were unwarranted.

The factory was a maze but thankfully Luke knew exactly where he was going. He followed the corridor back to the stairs and then darted down a side passage. Out of the corner of his eye, before the door shut behind him, he saw the receptionist again and the dark hair of a man he'd only ever seen on the television. Luke didn't need to see his face to know who it was.

He slipped through a door to the back stairs. He didn't want to be anywhere near Martin's office when he delivered that same message to his second driver.

Luke reached the white-painted concrete floor and walked through the fire door into the belly of the factory. It was busy and loud, mechanics working at their stations and machines building, heating and cooling the pieces that would make up his next championship challenger.

He skirted round the edge of the room until he saw someone he recognised. Jamie, one of his race team mechanics, was chatting to another guy he didn't know.

'Hey dude,' Jamie said when he spotted Luke walking towards him, a smile breaking out on his face. They clasped hands and Luke scanned the room for what he was looking for.

'Can I see it?' he asked his voice low. Jamie frowned but he had a twinkle in his eye. It wouldn't take much to make him cave, even though he wasn't allowed.

'I don't even know if it's assembled yet,' Jamie said but he was lying.

'Oh, come on, the launch is in a few days, we both know it's ready,' Luke said nudging Jamie to encourage him.

'Fine, but it wasn't me.'

'It wasn't you.' Luke pulled his thumb and forefinger across his lips as he pressed them shut.

He followed Jamie across the room, spying other members of his race team as he went but he kept his head low. They reached the rear wall and by the loading bay door, the WR19 was assembled and waiting for transport to the launch event.

Trying not to draw too much attention to himself, Luke skirted around the car covered by a white sheet. Jamie swayed on the balls of his feet, glancing around the room for any signs of a manager or Martin himself.

Luke squatted and gently lifted the sheet, peering beneath it. The car was black with purple stripes down either side, and the paint job was matt rather than gloss this year. The nose dove down to the floor, the front wing hovering only a few inches above the ground. He pulled the sheet back a bit more to unveil the whole front of the car.

'Dude, no, come on,' Jamie pleaded. 'You'll get me in trouble.'

'No, I won't, you can leave if you want. I'll take the blame.'

'I'm not leaving you,' he replied, and Luke shrugged but he smiled too.

The side pods ballooned out with the cooling vents. It looked fierce and Luke wanted nothing more than to climb in and take it for a spin.

There was nothing quite like the thrill of driving around a smooth track at one hundred and eighty miles per hour to make him feel alive.

He needed it. He needed it more than anything else in life.

Two

**Wilson Racing Car Launch – The Shard - London
February 12th**

The black cab crawled along with the London rush hour traffic. Luke jiggled his leg, tugged at his black t-shirt and ran a hand through his hair. He hated press events but what he hated more was being late.

He shuffled in his seat and willed the traffic to move. The driver looked in the rear view, his eyes assessing as Luke squirmed in the back seat. When Luke huffed loudly, he said, 'I'm doing my best man, this traffic's terrible.'

Luke nodded; he didn't need excuses.

'I would've thought a guy like you would prefer to drive himself.' The taxi driver laughed; his eyes still glued to Luke through the mirror.

'I was only round the corner,' Luke said with a slight

shrug.

'Surely the team could have paid for a driver?'

'Are you not a driver?' Luke quirked an eyebrow. 'How far away are we now?' In his head, he could hear his sister laughing and telling him to relax but his shoulders crawled towards his earlobes with every second that ticked by.

'About ten minutes with no traffic,' the driver said with a shrug. Luke pulled out his phone and checked Google Maps. He could walk it in five.

He leant forwards, stuffed a fifty into the driver's hand and darted out of the cab into the middle of the road. He dodged a bus by millimetres and made it to the pavement unharmed. He couldn't have been gladder that he said he'd change there as he stared down at his trainers. Although not designed for sprinting, they'd have to do.

Luke started running but it wasn't like being on the treadmill or the trails of Monaco. This was busy.

Commuters and tourists, staring at the sky or their phones. He hopped, skipped, and dodged people as fast as he could, his arms lifting so he didn't wipe out a little old lady weighed down with shopping bags.

'Isn't that Luke Anderson? You know the racing driver?' He heard the whispers as he dashed past.

He smiled to himself, but it was a reminder of why he rarely went out in public without a cap. There was no cap today, his blonde hair coiffed perfectly so he looked half decent in the videos and photos.

When he turned the corner, the glass building he was headed for came into view, like a beacon in the dusk. Lit up from the base of its triangular structure, all the way to its spikey top, it reflected the city in the tinted glass. Martin Clark wanted to make a splash in the world of Formula One and he hadn't held back on his first event of the year.

Luke reached the base and slowed to a walk, checking the

time before he strolled through the sliding doors.

'Luke!' He heard his name and spun to look for the owner of the voice. Jessie, their Head of Communications stood by the lift waiting for him. 'You're late.'

'Sorry,' he said, trying to calm his breathing. He was used to running long distances but not cold and not in inappropriate clothing. His chest heaved with the effort of it.

'You're here now, that's all that matters. Can't have a car launch without our star driver.'

'Don't let the other guy hear you say that,' he said, wiping his brow with the back of his hand.

'I know where my loyalty lies,' she said with a grin.

'Good to know.'

'Why are you sweating?' she said looking at him with a hint of disgust as they climbed into the lift.

'I ran here. Why are you looking so disgusted? You've seen me looking far worse, remember Singapore last year.' The memory of the sweat dripping down his back made him arch his spine.

'I do, I took five showers that night and every time I got out, I was drenched again. Let's hope it's cooler this year.'

'Fat chance,' he said, mopping the drips off his forehead with his t-shirt this time.

'Couldn't you have got a cab or something?' She looked at him like he was a smelly old sock.

'I was stuck in traffic, and I was under the impression I needed to be here.'

'You do,' she said as they reached the sixty-eighth floor, where she ushered him into a temporary back room that had been set up specifically for the event.

'Now hurry up.'

'How did you get the car up here?' he asked as he peered round the edge of the wall to the viewing platform. He'd been up here before, but it didn't look anything like the open space it had back then. The room was packed with chairs, a bar and canapés being prepared by waiters in whites. A raised platform was set up by the wall of glass where he knew there were unparalleled views of London sprawling out to the horizon.

'Get in there.' Jessie shoved him hard. Despite her small frame, she was strong. 'Get changed and I'll see you out here in two minutes. Got it?'

'Got it.' Luke gave her a captain's salute and Jessie shook her head with a chuckle before she disappeared.

With a deep breath, he ran his hand through his hair again and rolled his shoulders to release the tension. He'd made it, by the skin of his teeth which wasn't his usual style, but he'd made it.

Luke didn't notice anyone else in the room until he heard a rustling behind him. He spun around and his eyes landed on Tyler Finley.

His new teammate stood with his square jaw set and a smile showing off his straight white teeth. He looked like he had in all the videos Luke had poured over during the off-season, except the camera hadn't done him justice. His tanned complexion, the perfect partner to his jet-black hair, gave his face a glow the television hadn't captured.

Luke felt the instant surge of dislike.

He'd watched hours of Finley driving, of interviews where he took every opportunity to flirt with whoever was interviewing him, or when he wasn't in the mood, his words dripped with attitude. Luke knew his strengths and weaknesses on the track, and he despised what he saw off of it. He'd spent months seething over the fact that this guy had been gifted the best seat in F1 when Luke's parents had had to pick up extra jobs for years to help him get to where he was.

'Hi,' Tyler said with a bright smile. 'I'm Tyler.'

Luke's eyes grazed over Tyler's face before he turned back to his hanging overalls.

'I know who you are.' Luke sensed him take a step forward and instinctively turned back to face him. The cool shade of Tyler's blue eyes caught Luke's for a split second as Tyler searched his face.

'My reputation precedes me,' he said with a cheeky smirk that lit up his eyes. 'Hoping it's my racing talent that's caught your eye and not the headlines.'

Luke waited a beat before he replied.

'Would it matter?' His tone was emotionless, masking the irritation he felt. Tyler's easy smile faltered.

'If it's the latter, I'll have to show you what I can do behind the wheel of that car,' he said, nodding to the hidden WR19. A humourless laugh escaped Luke's mouth.

'Can't wait,' he replied flatly. The smile on Tyler's face slipped and he frowned, tilting his head to one side before he recovered.

'Congratulations by the way, on your championship. You dominated the season and that comeback from sixteenth in Belgium was very impressive.'

Luke turned away. Flattery wouldn't work on him. Tyler Finley might be able to charm everyone else and maybe in another lifetime Luke could have looked at him and appreciated how attractive he was but not in this one. All he saw was the competition, the man he had to beat at all costs. The man he wanted to bury out on track. Luke clenched his fists and swallowed down the words he wanted to say.

'Mind you, Vasquez probably has nothing on me.' Tyler smirked.

'Think a lot of yourself, don't you?' Luke snapped. 'Pedro Vasquez is a World Champion. When you've won a championship, maybe then you can talk.'

He turned away again, screwing his nose up, annoyed that

he'd bitten back. He wanted to forget about Tyler Finley but the irritation that clawed at his insides wouldn't let him. It was unnerving being in the same space as someone he had spent the winter dissecting. He'd almost convinced himself that Tyler Finley wasn't a real person, that he was an unknown entity that needed destroying but there he was, in flesh and blood, trying to understand why his new teammate wasn't falling at his feet.

'Maybe we can have this conversation again at the end of the season then,' Tyler replied and the steely edge to his voice wasn't unfamiliar. Luke had heard it plenty of times in interviews when Tyler had failed to score or finish a race.

'We'll see about that,' Luke muttered as he slipped his leg into his race suit. He cursed the warmth that started in his calves as his body heat radiated back in on itself. They could have made them less thick for the launch, it was always torture standing beneath the lights for an hour, the fireproof material like a radiator on a summer day.

Tyler peered at himself in the window, adjusting his hair and Luke looked beyond him to Tower Bridge glowing below them, sending a silent plea up to the skies that might make Martin Clark change his mind about Tyler Finley.

'Are you guys ready?' Jessie said from the other side of the wall. The noise from beyond grew with chatter and the famous singer Martin had hired crooned into the microphone.

'Yes,' Luke said, striding out of the room.

There were around three hundred members of the press sitting on chairs facing the podium where the WR19 was covered with a silk sheet of deep purple. The large display board with the Wilson logo and their racing numbers blocked the incredible view. Jessie handed him his helmet which he tucked under his arm, the smooth surface familiar and comforting for him.

'Don't be intimidated, their words can't hurt you,' Tyler whispered, his tone mocking as he waved to the crowd of journalists. Luke ignored him, he knew Tyler was trying to get under his skin and he wouldn't let him. 'If you need any pointers this season, with the car or the press, you let me know.'

A muscle in Luke's cheek tensed as he clamped his teeth together. He was never one for trash talk but if anyone could make him stoop that low, it would be Tyler Finley. Tyler's eyes twinkled under the artificial lighting that was meant to create a cosy atmosphere, seemingly pleased with himself. A shiver ran up Luke's spine as the lights at the bottom of the podium twirled, casting shadows across the covered car.

The music ramped up, the singer finished and Martin Clark, clad in a purple polo with the Wilson logo on the breast hopped onto the stage as one of the events team handed him a microphone.

'Hello everybody and welcome to the launch of the Wilson Racing WR19,' he boomed. 'It's been years since car launches like this have been a thing, but I think they're part of the tradition of F1. A worthy expense despite the budget cap. It's not the Spice Girls,' he said referring to a launch from two decades ago, 'but I don't see anyone else getting a two-metre wide, eight-hundred-kilo car to the top of the Shard.' He chuckled and Luke groaned as the sea of journalists looked on unimpressed but more than happy to indulge in the free champagne.

Luke was momentarily distracted from Tyler beside him as he stared out to the crowd, spotting journos, some he knew and liked and a bunch he didn't. But he couldn't ignore Tyler when his arm rubbed against Luke's as they walked onto the podium at Martin's invitation. They stood side by side behind the car, their helmets tucked under their arms, smiling at the flashing cameras.

'Why are you staring?' Tyler said catching Luke stealing another glance at him. 'We've got a job to do. I thought you were a pro at this kind of stuff.'

Luke straightened his back and turned his gaze back to the people in front of him, his jaw twitching again. He didn't want to admit to himself that Tyler Finley was much better looking in person, sadly nothing could make up for his personality. Not his sharp cheekbones, not his straight nose or his lips that were the same shade of pink as rhubarb and custard sweets.

'Get over yourself,' Luke muttered, thanking his lucky stars that Martin was hogging the microphone and didn't seem in the slightest bit ready to hand over to his drivers.

'I'd rather get over her.' Tyler nodded towards someone in the crowd, but Luke refused to yield. He held his composure, his eyes focused straight ahead.

Martin chatted about the car, the team and their plan for this year to a disinterested crowd and Luke itched to get off the stage. The lights were too bright, the volume too loud and the hundreds of pairs of eyes that devoured him were irritating him too.

A fake drum roll came over the speakers as he and Tyler walked to the sloped front end of the car. Together, they grabbed the fabric and tugged.

It slid onto the floor in a pool, revealing the car to muted applause. Luke fingered his race suit collar, trying to let some cool air in as he waited for it to die down. The cameras flashed in their direction, and the social media team hung around sidestage trying to catch all the reactions for behind-the-scenes content. The lights suffocated them with heat and Tyler Finley made no effort to keep his distance.

Luke could feel the sweat beading on his forehead as Martin talked into the mic again.

'Boys, what do we think?' As Luke was about to reply,

Tyler leant over in front of him and put his lips on the microphone.

'Looks like a race winner to me,' he said, his private school education bouncing off each word.

'You wouldn't know a fast car if it hit you in the face,' Luke muttered before he could stop himself. He hoped no one had heard but Tyler's head swung round, his blue eyes like ice as his eyebrows knitted together. Before Tyler could bite back, Martin thrust the microphone in front of Luke.

'Let's see what it's like in testing, then I'll let you know what I think of it.' He smiled at the crowd, slipping into the persona he had crafted for the media.

'I own a Bugatti Chiron Sport, I'll have you know,' Tyler hissed, his nose pointing towards the ceiling once the microphone had vanished.

'Of course, you do, did Daddy buy that for you too?' Luke tutted and rolled his eyes. He was being juvenile, but he couldn't help it, there was something about Tyler Finley that got on his nerves. He turned his gaze away and felt a strange heat crawling up his neck.

'It's the fastest road car in production.'

If he was trying to impress Luke with that statement, he'd picked the wrong guy.

'Bet that's really handy on the M25.'

Martin walked back across the stage towards them which shut them both up, but Luke could see Tyler losing his buoyancy.

'I do think we have the two fastest guys on the grid,' Martin said to the crowd and Luke huffed in derision.

'Certainly the most cantankerous,' Tyler shot under his breath. Luke didn't have a chance to counter as the formal presentation came to an end.

Another dull ripple of applause travelled across the audience before the music turned up and the journalists went back to the free bar. Luke left his helmet on the podium and jumped down. A swarm of reporters found him and he fielded questions, dropping all the positive keywords in, with his media smile in place.

He spotted Tyler across the room, chatting to a smaller group and Martin doing his best to change everyone's opinion of him. Jessie was by the bar grabbing herself a well-deserved sip of champagne. Once free of his duties, he wandered over to her.

'How much extra work has tonight made for you?' Luke asked as he sat down beside her. She sighed and looked up at the ceiling.

'I don't want to say something I'll regret,' she said, glancing over at Martin. 'I miss David Crosby.'

'I miss Pedro Vasquez,' Luke said.

'What was all that on the podium?' she asked, her eyes narrowing and searching his face.

'I don't know what you mean.'

'With Tyler?' She rubbed her hands over her face. 'I beg of you Luke, do not make my life hard this year. I've had the most stressful off-season and I would like it to be better from now on.'

'Scouts honour,' Luke said with a smile. He had no intention of getting anywhere near Tyler Finley, whether on track or not, so that wouldn't be a problem.

'Go mingle, give some good quotes about the car and the season, then you can go home.' She sipped the pale gold liquid like it could make her life ten times better.

'Looks like Finley's doing a good job of that already,' Luke said as he scanned the crowd and found Tyler standing too close to a journalist for it to be classed as professional. Tyler's hand skimmed her arm and she giggled at his comment.

'Oh god,' Jessie said, downing her champagne and making a beeline for him. With a smirk on his face, Luke watched

Jessie pull Tyler away from the girl he'd been talking to, then bawl him out with a look that wiped the grin straight off his handsome face.

Luke ordered a beer from the barman, his back to the crowd again. He smoothed his hand down the side of his face, grateful he'd be out of the race suit soon. He didn't usually stay up late, and he was looking forward to getting back to the hotel and his bed.

He felt the presence before he caught a glimpse of Tyler's profile slide onto the bar stool next to him, his shoulders slumped as he leant onto the white marble top.

'That Jessie's a right ball buster,' he murmured so no one else could hear.

'You won't be saying that when she's saving your arse every time you fuck up this season. Unless you get Daddy to pay off the newspapers too.' Tyler stared at him hard, his face unmoving apart from a twitch in his jaw.

'Wow, are you always such an arsehole?' he said, a trace of surprise flashing in his eyes.

'First day on the job too hard for you?' Luke quipped, leaving the beer he'd been given and walking away.

'Go to hell.' Tyler drained it in one go.

Tyler Finley had a lot to learn about the way a Formula One team ran, and Luke would enjoy every moment of his downfall.

Three

Towcester - Northamptonshire
February 13th

The muscles in Luke's neck felt sore as he drove through the historic high street. The buildings rose on either side of the road, unusually quiet for this time on a Wednesday night. Luke loved this town, not far from iconic Silverstone but also close to his family who only lived half an hour away, across the border into Oxfordshire.

He rubbed his neck distractedly, his mind still doing laps of Catalunya from his day in the simulator, his other hand held onto the steering wheel to make sure he stayed on the road. After a day spent in a dark room at the factory, it felt nice to catch the last rays of the evening sun as he pulled into the pub car park.

The cold air crept through his layers as he made his way to

the door of The Folly Inn, he wasn't used to England's temperamental weather anymore. He walked into the pub, ducking to avoid hitting his head on the low beam above the door and scanned the room. His eyes were drawn to her straight away, the sandy blonde of her hair the same shade as his and the deep velvety brown of her eyes sparkled as they found his face. Luke smiled and walked towards his sister, ignoring the odd looks he got from the two men sitting at the bar nursing their pints.

They greeted each other with a hug and a long squeeze before Luke sat down opposite Nick and eyed up the martini on the table between them.

'It's been a rough week alright,' she said, her round cheeks quirking up as she grinned.

'It's Wednesday.'

'What's your excuse?' she asked looking at his outfit.

'What d'you mean?' He looked down at himself, wondering what was wrong with his plain grey t-shirt and blue jeans.

'Where did you even get that t-shirt?'

'I don't know, Next? Wherever Mum picked it up from,' Luke said leaning back into his seat, enjoying the casual teasing, the familiar and comforting feeling of being around someone who knew him inside and out.

'You must earn at least...actually, I don't even want to think about how much you earn, and yet you only wear the stuff Mum sends you? Aren't you supposed to be wearing, I don't know Gucci or something?'

Luke rolled his eyes, but the smile didn't leave his lips.

'Am I?'

'You're World Champion, don't you have an image to uphold?'

'Not with you I don't.' He smiled that real smile, the one he reserved for the people he cared about most, not the flashy fake smile he gave the media. The one that showed up the slight green in his brown eyes, that lit up his face like God was shining a light on him, that made the crow's feet appear at the side of his eyes.

'Ah, I've missed you,' Nick said.

The landlady came over and Luke ordered a pint (what Johan didn't know couldn't hurt him) and fish and chips to Nicola's steak and ale pie. He relaxed with the slow pace of the country pub, the tension leaving his shoulders as each second ticked past.

Beside their table, the fireplace was cold and dark, not having been lit in years. The comfy corner booth and the hard-wooden chairs reminded him of Sunday lunches down their local with his grandparents whenever he had a weekend off racing. The lazy afternoons running around pub gardens whilst his parents and their friends enjoyed the sunshine with a beer.

'How's everything going?' Luke asked. 'How's work?'

'I don't want to talk work, Lord knows work sucks.'

'No better?' He gave her a sympathetic look. She shook her head with a deep sigh. 'If it's money you need, you know I can help you.'

'Thank you, but the house was enough. In fact, the house was too much. You keep your well-earned money.'

'What do I need it for?' he said, his features reflecting what he had said.

'It'll be fine. I'll find something else, I'm sure. If not, I'll endure it, like you'll have to endure working with that gorgeous thing of a man…'

'Okay, thanks, I don't want to talk about him.'

She searched his face for a moment then changed tracks.

'Have you heard from Drew?' She grinned, a mischievous glint in her eye. He remembered the text he'd received at the factory a week earlier.

'Yes.' He took a sip of his pint so he didn't have to elaborate.

'And?'

'And… nothing. I don't want a relationship.'

'You think you don't want a relationship,' she said. 'Come on, you need to take one for the team here, Mum's been nagging me about kids again. I don't understand why it should all be on me. Just because I've been with Dan for more than two years, doesn't mean we need to be settling down, getting married and having a family.' She huffed, and Luke couldn't help but laugh. 'I need you to step up. You're the oldest and quite frankly it's your responsibility to get married and have kids first. So, get to it.' She clapped her hands and smiled to show that she was joking, but only half.

'It's not happening, I don't have time for it,' Luke said as the waitress brought over their food.

'Come on, who doesn't have time for love? It's a wonderful thing, warms you right up like a big ball of sunshine in your chest. Most of the time anyway.'

'And where would I meet someone? I'm never in one place long enough.'

'That's why I introduced you to Drew.'

'He's not my type,' Luke said gruffly.

'Tinder then?'

Luke nearly spat out his beer.

'You want me to go on Tinder?!'

'You're right that's stupid. According to Cosmopolitan, you're one of the UK's most eligible bachelors and I think The Sun put you at number one for their hottest sports personality last year.'

'Oh, for goodness' sake.'

'You could have your pick, I'm sure there are enough people out there who would sell their soul for a date with you.'

'I don't think there is.'

'You need to take those racing blinkers off then. There's a whole life outside of that car you know.' She waved her hand around in front of her face, dismissing Luke's attempts to deny it. 'And I need you to find love so Mum gets off my back.'

'She knows I'm a lost cause.'

'How are you a lost cause? It's only because you want to be. Fine, I'll keep batting her off. If only I had won a world championship, or been a boy, maybe then she wouldn't be so obsessed with me procreating.'

'Is she bored? Are the WI not giving her enough to do at the moment?'

'Maybe she needs a hobby. Ooh, you could send them on a long holiday, like a year or two, that would do it!' Nick said, her eyes twinkling with mischief, like they had every time she came up with a scheme. When they were younger it often involved Luke doing something he didn't want to, like lying about where Nick was, or buying her wine when she was underage.

'I don't know why you're worrying about it, let her say whatever she wants. We're no longer in the medieval times and we're young, we don't need to be settling down at twenty-five. We've barely figured out who we are.'

'Exactly, thank you, brother. Women want careers and to enjoy their life before they have to push little tiny humans out of their hoo-ha and dedicate themselves to keeping them alive. If she's not worried about you being twenty-six and single, I don't know why she's so concerned about me.'

'I agree, you do what you want to do and don't worry about Mum.'

'Now if you could tell her that as the favourite child that would be great.' She grinned, knowing how much Luke hated being called that. His success didn't make him a better child than her, but the world outside deemed his accomplishments to be superior. The way he saw it, she was happy, in love and having a blast in her twenties, surely, she was the one that had won at life?

Nicola polished off her last chip and the dregs of her martini, then turned her dark eyes back to her brother with a look that told him enough to try and wrap up the evening.

'I know you don't want to talk about it, but I can't hold it in anymore. I wanna know everything, have you met him yet? Is he as vile as you thought? He's so gorgeous.' Her eyes clouded over dreamily as she pictured him in her mind's eye. 'He seems to have a lot of fans, although it's very divided. I can't believe he's this terrible rich kid, living off Daddy's cash and buying his way into everything.'

'Nick, do we have to?' Luke groaned.

'We do.' She lifted herself off the chair and stalked to the bar, her black dress swinging behind her. She came back shortly after with another pint for him and a martini for her.

'I can't stay too long, I have a flight at ten,' he said eyeing up the pint, knowing he'd had too much to drink already.

'It's not even seven thirty, we've got time,' she said, not budging an inch. 'So, Tyler Finley?'

'What about him?' Luke clammed up, he had spent the best part of the winter pretending that name didn't exist and the last twenty-four hours banishing the image of him from his mind.

'He's a bit old to be making his debut in F1, no?'

'I don't care,' he said, trying to block her out.

'I read on Wikipedia that he's twenty-four this year.' Luke didn't utter a word, but he nodded with his eyes to the heavens, holding in the roll. 'Is he really that annoying?' She leaned in, keen to hear all the juicy gossip straight from the horse's mouth.

Luke didn't reply, he eyed up the beer instead but knew he

had to drive to the airport soon.

'He can come across as very charming in interviews when he's not upset or pissed off. The bad boy thing seems to work well for him though. And I don't get the impression he likes living off his dad's money. He seems to want to do things his way.'

'Good for him.'

'Come on, give me something. He certainly seems like he's going to give you a run for your money.' She waggled her eyebrows, and he couldn't help but smile in an irritated kind of way.

'Is he single? Because I do love Dan, but I could make myself available if needed.'

'No thanks, I don't want him in the family. I'll keep Dan, ta.'

'But those cheekbones, those eyes.' Luke didn't think she could look any more like the heart-eye emoji if she tried. 'And his hair, it always looks so glossy and thick. Have you touched it?'

'What? No, I haven't touched it!' He said a little disgusted, but it had looked very thick and glossy under the dim lighting of the Shard.

'Oh, have you seen him naked?' she said the idea coming to her.

'What was in that martini, Nick? We don't walk around the paddock without our clothes on, it's not a nudist paddock.'

'Not like fully naked, but topless, surely, you've seen him topless? I bet he's super chiselled and has the most glorious abs.'

'You can stop now. I haven't seen his abs and nor do I care to. Google it if you're that desperate.' He sipped the beer for something to do, trying to forget the exact shade of blue of Tyler's eyes.

In racing, there was no one you wanted to beat more than

your teammate, he didn't want to think of Tyler Finley as anything other than the enemy.

'That's a good idea, how did I not think of that.' Nicola pulled her phone out and started tapping away at the screen. Luke checked his watch and did some backward maths to figure out what time he needed to leave so he didn't miss his flight. He still had to return the rental car and get through security.

He took another sip of his drink as Nick squealed with delight. She turned her phone so he had no choice but to stare at the naked chest of Tyler Finley.

As Nick had suggested, he had a sheet of abs that looked as solid as a rock and as perfectly carved as sand ridges. Luke stared at the deep golden skin that covered Tyler's body. He was bulky and athletic more akin to a Greek statue than the lean skinny frame of other drivers.

'I need to get going,' he said, and he could hear the slight strangle in his voice as his breath got caught in his chest.

'You can't pretend that this guy is not the best-looking thing you've ever seen,' she said ignoring his comment. 'Do you think he's gay? Oh my gosh, you two could be like a Formula One power couple.'

Luke stood up, the chair scraping across the tiled floor of the pub.

'Over my dead body.'

Four

Pre-Season Testing – Circuit de Barcelona-Catalunya - Montmeló
February 18th

Luke scanned his ID badge at the gate, pushed his muscly thighs into the turnstile and walked into the paddock. It was early morning and the grey clouds swirled overhead, not a promising start to the first test of the season.

Clad head to toe in purple and black, he wore the same team colours as he had for the last three years. They washed him out a bit with his sandy hair and fair skin but that wasn't why he'd signed with them. They'd promised him a championship-winning car and boy had they delivered. Part of him had expected it to feel different walking into the paddock today, but it felt the same.

The same long row of motorhomes in shiny colours down

one side, the back end of the pits down the other. The purple and black one, home of Wilson Racing, was the first in line as the current World Champions and it was already a hub of activity despite the early hour.

'Morning Champ,' said Vicki, his chief mechanic, as she crossed the concrete river from the motorhome to the pits. Her blonde hair pulled into a high ponytail and her eyes focused straight ahead as she vanished through the small entrance to their garage.

'Does it feel weird?' Johan asked from beside him, drowning beneath backpacks and sporting equipment. His hair was so blonde it was almost white, melting into the creaminess of his Scandinavian skin.

'The Champ bit maybe, the rest, not so much,' Luke said, trying not to make eye contact with anyone else roaming the paddock.

Despite the extra money from winning the championship, the motorhome was no different, it felt like it had done all the other times he'd crossed the threshold. He followed Johan to his driver's room, the floor still as springy as last season.

The two men squashed themselves into the small room, with the bench down one side, and Johan dropped his stuff on the desk in the back corner.

'Could've at least given you a bigger room,' he joked, his Finnish accent keeping the sentence monotonous despite the humour. Johan had been with Luke since the very beginning. Two years his senior, he wasn't just his trainer but his friend too. He'd always been a part of Luke's journey and this championship may be in Luke's name, but it belonged to all of them, especially to Johan.

'I know right, I guess it wasn't in the contract. I'll have to chat to my manager before the end of the season if we're planning on winning another,' Luke replied, pulling off the purple waterproof and slinging it over the back of a chair. He sat down on the bench, resting his feet on the wall opposite and pulled out his water bottle, taking a long drag on the straw.

'And that definitely is the plan.' Johan grinned.

There was a soft knock on the door before it opened, revealing a short woman in her late forties with jet-black hair cut into a sharp bob and the same purple shirt with the Wilson logo on her chest under her coat.

'Morning,' she said, coming in and leaning up against the doorframe, clutching a clipboard.

'How's it going, Em?' Luke said lazily.

'It's bloody freezing, I thought Spain was supposed to be hot,' his press officer grumbled, pulling her coat around herself as if to prove a point.

'They'll be moving testing to a hotter country if it doesn't change,' Johan said from his spot at the desk. He pulled out his laptop and tapped away. When he wasn't with Luke he ran his own business, wellness retreats in the wilderness of Finland.

'Probably. You won't catch me complaining. I don't like starting the season without a tan, with all those cameras around.' She shuddered at the thought like it was a fate worse than death. Luke's lips gently pulled up at the corners, a slow huff leaving his mouth in amusement.

'Right, World Champion, let's get down to business,' she said, unfolding the sheets of paper she was holding. 'As you can imagine, you're in hot demand today, I'm almost glad they didn't put you in the car first because then we can get it all over and done with. And get you back to focusing on what you do best eh? Winning championships.'

Best intentions aside, Luke would have rather been in the car first, and not letting Tyler get the upper hand with the new machine. As his thoughts drifted to Tyler again, he shook his head to rid himself of them.

'Cheers, Em.'

Emma Bacon had been his press officer from the moment he'd started with the team, she was like his second mum, but he would never tell her that for fear of losing his manhood in an ugly accident. She was not a woman to be messed with. Which was why she was so good at her job. She was his gatekeeper and there wasn't much that slipped past her. Most of the press were constantly trying to get on her good side because if you were friendly with Emma then you stood half a chance of getting that coveted interview with the paddock's most in-demand driver.

'You're scheduled for your official photo shoot this morning,' she said looking down at her sheet. When she looked up, she appraised him. 'I see you did your hair then?' Her pencil-thin eyebrow reached for her hairline.

Luke ran his hands through his thick hair which the wind and rain had messed up on his walk from the car park to the motorhome.

'Here.' Johan chucked him a comb.

'You'll need your overalls and your helmet, I think.'

'I've got it, it's fine. I've done a few of these before.' He smiled. He'd been in Formula One for eight years now, joining the elite class at the tender age of eighteen, fresh out of his F2 championship win. He knew what he was doing.

'But you're the World Champion now,' she said grinning, taking every opportunity to remind him.

'Does that mean I have to do something different? Like an icier glare into the camera or something?'

'Is that even possible?' Johan laughed from beside him, not lifting his eyes from his laptop. Luke glared at him.

'I have no idea what they'll ask of you if I'm being honest. You're going to have to make it up,' Emma continued.

'Don't I always,' he muttered, staring down at his nail-bitten fingers.

'You always look drop dead honey and don't be giving me any of that sass or I'll release Petra on you.' She waggled her finger at him like a teacher telling off a school kid.

'You wouldn't dare,' Luke said trying to suss out whether she was being serious.

Petra had been after him for years now, all that flirting had him avoiding her like the plague. She was the lead presenter of RTL Germany; she was beautiful and if he swung that way he might even have gone there. She had legs longer than was humanly possible in his opinion and the glossiest brown hair which always looked like it had been blow-dried, it didn't matter whether it was forty degrees and everyone else was melting or if a hurricane was belting past, she always looked perfect.

'I wouldn't, I don't trust the woman,' Emma said, waving her hand in the air to dismiss the topic. 'Speaking of people I don't trust, after the photoshoot you've got a sit down with Sara from CultRacing. The one who has been slating Martin in the press all winter. You've met her before, she's the one with the curly hair.' Emma's hand waved around beside her head, illustrating how curly Sara's hair was.

'Why am I sitting down with her then?'

'Martin insisted, he needs you to smooth things over for him, you know, make a good impression,' she said with a pointed look. 'Talk highly of him and be positive about the team. You're a pro at this, rub some of that Luke magic over the situation. Anyway, after that...'

Luke didn't like being dragged into Martin's problems and the idea that he would need to work extra hard in this interview irritated him. Another way Tyler Finley was making his life hard. He switched off, not wanting to think about his teammate and let his mind run through the 4.655km of the Catalunya circuit. That drag down to the first corner, a right-hander, swooping into turn two, the big curve of turn three…

'Are you listening to me?' Emma's voice cut through his train of thought.

'Hmm?' he said, tearing his gaze away from his hands and back to her face, her blue eyes twinkling with both irritation and amusement.

'God, I'll be glad to see the back of you when you leave,' she said smiling. He knew she didn't mean it. He remembered the first time he'd met Emma; she scared him a bit, especially when he said something stupid in an interview after a race. Not that he made that mistake too many times because Emma's icy glare was enough to put anyone back in their place. 'I said this afternoon you've got an interview with Sky Sports F1, it's filmed. As far as I know, they aren't planning anything crazy, but you never know with those guys.'

'They'll probably have you ice skating around the circuit it's so cold,' Johan piped up, his eyes still focused on the laptop.

'And at the end of the day, we've got a team meeting upstairs. Right, that's it, I'll leave you to it,' she finished up, handing him the schedule. 'Oh actually, I think it's likely they'll ask you about your new teammate. Maybe we should go over what you'll say on that, we all know it was a controversial decision to sign him, so we need to stay positive about it and not add to the rumours.'

'I don't know anything about him,' Luke said, his shoulders tensing. Like the other nineteen drivers on the grid, Luke would much rather have the whole team working for him but alas that wasn't how it worked. His previous teammate had retired after fifteen years of racing and two championships under his belt, he'd been so absorbed in his former glory that he had little to no time for Luke which suited him. They both stayed on their side of the garage, only seeing each other at team meetings and when they were battling it out on the circuit, which last year wasn't all that much since Vásquez trailed him in most races and came fifth in the championship despite them having the best car on the grid.

'Do you know his name at least?' she said her eyes narrowing.

'Yes Emma, I don't live under a rock,' he shot back, his brown eyes narrowing to match hers.

'And you know the rumours that surround his signing?'

'Vaguely,' he said, not wanting to concern himself with whoever's problem this was because it sure as hell wasn't his.

'Well, you know how to handle it, bring the conversation back to you, stay neutral about him and you'll be just fine.' Emma opened the door back out onto the atrium of the motorhome.

'Just fine,' he repeated as she closed it behind her.

Sara's hair was indeed very curly, and also flaming red, not unlike Merida from *Brave*. He only knew that because he'd watched it a few too many times with Johan's nephew. Okay, he may have also watched it a few times alone since, on a boring flight or one night in a hotel room a long way from home. Sara had a sweet smile, like you could trust her but one glance at her steely eyes and he knew she meant business.

Luke fidgeted in his seat, feeling a little sweaty in the overheated press room. She shuffled the papers on her lap and set down the recorder on the table between them.

'Ready?' she asked, her eyes meeting his. He nodded once and slid on his media game face. He forced a smile onto his face, the one he reserved for interviews, media appearances or in the pen after the race. His "winning" smile but one that always looked a little alien to him when he saw himself wearing it in photos.

'So, new season, same team and a championship under your belt. How do you feel?'

'I feel good, I've had some downtime over the winter and we've been back training since January. I've been working hard on getting into the best shape possible for this year.'

'And winning a championship, finally after eight years, how does that feel?'

'I mean, it feels great. It's what I've been working on and dreaming of since I was a kid. It's taken a lot of hard work and sacrifice by a lot of people for us to get here, so yeah, of course, it feels fantastic to finally have achieved that.'

'You were branded as the most promising talent in F1 in your first season and after a tough couple of years with a different team, you came to Wilson Racing. Does it feel even better to have achieved it with them?'

'It would have felt amazing wherever I'd been but yes, these guys and girls are like a second family to me, we spend so much time together throughout the year. I'm glad we achieved it together.'

Sara paused a moment and Luke took a chance to have a drink. It's not that he didn't like interviews, but he preferred to let his driving do the talking. He always knew that if he won the championship there'd be more media attention on him and he was okay with that, it was worth it for that feeling he had when he stood on the podium, knowing that the season was over and that the season was his. He could still remember it now, as he sat in the white box of a room, opposite redhead Sara.

The season had been long, but the title challenge hadn't been that tough, once Vásquez was out of the running, he wrapped it up before the last few races. But standing up there, his whole team cheering for him because he had secured the driver's championship for Wilson Racing for the first time in twenty years, he had felt his heart soar. The elation, the goosebumps and the relief, there was nothing quite like it.

'What's the plan for this year then? Another championship?' Sara resumed.

'Of course, being World Champion is great, being two times World Champion is even better.' He laughed the fake laugh he reserved specifically for these moments.

'And this year, there are some changes in the team, new Team Principal and new teammate?'

'That's right,' he said, knowing this was where Emma's warning came into effect.

'There's been some controversy around the signing of Tyler Finley. Wilson Racing's new Team Principal is good friends with Finley's father I believe and there are rumours around the paddock that Finley secured his seat due to a large financial contribution from his father's company. Were you involved in those talks?' Sara pressed but Luke kept his features in a neutral position.

'I don't have any say in who my teammate is, I trust the team and management to be signing the best driver for the job so that the team can secure another championship because that's what we're all working towards.'

'Do you think Finley's talented enough to take you on? You wiped the floor with Vásquez last year, do you plan on doing the same?'

'I honestly don't know a lot about him, I don't concern myself with what my teammates are doing unless they're beating me. I want to focus on the job I've got to do, get the best out of the car and help the team improve each race so that we come out on top.'

'You could argue that Finley has some talent as he did come second in last year's Formula 2 series but is it enough to merit a seat at a top team like Wilson Racing?' Sara's steely eyes bore into Luke's soul, willing him to give her some sort of scoop for a decent story. Martin was an idiot to have given her the first interview after the winter break, clearly, she had no interest in making things better for him and she'd be dammed if she left with nothing.

'I can't say, I've not followed his career. Aside from his name, I know very little about him. As I said, I trust the team to do what's best so that we can continue with our winning streak.'

'You mean to say you haven't done any research into who will be your main competition this year? You haven't checked his stats, his driving style, his strengths and weaknesses?' Luke shrugged. 'Doesn't that seem a little foolish, almost reckless?'

She wasn't giving it up and Luke knew what he had to do. He pulled out his best panty-dropping smile, the one he always saw when he was being described as a heartthrob in the UK tabloids, leant forwards like he was about to tell her his biggest secret and lowered his voice.

'Is there something I should know?' he asked, giving his voice a little lilt that melted the edge of her glare. 'Do you have inside intel? Should I be worried?' He then gave her the stare, the one he hoped would melt her cold heart and have her giggling like a schoolgirl.

'You tell me,' she countered.

Dammit.

Five

Pre-Season Testing – Circuit de Barcelona-Catalunya - Montmeló
February 19th

Luke knew a hell of a lot more about Tyler Finley than he had let on the day before to Sara Holdsworth. He had, in fact, been one of the most vocal to David Crosby against signing the driver during the last season. He didn't like bought seats; money shouldn't have a say in who gets to drive but he knew it wasn't smart business to look a gift horse in the mouth. Finley was somewhat fast, he'd checked his stats, watched him race, but to him, it looked like Finley had had his way paved in gold from the moment he started karting. His billionaire father throwing money around, opening doors, or vacating seats for him, despite what Luke's sister might think. Finley had jumped around the racing world, from

America to Europe, trying his hand at everything and now he was in one of the most coveted seats in Formula One because Daddy had waved a cheque book at the new man in charge.

Luke had spent his whole life trying to prove to everyone that just because he didn't come from money, he could still drive. His parents had sacrificed so much, working extra-long days and jobs so he could compete. He wasn't about to let some rich boy waltz in there and beat him.

Once Luke had found out that David Crosby was out and Martin Clark was in, he knew he didn't stand a chance of stopping the signing but he'd be damned if anyone knew quite how pissed about it he was.

He exited the motor home in his brand-new purple overalls, done up to the chin with his waterproof over the top because the weather hadn't improved since the day before. The rain lashed down and he wondered if he'd even get a spin in the new WR19.

The garage was pristine, decked out with the team logo and colours, the partition walls in a high gloss white, not a single mark on them. Luke walked past the back office which was a hive of activity and out into his side of the garage. His car sat up on a jack, with no tyres and no front wing, his team working on it, getting it ready for its first outing of the season.

'Morning all.' He strolled over to Vicki, his chief mechanic, who was working at the computer station to the side of the car. 'Vicki.'

'Lucas,' she said, not taking her eyes off the screen, fully focused. He arched a sandy eyebrow. 'I'm looking at Tyler's data from yesterday.'

'It's Luke.'

'Yes, I know Anderson, I'm pushing your buttons.' She laughed and finally turned around. She punched him lightly on the arm. 'How were your media duties yesterday?'

'Let's just say I'm happier to be in the car today.' He smiled, relaxing a little more. He glanced over at his new baby and felt that itch to get going, but another look out of the open doors onto the pit lane and he knew it wouldn't be soon. The huge drops of rain pelted the floor, springing back up off the tarmac like bouncy balls. All the water had created rivulets across the surface of the road, very dangerous when driving at such high speeds.

'That's if we get a run in,' Jamie said over Luke's shoulder, twirling a screwdriver in his hand. His side of the garage comprised of fourteen mechanics, both men and women who were exceptional at their jobs. Luke snatched the screwdriver off Jamie and threw it into the air before catching it at the last second.

'I feel sorry for the poor fans out there,' Vicki said nodding to the grandstands visible over the pit wall, but it sounded distant to Luke because someone had caught his attention on the other side of the garage. Like metal to a magnet, his eyes were drawn to Tyler as he strode in, relaxed and laughing with one of his mechanics. He wore the team's branded polo shirt and black jeans that hugged his thighs. Luke shook his head as he tried to ignore him.

'I don't know why they do it, especially not for testing,' Jamie replied as raucous laughter erupted beyond the partition catching all of their attention.

'To get a glimpse of you,' Vicki said. She nudged Luke with a mischievous twinkle in her eyes and he half laughed, knowing she was right but finding it ridiculous.

Tyler's presence made Luke fidgety. His eyes flicked in Tyler's direction as his skin prickled with irritation. They turned up the music, the laughter continuing, and Luke needed to escape. He didn't want to be anywhere near Tyler or his obnoxious personality.

He made his way over to the front of the garage, lifted his

hood back over his head and walked over to the pit wall. He spotted the group of fans straight away, purple caps on, huddled together under a blanket, a Union Jack hanging from the railing in front of them with "Luke #1" written on it. He found the gap in the fencing he was looking for and climbed onto the wall. They spotted him, one of the girls pointing him out to the rest and they all cheered. He waved and grinned boyishly, the water dripping off his hood and onto his nose.

He hopped down and walked the few metres over to his team's pit wall, where Martin sat with his back to the garage, wrapped up in all the layers and a team beanie. He was bent over talking in hushed tones to Finley's race engineer.

Luke put his hand on his shoulder.

'Morning Martin.' He may dislike the way Clark signed up drivers, but he would put on the charm offensive if needed.

'Ah, our star driver,' Clark said with a wide smile. Luke saw straight away that it didn't reach his eyes and he knew Clark was stroking his ego.

'How's the weather looking?'

'Not great but it's meant to clear up. We managed to do twenty laps yesterday with Tyler, so hopefully we can do the same if not more a little later.'

Luke nodded, the fire to beat his teammate lit in his stomach even though it was only testing. They were supposed to be working together right now to get the car in the best possible shape before the season opener in Melbourne, but it was part of him. It always had been, from the minute he'd learnt to ride a bike, he had to be the fastest, the strongest, the best. Then he got his first taste of karting and that was it, there was no stopping him. The fire that burnt in him, the desire, the need to succeed, it never dulled. Even after achieving his biggest dream, Luke was hungry for more. He wanted a second title more than anything and he wouldn't let anyone derail him. Certainly not a cocky twenty-four-year-old who was only there because Daddy had paid for it.

Late afternoon, Luke guided the car back into his pit box, his mechanics racing out to meet him. They put the car up on jacks, wheeled the trolley underneath it and rolled him back into the garage. Luke lifted his visor and couldn't help the grin that spread over his face. The car was good, he knew it, he could feel it in his bones. Throwing it around the corners of the circuit, it felt incredible underneath him and he knew that this was a championship-contending car. He hopped out, Vicki giving him the thumbs up from the computer and Martin watching from the pit wall. At the back, Johan waited beside his driver's seat, ready with his water bottle and a towel to wipe off the sweat.

'Good?' he asked in his emotionless voice. Luke grinned again but the helmet hid it from view. He pulled it off, the comms cables hanging down and dragged his balaclava over his face. He knew he was red and sweaty and without even asking, Johan handed him the towel. He wiped his face and took the smile away with it.

'The car felt good,' he said with a shrug, he didn't want anyone relaxing because they had delivered a great car, he wanted them to keep pushing, always pushing, always striving for more. That was the name of the game because you could bet their nearest rivals, the boys in red, wouldn't be sitting around patting themselves on the back for a job well done. Everyone, up and down the pit lane, was working hard, trying to find that extra tenth of a second that might gain them one or two extra places on qualifying day.

As Luke sipped on his drink, ready to head over to Martin to make sure he was happy, he heard something that made his head whip around faster than he had taken turn one earlier today. Vicki was on the border between his side of the garage and the other and if his eyes didn't deceive him, she was giggling. Full on giggling like a schoolgirl whose crush had said "hi" to her. Did she flick her hair? Was she…flirting?

He took a couple of steps towards her because he couldn't see who she was talking to from his spot at the back. Johan followed his gaze and the two men exchanged a confused look. It's not that Vicki didn't laugh, of course she did, but not like this.

Vicki took a step forward and rested against the column, tilting her head to the side, batting her eyelashes and before Luke knew what he was doing, he walked past his new car towards her.

As he approached, he skirted around her so he could glance back to see who she was talking to. A few feet away from her, Finley stood with a smile dancing on his tanned face as Vicki spun around, eyes wide like she had been caught doing something naughty.

'Everything okay?' she questioned, resuming her professionalism. Luke nodded and turned his head back towards the pit lane, not wanting to get involved any further. 'Lucas, Tyler was saying that some of them were heading out to dinner tonight.' He stopped in his tracks.

'That was supposed to be between you and me, Vickster.' Tyler's tone was light and flirty.

Luke took a deep breath, wishing he could keep walking, but he couldn't ignore her. He composed himself and then turned, his face impassive.

Tyler Finley stared back at him, his blue eyes wide and a slight rise to his bushy black eyebrows.

Vicki blushed. Luke shook his head and closed his eyes, the woman who could make a whole team of grown-arse men cower with one look was blushing.

When he opened them, Finley was still staring at him.

'It's Luke,' he said again to Vicki. His voice was flat and his features remained neutral, not wanting to give away quite how much his new teammate irritated him. Vicki looked between the two men, the laughter having long since died on her lips with the change in the atmosphere.

'You should join us, Lucas,' Tyler said, a glint of mischief in his eye.

'It's Luke.'

Luke glared at Vicki, who looked sheepish.

'Of course, the mighty Luke Anderson,' Tyler continued, and Luke couldn't tell if he was being sarcastic. The air between them dropped a good ten degrees, Vicki caught in the middle of Luke's impassive stare and Tyler's provocative posture.

'Right, we should get back to work,' Vicki said, clearing her throat and shuffling from one foot to another. 'See you later Tyler.'

'And you lovely Vicki. Watch out buddy, I might steal her from under you,' Tyler added, flashing Luke a cheeky smile that did nothing but reinforce how much Luke disliked him.

'He's quite a character,' Johan said when Luke made it back to his chair.

'He's a prick.' He slipped on his waterproofs as Johan picked up his helmet and they left the garage.

Halfway across the road back to the motorhome, Luke heard his name being called above the sound of the rain. It had increased again, creating a symphony as it hit the metal and glass of the motorhomes, the tarmac of the floor, and the concrete of the building behind him. Luke stopped and looked for the person who had called him. Inside their team garage, Tyler pulled his hood over his head and jogged to catch up with Luke and Johan.

'I'll see you inside,' Johan muttered, leaving Luke exposed and having to talk to his teammate.

Luke narrowed his eyes and waited for Tyler to get closer.

The latter paused for a moment as he took in Luke's expression but appeared undeterred.

'How are you?' he said now that they were face to face. His earlier bravado left him as he shuffled from foot to foot.

'Wet,' Luke said losing patience. He was cold and tired, his body bruise from spending the afternoon in the new car, no longer used to the G forces from a winter off. Tyler stared at him for a moment as if trying to remember what he had come to say. 'What do you want?' Luke said and it came out harsher than he had meant it to.

'Dinner,' he started, then stopped, his lips parted in a silent o. 'It'd be great if you could join us.'

Luke narrowed his eyes further; he didn't want to go to dinner. He did breakfast with the team every Thursday morning before each race, he remembered his team's birthdays and partner's names, and he worked hard and encouraged them which was why they won last year. Tyler could do his own work on his own time.

'I can't. I've got a flight to catch.'

Tyler nodded slowly and Luke turned to leave, his waterproof saturated and in danger of soaking through. He felt the hand before he heard the words. His senses zeroed in on the touch of Tyler's hand through his clothes. It was fleeting, the minute Luke looked down at the point of contact, Tyler let go.

'I know I'm new here, and I don't know how these things work yet but I was hoping we could, I don't know, bond.'

'Bond?' Luke repeated.

'Yeah, like get to know each other, I don't know. Become a team.'

Luke raised an eyebrow.

'We're already a team.'

Tyler must have realised Luke wouldn't budge, so he took a step back as if he'd been slapped. His face changed, it wasn't open and receptive anymore. His eyebrows knitted together, his cheekbones looking sharper somehow.

'If that's how you feel,' Tyler said before spinning on his heels and heading back towards the garage.

Luke didn't feel bad, he didn't want to be friends with him. He didn't want to get to know him. He wanted to drive a car fast and win championships.

Six

**Australian Grand Prix - Albert Park Circuit – Melbourne
March 17th**

'Radio check?'
'Yeah I can hear you fine,' Luke replied from the front spot on the grid. The purple car of his teammate lined up beside him but a few metres back. The mechanics moved away, taking all the equipment with them, leaving the twenty cars lined up alone, Melbourne City rising in the background behind the sea of people in the grandstands. Mostly clad in black and gold, supporting their local boy, Kyle Kelly but amongst them pockets of purple, the Anderson Army as they called themselves coming out to support their World Champion.

He was alone with his thoughts until after the race start, Dash not able to talk to him on the radio anymore whilst they did the formation lap. Luke took a deep breath.

The first race of the season. He wanted to win. He needed to win.

The lights went out, he released the clutch and started the long way down the straight to the first corner, bumping along, weaving to warm his tyres up. Each new season he could hardly believe he was here. Years of sacrifice, hard work, failure and finally success to get to where he was. He still felt like that little boy, the first time he went to a karting track and felt the power underneath him as he squeezed the accelerator.

The track owner, a retired driver himself, had been impressed. Luke remembered him telling his parents that he would go far if he was disciplined enough. Those words had always echoed around his head, whenever he'd felt a streak of laziness course through him, when he was a teenager, watching all the other boys playing football or hanging out on the weekends. He was at the track, in the gym, working. His discipline, his dedication and his hard work had landed him here. About to start this season as the World Champion.

The pressure to equal or do better than he had last year rolled off of him like water off a duck's back. A journalist once said he was impermeable and he kind of liked that. The notion that nothing could touch him.

It was easy to let emotions ruin everything, so he tried to keep his locked away, staying impassive, not letting anyone see how he felt. Not the simmering rage when someone took him out, or the exhilarating happiness of standing on that top step. He kept all of his emotions measured, in check, only ever showing enough and never too much.

He rounded the last corner, the white grid lines shining in the late afternoon sun. He weaved a little more, stopped inside his slot and waited. That long wait until everyone else was positioned in their slots. He took a few more deep breaths, slowing his heart rate, keeping his eyes focused on the lights above him, not even blinking.

The red lights came on, one at a time until all five were alight and then they were gone. Luke released the clutch and fired his car forward, his foot to the floor. He checked the tiny mirrors on either side and was relieved to see Lewandowski quite far back. The tall Pole was a force to be reckoned with. They'd known each other since their Formula 3 days, they had a lot of respect for each other and last year Lewandowski had put up a tough battle but didn't quite make it close enough to contend for the championship. Luke knew he would be even fiercer this year, he hadn't achieved what he wanted in F1 and his career was looking dubious after a few rough years. His contract was ending at the end of the season and he was a desperate man. He was also fast and precise; Luke knew he'd have a battle on his hands because the Ferrari looked quick.

Finley was within view but neither were close enough to fill the small vanity mirrors. He braked, turned right and nailed the first corner, everyone else filing in behind him.

Albert Park wasn't renowned for good overtaking opportunities, in fact, the previous year had only seen two on-track overtakes, which, as boring as that was for the fans and irritating for those behind him, was a good place for Luke to be.

'Great start buddy,' his race engineer, Dash's voice came over the radio, cutting through the roar of the engine. 'Head down, let's save those tyres. Plan A.'

Luke didn't bother to reply, he got his head down as instructed and kept aiming for the lap times the team wanted. Finley matched his pace for the first half of the race, never more than a few seconds behind him, always in his mirrors. Luke had to give it to him, he was certainly making a splash in the big boy pool. His first race in Formula One and he was right up there, on the pace with the World Champion. Luke's mind flashed back to the day before, the angry frown that graced Tyler's otherwise flawless face when he hadn't got pole, the resigned form of his body after he'd bawled out his race engineer in his driver's room. Luke hoped that whatever was going on didn't affect him or the team. He needed them all focused on the racing, on improving the car and making sure Luke came out on top again.

He took a few stifled breaths behind the visor, not wanting to let the irritation and worry get through his skin. Luke refocused on the road ahead when Dash's voice came over the radio again.

'Right, push push, give it all you've got.'

Luke did as he was told, putting his foot down and using up the rest of his tyres, leaving Finley in the turbulent air and unable to keep up.

'And box box,' Dash said a few laps later and Luke obeyed, peeling off at the last corner and heading down the pitlane. Pressing the limiter, he trundled down to his pit box. He swooped in, hitting his marks as the team got to work. Within seconds he was out and heading back to the track.

'Quick lap, the other car is about to box so it'll be close,' Dash said and Luke felt the competitive buzz zip through him. There was no way this guy was going to get him at the pit stop. He slung his car around the corners, fuelled by the desire to win, keeping calm as he did, so he wouldn't over drive it. As he hurtled down the straight again, he saw the sister car pull out of the pits ahead of him. He had a few seconds in hand whilst Finley got up to speed but he knew it would be tight. They were side by side as they approached the first corner, the purple machine filling his mirrors now. He had the racing line ,and he was half a car ahead as they turned in.

He had it. He'd beaten him to it.

The sickening crunch of carbon fibre accompanied the shock of being shunted and spun around. It all happened so fast but Luke still saw Finley's car heading for the wall. He didn't stop to worry, he needed to save his race as he saw the unmistakable red Ferrari of Lewandowski tiptoe around the mess their two Wilsons had made.

Luke put it back into gear and regained the track as Dash's voice filled his ears.

'Are you okay mate?'

'What the fuck was he doing?' Luke exploded, not able to keep his voice as calm as he would have liked. 'Man, he's ruined our race!'

'Copy, are you okay?' Dash repeated, not wanting to get into it over the radio where everyone could hear them. The safety car signs came out and Luke slowed down.

'I'm fine,' Luke replied, keeping the anger out of his voice this time. 'How's the car?'

'There's a scrape on the side pod but everything else looks good. Close up behind Lewandowski, we can still do this.'

They could, as long as the car was okay and as long as Luke could overtake Lewandowski on track, neither of which had high probability rates.

'Finley's out of the race.'

'I saw,' Luke said as he filed in behind the Ferrari and the flashing lights of the safety car. 'I had the line Dash, I was ahead.'

'Yeah, copy. Let's concentrate on winning this race.'

Luke nodded inside the cockpit; his jaw clenched.

Despite his best efforts, Luke couldn't get past Lewandowski and finished the race on the second step of the podium. He couldn't help but rue the loss of an easy win and a one-two for the team. He smiled for the cameras, waved for the fans, replaying in his mind what had happened, for a split-second questioning himself but knowing he was right.

He'd had the line; he was ahead and Finley should have backed out. Whether his inexperience or his arrogance made him not, Luke didn't know but either way, he felt the anger bubbling inside of him as the podium interviewer asked him for his take on the accident.

'I don't know what happened,' Luke said through his smile. He looked out at the sea of fans, those with the purple merch crowding around the bottom of the podium, waving flags and banners at him. 'I'd need to review the footage to see for sure, but I'm delighted with second place, it's a great start for the team.'

'Arguably, your teammate threw away a one-two there,' the interviewer pushed but Luke wouldn't be swayed.

'That's racing,' he said, still smiling, waving down to the fans. 'You know all about that eh?' He grinned, trying to deflect. The interviewer laughed.

'Yeah, I've had my fair share of torpedo teammates. Well done, Luke, and good luck for the rest of the season.' Luke nodded, pulled his cap low and picked up his trophy and champagne bottle, leaving the podium by the back door not waiting to hear what Lewandowski had to say about his opportunistic win.

Luke felt exhausted. The race had been hard, chasing down someone he knew he had little chance of being able to overtake and it being the first race of the season. His body felt heavy and weighed down and if he was being honest the thought of doing more interviews and a race debrief didn't fill him with joy.

'Dude, what even was that?' Johan asked the minute he saw him after the podium.

'Fuck knows.' Luke sighed. 'What did it look like on TV?'

'It looked like you had the line and he sling-shotted it down the inside when you were clearly ahead and there was no space.' Johan's eyes narrowed and his jaw twitched as he too tried not to lose it in the very public space of the team motorhome. They walked through the main atrium over to the driver rooms and Luke was relieved that Tyler's door was shut.

'It'll be an interesting debrief then,' Luke said, raising an eyebrow as he took off his champagne-soaked overalls.

Back in his team polo shirt and jeans two hours after the end of the race, Luke left his driver's room at the same time as Tyler Finley. The two men came face to face; Luke stayed impassive but Tyler's eyes burnt with fury. He pushed past Luke and started down the corridor towards the front door, his shoulders creeping towards his earlobes. Luke pulled out his phone for something else to look at, scrolling through his unread messages of congratulations, from his sister, his mother, his mate from back home and a bunch of other random people he didn't remember giving his number to.

He hit something hard and when he looked up, he was face to face with Finley by the open motorhome doors.

'Do you make a habit of it?' Finley said, his voice low and threatening, his brow pulled together and his blue eyes flashing danger.

'I beg your pardon?' Luke kept his face as neutral as possible, his eyes scanning the crowds outside who were drawn to drivers.

'Not giving people space, cutting people off, causing very dangerous accidents?' Tyler's voice grew louder with every word he said, not even trying to hide how angry he was. 'Ruining people's races, costing the team millions of pounds?' He was shouting now, and Luke could see people gathering around, journalists, fans, and other team members.

He knew this was a conversation for another time, he knew they should be doing this behind closed doors, that they should be presenting a united front for the team, especially after what had happened today but for some reason, he couldn't move. He was pinned there by the look of utter fury on Tyler's face and Luke was sure he had never seen anyone this angry before. Never in his goodness knows how many years of racing, of competing had he ever seen someone react like this.

'I'm not talking about this,' Luke said pushing past him into the paddock, where the crowd was increasing by the second. 'Even a blind man could have seen I had that corner.'

'Of course not, dick!' Finley shouted from the top step of the motorhome. That last word pinged something in Luke and his anger exploded inside of him like fireworks on the fourth of July. He spun on his heels, reeling. His calm disposition was lost in the flames of his anger.

'What did you say to me?' It was his turn to lower his voice as he advanced on his teammate who only showed a flicker of doubt at what he had started. Drawn up ready for battle, Luke was about three inches taller than his rival, muscles tensed as if ready to strike as they glared at each other.

'You,' Luke said, jabbing his finger into Tyler's shoulder, 'are the one who caused that collision. You,' he poked again, 'should be apologising to the team and to me.'

He turned, ready to walk away. He knew the press was watching and he had to think of the team, he had to think of the reputation he had built up of this cool, calm, laidback bloke, a fair and honest driver and opponent.

'You fucking arsehole, just because you're World Champion doesn't mean you're any good.' Tyler continued to shout from the top step, Luke now at the bottom in the swamp of journalists, their Dictaphones out, their cameras rolling, fans with their phones held up high, filming the altercation. But Luke didn't see any of it. All he heard were Finley's words echoing around his head and the bubbling anger that couldn't be held back anymore and it exploded as he replied, his voice hard and cutting:

'At least I didn't bribe my way into the sport.'

'Yep, okay, that's enough thank you,' came Emma's voice from somewhere nearby. She grabbed his arm and pulled him into the back of the garage, away from the prying eyes. Away from Finley.

'What in the name of the good lord was that about?' she asked, turning her own blazing eyes to him and Luke had the decency to look ashamed.

'Em, I'm sorry…'

'Save it!'

THE BIGGEST RIVALRY OF OUR TIME: ANDERSON VS. FINLEY

Are we witnessing the biggest rivalry in modern Formula One?

By Sara Holdsworth

Date published: April 9th

With only two races under his belt, rookie Tyler Finley looks set to challenge his teammate Luke Anderson for this year's Formula One World Championship. As it stands the rookie is only eleven points behind the two main contenders, no mean feat considering he is up against two veterans of the sport.

Anderson leads with a total of thirty-six points, after his two second places and Lewandowski, the third title contender sits second with thirty-five, the Pole only managing fifth in Bahrain after his win in Melbourne.

Finley, 24 and son of British billionaire Joseph Finley secured his first win in Bahrain, only his second race in Formula One, beating Anderson to the line by a mere five-tenths of a second. The teammates battled it out around the Sakhir circuit, each determined to secure the win under the lights.

Finley got off the line cleanly from third and overtook Schulz at the first corner, leaving him to chase down Anderson for most of the race until a daring lunge propelled him into first place. The on-track action was fierce with some close calls, but both drivers kept it clean in the end to bring home the first Wilson Racing one-two of the season.

Jan Schulz, who has been with Ferrari for four seasons now and shared the podium with the two men, described the atmosphere up there as "frosty".

At the last round in Melbourne, the teammates collided, robbing Anderson of his first win of the year and ending Finley's race prematurely. The dispute between the two drivers escalated into a well-publicised altercation in the paddock, with Anderson not mincing his words when it came to how Finley secured his seat at Wilson in the first place (to watch the viral video, please click here).

The billionaire heir has already divided the paddock with his promotion to the highest league of motor racing, many believing he doesn't deserve the spot over others who have made it on merit alone. However, his performance so far is arguably one of the most impressive starts to an F1 career. No rookie has ever scored this many points, let alone a win in their first season. Finley has ensured his name makes it into the history books alongside his World Champion teammate.

New Team Principal Martin Clark, a well-known friend of the previously mentioned Joseph Finley, has a lot on his hands with his two drivers. "The rivalry between the two is good old-fashioned racing if you ask me. I wouldn't want them to be any less than they are," he stated after the team's one-two in Bahrain.

Anderson is renowned for his laidback, effortless driving style, a huge contrast to Finley's aggressive and possessive attack of every line. The two could not be more different both on and off track. They divide not only the British fans but also the other drivers.

Matteo Brambilla, Lotus driver and previous teammate of Finley believes neither will concede if it comes down to a championship between the two. "We've all seen how hard Anderson will fight to win, last year he was lethal in his approach to every race, and he wiped the floor with Vasquez and Lewandowski, but I've raced against Tyler. I've been his teammate. There's nothing he wouldn't do to make sure he comes out on top."

Finley's father, often present at the races cheering on his son, couldn't help but brag about his prodigy. "Tyler is single-handedly the most talented driver I have ever seen. There's a lot riding on him to do well this season, and nothing less than a Championship will be good enough."

Even this early on in the season, it is lining up to be a corker of a championship if the two drivers keep up this level of entertainment. Throw in Lewandowski in the Ferrari and his teammate Schulz, who showed good form last year, then it promises to be as exciting the whole way through as it was at the first two races.

The teams head off to Shanghai next for the Chinese Grand Prix and all bets are off on who might come out on top. Although this rivalry, with airs of Senna vs Prost, is simmering at the moment, it seems it won't be long before it explodes into something far more perilous.

Formula One is a dangerous sport, with cars hitting speeds of up to 160 miles per hour, it's often lives hanging in the balance of one wrong move. The ruthless, unyielding approach both drivers have will no doubt see more crashes like Melbourne as the pressure increases.

Wilson's publicists can push the "mutual respect" narrative as much as they like, but everyone looking can see fireworks are being lit and it's exactly what the F1 community has been asking for.

The most burning question is, are you #teamluke or #teamtyler?

Seven

Chinese Grand Prix – Shanghai International Circuit – Shanghai
April 11th

Luke hated the early start on a Thursday. He stifled a yawn as he guided the Mercedes GLE SUV into the car park beside the paddock entrance. Nick's voice was too loud in the empty car and thick with sleep as she battled to stay awake.

'You were the one who took it too far,' she reminded him but he didn't want to hear it.

'I already know what you think of my choice of words, we've talked about it and I don't want to rehash it today,' he said hoping that would shut her up but he should have known better.

'You need to try harder.'

'But he crashed into me.' Luke knew he sounded whiny

but he couldn't help it. After Bahrain, things had gotten progressively frostier inside the garage and Luke was still seething that Tyler had secured a win before he had.

'And I punctured your kart wheel on purpose because I was mad that we were spending another weekend doing what you wanted to do, yet you still love me.'

'You did what?' He heard her laughing at her confession. 'That was you? Nick, that's terrible!'

'And so was telling your teammate he bribed his way into the sport. Build a wall and get over it.'

'Cheers.' He rolled his eyes as he parked up in his dedicated spot. 'I've got to go, get some sleep.'

Luke jumped out of the car, grabbed his backpack from the back seat, and walked over to the gate. He looked at the space beside him where Johan usually was; he'd stayed back at the hotel for a meeting about his next retreat and planned on joining Luke later.

He headed straight for his driver's room to drop off his things, then met the rest of the crew for breakfast. It made them stronger and willing to work harder. Luke was a great leader, a great motivator, and a good friend to all of the people around him. They always gave extra for him, they always pushed harder because they believed in him and he made them feel like they were all in this together.

It took Luke a moment to realise that the table wasn't as full as usual. Like the first two races, Tyler hadn't joined them but this time it looked like some of his mechanics were missing too. He tried not to think too much about it but it niggled at him as he grabbed a takeaway coffee to take into his first meeting of the day. He made a mental note to talk to some of the guys about it later.

The small upstairs corridor was quiet and deserted. Martin wasn't in his office yet and the top floor lay empty. He was early.

Luke tried the door but it was locked, so he sipped his scalding coffee hoping it would keep him awake for the duration of the press meeting.

'Hi,' a voice said from behind, startling him. He spun around to find Tyler lurking by the top step. Luke felt himself freeze, draw up a little taller but there was nothing combative about Tyler today. He lent up against the handrail which wobbled against his weight, the temporary structure not that stable. 'Early too huh?' he said, taking his ice-blue eyes off Luke and down to his feet. His arms were crossed over his broad chest, the muscles pulling and flexing under his skin.

Luke was stunned and left Tyler's question hanging in the balance. He heard his sister's comment about being friendly in his mind, but his face stayed stony as he looked wide-eyed past his rival and down the stairs, almost begging someone to arrive so he didn't have to think of what to say.

There was something about Tyler that made him clam up, even when he wasn't in one of his moods, Luke didn't know what to say to him. He stared into the distance, the silence expanding, not able to pinpoint what was going on in his head as he saw Tyler's lean body shift in discomfort.

'I'm still getting used to the jam-packed schedules, it's a lot busier than I thought,' Tyler said, filling the silence, trying to rid the space of the tension that was palpable. He let out a strangled sort of chuckle and when Luke didn't return it, the small smile dropped from his handsome face.

Luke turned his eyes to his teammate, confusion swirled in his head at what was going on and still he remained quiet, not sure what he should or wanted to say.

'Hey, I meant to catch you last time out. I wanted to…' His words got lost in his throat as Emma's joyful face came bobbing up the stairs, her arms full of sheets of paper, pens and her phone balancing on top. Tyler shifted out of her way, his fingers finding his dark hair, tugging at it as he looked down the stairs.

'Morning,' she said smiling. She glanced at Tyler then her eyes settled on Luke. 'You alright champ?' she said, squeezing past him and unlocking the meeting room.

Luke followed her in and took the spot right by the door, ready for a quick escape. Emma dumped her stuff beside him and Tyler settled on the other side. Shortly after, Jessie joined the group, taking her seat at the head of the table.

'Looks like the weather might be good this weekend,' Jessie said as she arranged her paperwork.

Luke could feel Tyler's eyes on him but purposefully ignored him, feeling the tension between them like a thin thread of elastic.

'Nice to see we're all chirpy today,' Jessie continued when no one replied.

'Sorry Jess,' Luke finally said, his mouth feeling dry. 'Rough night last night.'

'We heard about Petra,' Emma said, stifling a laugh. 'I told you she wasn't good news.'

'What happened with Petra?' Jessie asked, her ears pricking up at the mention of the notorious journalist.

'I believe she was hoping Luke might be up for a little sleepover.' Emma giggled this time, not able to hold it in.

'Oh god, what did you say to her?' Jessie stopped what she was doing and stared at Luke with a look that told him he best not have messed up.

'Not a lot, I politely declined her request and when she fell over, I offered to walk her back to her room,' he explained, still very aware that Tyler was staring at him. Irritation prickled at him again.

'Always a gentleman, our Luke,' Emma said and Tyler snorted from across the room. All eyes flew to him. He had the decency to look embarrassed but it was too late. Luke felt a bubble of red-hot lava growing inside of him as his eyes narrowed. He wanted Tyler to go away, to disappear and not be part of his world anymore. He'd never disliked anyone quite so much and he hated it.

'Sorry I'm late,' Martin said rushing into the room. He took a seat beside Tyler and the atmosphere simmered down with his presence.

'Here are your schedules. It's a busy one,' Jessie started, as she handed out sheets to the two drivers and Team Principal.

'Wow, do I have time to visit the gents today?' Tyler said with humour as his eyes travelled down the long list of interviews planned.

Jessie pinned Tyler with a look Luke knew well. *Don't mess with me. Not today.*

Tyler slouched down, showing how new he was to all of this and Martin checked his watch every two seconds like he had somewhere better to be. Emma fiddled with her pen and notebook, her phone open on Twitter too as she scrolled the feed.

'I'm sure you've all seen Sara Holdsworth's article that came out a few days ago?' Jessie continued, ignoring Tyler. Luke looked to Emma confused. He hadn't seen the article, he had no idea what they were talking about. Silently, Emma handed him a printout of it.

'Have you been neglecting your social media again?' she asked half berating, half amused.

'I've told you, you can have the password and you can do it. I hate it, you know I do,' Luke replied as he scanned the article, his features getting harder as he took in the words of Sara Holdsworth.

'We thought we'd put a pin in the whole rivalry narrative but the article has got a lot of traction online and that video seems to be doing the rounds again. Needless to say, the last race didn't help things.' Jessie looked between Luke and Tyler. Luke stared at the blank wall behind her head, the muscle in his jaw twitching as Tyler continued to stare at the schedule. He wasn't reading it, his eyes not moving and glazed over.

'We won't ask you to be best friends but you guys need to put on a front. I don't care how painful it is for you but the reputation of the team is on the line. The whole "paid for seat" is damaging to us and our sponsors and I don't want to hear another word about it to the press. Say and do what you have to so it looks like you're getting along.'

'We don't care what happens behind closed doors but outside of these walls, you two are buddies. Understood?' Martin interjected and Jessie gave a sharp nod.

Tyler finally looked up, his eyes searching Luke's face for something. It was intense enough to make Luke turn away.

'What kind of rubbish is this?' Tyler asked, chucking his schedule on the table with disgust. 'We're racers, we're competitors, they would never expect us to be friends. It seems ridiculous to try and pretend that we are when we very clearly aren't.' He said the last words with a probing stare at Luke like he was challenging him to disagree.

Despite the rising anger in him, Luke kept his face impassive, his stare hard as he looked past his teammate and out of the window.

He'd never had a teammate he'd despised. It changed the dynamics of the team completely and it put him off-kilter, never quite sure where the floor was when he took a step. Sure, he and Vasquez had had their moments, but nothing like this. Even when he was partnered with Schulz at the beginning of his career there was always respect even if they didn't get on off track. The racing between them was hard but the stakes had never been this high. It had never mattered that they didn't see eye to eye because there was always respect, mutual understanding and fairness. But Finley was chucking the rule book out of the window with his egotism, everything had to be about him. But through hard work and success, everything this year was about Luke and Tyler could not stand that, too used to being the centre of Daddy's attention, too used to Daddy's money making him the most important thing.

'Just don't talk about each other, yeah? Deflect, change the subject, charm them, laugh about it, I don't care, flirt if you have to.' She said the last bit looking at Luke but he ignored her.

'Are we done?' Luke said, standing up from his seat leaving Jessie no option but to agree.

'Thanks, guys,' Martin said as he shuffled past Luke and out of the door first.

Emma followed Luke back down to the ground floor and his room.

'Let's not pretend Petra won't be out for blood today,' she said as she opened the door to Johan squished up against the wall at the little desk.

'Oh she will,' Johan said laughing, already enjoying the pain he knew was coming Luke's way.

'I can't pretend to be friends with that guy, no one in their right mind would like him,' Luke said taking a seat on the bench.

'Oh, come on, he's not that bad. I know he's a little rough around the edges and you do seem to get the brunt of his attitude but when it comes to the press, pretend he's any other guy on the grid. When you want to, you can make a turd look attractive Luke.'

'She's not wrong,' Johan interjected again, reclining in his seat and watching the exchange.

'Give them that beautiful smile and do your best. It's not you Jessie is worried about, it's him. She knows that outburst in Australia was out of character, she knows it's not you.'

Wasn't it? Maybe this was the person he was becoming

because of Tyler, incapable of mastering his emotions. He felt his steely composure shake whenever he was within Tyler's vicinity and he didn't like it one bit.

He sighed, he had other things to worry about, like the fact that it was the third race of the season and he hadn't won yet. He needed to focus on the weekend ahead and not be distracted by all the Tyler Finley chatter and the press making things up for a quick story. That wasn't what was important. What happened out on track was what mattered, and he would always fight hard and fair. He would continue to do that because that was who he was. He would win again with his head held high, being proud of how he had held himself throughout and not having stolen, barged and swindled his way there.

Tyler Finley would not be his greatest rival. He had more talent and hard work in his little finger than that guy did in his whole body and he would not let the media dictate the narrative around this championship. Lewandowski was also a threat, and he hadn't discounted Schulz either, the Ferrari looked strong. He needed to focus on the work they still needed to do, how they could improve the car and find that extra half a tenth. He wanted this second championship; he wanted it with every fibre of his body.

Emma left them and Luke plugged his air pods in, blocking out the world for a moment to calm his heart rate and get ready for the day ahead of pretending the guy across the hall wasn't so much a foe but a friend.

Eight

Somewhere over the Mediterranean – Turkish Airlines First Class
April 24th

Even at thirty-five thousand feet, Luke couldn't escape his teammate. Each time he closed his eyes Tyler's face swam on the back of his lids. The arrogant twinkle in his eye, the angry frown, and then the look he'd worn when they'd been alone on the stairs outside that meeting room. A feeling crept over his skin, a whisper of something that wasn't the anger he'd felt up until then but he ignored it.

As requested, Luke had pretended that there was no feud between them to the press, though he hated the deceit of it. Even standing on the podium as Luke took away his first win of the season in China, they'd shaken hands, smiled and pretended to be happy for one another even though Luke knew Tyler was seething at having finished so close to first place.

He'd had a whole week off and now they were on their way to Baku for the next race, he'd be dammed if he spent another weekend thinking about Tyler Finley.

He looked over to the pod beside him, the door pulled shut hiding Johan from the rest of the passengers around them, giving them the privacy that only first-class afforded you.

Abandoning the idea of sleep, he lifted the blind on the window and the sun poured in, glinting off the gold trim around the table, door and TV screen. It was obscene and so far from the small semi he'd grown up in in Buckinghamshire, even from his two-bed flat in Monaco. The opulence and the luxury were unnecessary in his eyes. He bet Tyler didn't think so, having grown up in a huge mansion with maids and a driver.

There he went again, thinking about him. He felt heat seep through him, half annoyed at Finley, half annoyed at himself for letting his mind wander.

He couldn't be trusted to be alone with his thoughts.

He yanked the screen down separating his seat from Johan's.

The top of his white blonde hair rippled under the jet of cool air coming from the vent above them. Johan had headphones on and was intently watching the screen and hadn't heard Luke.

Luke reached over and tapped his friend on the shoulder. Johan jerked and his head spun round. His clear blue eyes were wide but crinkled at the side when he saw it was Luke.

'You scared the crap out of me.' He laughed taking the headphones off. 'What's up?'

Before Luke could answer an air attendant appeared, her pretty teeth revealed as she smiled. She held a pen and pad in her hand ready to take their order.

'An iced mocha please,' Luke said as Johan quirked an eyebrow at the order. 'Oh, give me a break.'

'If I did, you wouldn't be World Champion,' he replied but he was smiling. 'An Americano please.'

She cast an appreciative look over Luke before wandering off down the aisle to fulfil their request.

'What's on your mind?' Johan asked the moment she'd gone.

Luke sighed, one hand on his drink, the other running through his thick sandy hair.

'You've won your first race of the season, aren't you happy about that?' Johan continued in his silence, trying to tease Luke out of his head, something only he was capable of.

'It's not that, of course, I'm happy but it's a long season. It's not the racing, it's…it's the other stuff. There's a lot of… noise, other things going on. Drama. You know how much I hate drama. I want to drive, I want to be able to do my work and not have to worry about what else's going on, you know?'

'I do know,' Johan said thoughtfully. 'You're struggling to focus. But it's noise. You need to shut it out.'

'I wish they'd never bloody signed him,' Luke huffed, wondering if there was more he could have done to influence that decision.

'They did and now, we need to rise above it. Let Finley throw his toys out of the pram, let Finley have his meltdowns. You, Luke Anderson, are the World Champion. You are the one to beat. You're stronger than that, you can rise above the noise. You are my headphones.'

'What?' Luke said spluttering on his iced coffee. Johan's face remained deadpan as Luke tried not to laugh.

'Noise cancelling,' he replied, shrugging like it was obvious.

'Right.' Luke's lips curled up at the side despite his best

efforts to not let them.

'Dig deep, ignore the noise, focus on you, that's what's important.'

Luke nodded but he wished it was that easy.

A week away from the circus of Formula One hadn't helped him like he thought it would. Back in his flat, away from the press, from the team, he'd thought he could regroup, train and get to a better place in his head but here he was, still struggling to focus on that one thing that mattered to him.

The plane jolted and the seatbelt sign came back on. The two men lapsed into silence.

Johan was right, he needed to block out the noise. Whatever his teammate did was none of his business. Luke needed to keep up appearances in front of the press and then make sure there was always enough air between them, both on and off track, that his presence didn't affect him in any way. He could do that.

Luke and Johan walked across the tarmac with the rest of the first-class passengers and entered the terminal. Baku was warm for April, the air-conditioning welcome on their skin even from that short walk. With his black baseball cap pulled low, his sunglasses in place he hoped no one knew they'd be landing today. He wasn't up for photos and crowds; his name being screamed across concourses, he longed for anonymity for a moment, but it was a by-product of the career he had chosen.

They picked up the hire car the team had arranged for them and headed to their hotel in the city centre. Luke drove as the skyscrapers flashed past and Johan flicked through his phone in the passenger seat.

'Have you seen this?' he held up his phone which showed a photo on Instagram. Luke and Tyler on the podium, shaking hands, both smiling, holding their trophies.

'What about it?' asked Luke turning away, focusing on the busy road. There'd be thousands of posts like it all over the internet, it was nothing new.

'Finley posted it,' Johan started but Luke interrupted him.

'I don't care,' he snapped, had they not agreed to rise above all this.

'Someone has commented on it, "Playing happy families for Daddy Clark?" and Sara, that woman from CultRacing has said "I wouldn't be surprised",' he finished.

'I don't care,' Luke said again. 'Don't show me that stuff.'

'I know we said let's rise above it, but you still need to know what's being said. Jessie won't be pleased.'

Luke knew better than to bite back. Emma would say the way to control the narrative was by knowing what was happening but Luke didn't want to be consumed with a woman's attempt to make a story out of nothing. Okay, well maybe not nothing but that argument was old news. Australia felt like a lifetime ago, he wanted to move on. The show had moved on. He had beaten Tyler out on track where it mattered and that was it.

At the track on Thursday, Luke walked into the motorhome ahead of the press day and settled at the table where the rest of his mechanics were tucking into eggs and toast. The group was smaller again and a quick scan of the faces there told Luke exactly who was missing.

'What's going on?' Luke asked Jamie in a stage whisper as one of the catering staff brought over his breakfast. Jamie looked up from his plate and looked around the room with wide, innocent eyes.

'I don't know what you mean.'

'Come on, cough up. Or I'll tell Clark you're the one who showed me the car pre-season.'

Jamie looked mock-shocked and cracked a smile.

'Some people within the team...' Jamie looked over his shoulder as one of Tyler's mechanics came in, glanced at the table, then headed in the opposite direction, 'think that sharing information and socialising with the other side of the garage will damage their chances of winning.'

Luke stared at him blankly.

'Are you serious?'

Jamie shrugged and Luke shook his head, he couldn't believe it. He knew the best tactic for winning this championship was having the team working as one, not divided down the middle. He wondered if this was Tyler's idea. Did he hate Luke so much that he wanted to create two different teams within Wilson Racing? The thought prickled at his skin.

Luke finished up his breakfast, not engaging in the usual banter as the small group dispersed back to their stations. When Luke walked into his room, he tugged his bag off the bench, changed into his trainers and pulled some shorts on.

'I'm going for a run,' he said without waiting for an answer from Johan and headed out of the door.

He walked to the edge of the paddock with long, powerful strides full of intent, the Caspian Sea sprawled out in front of him, dotted with white yachts and sailboats. The sky almost merged with the water at the horizon, both a brilliant shade of blue.

He skipped into the first step of his run and the wind rushed past his ears, drowning out the sound of the city behind him. It felt good to be moving after spending the last two days on flights. Letting his muscles stretch and contract at the physical effort of running along the coastal path. He pounded the pavement, letting go of his frustrations, the thoughts that had sat with him since China.

It had been a tough race, Tyler pushing him right until the

very end but he had come out on top, for the first time this season. He finally had a win under his belt and he felt better for it. The doubt that had nestled its way into his mind, reinforced by the rumours, the articles, the constant questions. Was Tyler Finley better than him?

Luke didn't like self-doubt, it was a weakness in his eyes, an emotional response. He would never get to where he wanted to go if he let his feelings take the lead. There was no room for the wants of the heart in motor racing, he had to think with his head, critically, analytically, logically. That's how you became World Champion. He knew it worked because look at him now, World Champion and leading this year's championship too.

The soles of his shoes met the pavement rhythmically as he continued pushing and sucking air into his lungs. He checked his smartwatch to see if his heart rate was in the optimum range and when he looked back up he saw Brambilla running towards him. The unmistakable limp on his left leg from the bad crash he'd had a few years ago was still obvious even after all this time. Luke sped up, not in the mood for a chat. He should have known better than to seek solitude on the running trails on a Grand Prix weekend. Most used exercise as an outlet too.

He dipped his head, looked out to the sea and continued on his route, barely lifting his hand in greeting as he sped past the Italian.

He couldn't believe that Finley would resort to destroying the harmony Luke had spent years forming inside the team. Yes, the two sides of the garage were in competition but they were also a team and a team worked together to achieve their goals.

He needed them, he needed all of them to get to where he wanted to go. As much as he hated to admit it, he needed Tyler Finley too. Luke needed his data, his setup details, everything.

There was so much more he wanted to achieve in this sport, so much more he wanted for his legacy. He was World Champion but he wanted more and that came with sacrifice.

He would have to pull this team back together if he wanted to win, there was no doubt about it. He would need to put his frustrations about Tyler Finley aside and start building bridges.

The Internet – Twitter
April 29th

FIA ✓ @fia · Apr 29
#F1 Following an investigation the stewards deem car #24 did not breach the regulations and will be able to keep first place at the Azerbaijan Grand Prix.

💬 13   🔁 26   ♡ 312

Luke's Girl @Lukesgirl · Apr 29
Whaaaat? You've got to be shitting me. He pushed Lewandowski straight into the wall.

💬   🔁 1   ♡ 3

Mrs Finley @f1girl1245673 · Apr 29
He didn't. Tyler had the line, Lewandowski was being opportunistic

💬   🔁   ♡ 13

Baz @bazracingfan · Apr 29
Just be happy it wasn't Anderson in that wall, would've been if I was driving

💬 1   🔁   ♡ 1

Aaron Zoooom @Brambifan · Apr 29
Pipe down Baz, you probably couldn't manoeuvre a scooter without falling off.

💬   🔁   ♡

Aaron Zoooom @Brambifan · Apr 29
He definitely pushed him into the wall. This guy is a loose cannon.

💬   🔁   ♡ 5

Mrs Finley @f1girl1245673 · Apr 29
Oh shut up. He could drive circles round Brambilla, that guy needs to re-ti-re. Tyler Finley is the best driver on that grid.

💬   🔁   ♡ 2

Aaron Zoooom @Brambifan · Apr 29
Let's agree to disagree. Finley is just in the best car. Put him in that McLaren and he'd be plumb last. Unless Daddy paid for him to win.

💬   🔁   ♡ 1

Sara Holdsworth ✓ @saracultracing · Apr 29

That's a turn up for the books. Finley gets to keep his first place after arguably shunting title contender Lewandowski into the wall in Azerbaijan.

♡ 157   ↻ 37   ♡ 759

Jared @badboyf1bants · Apr 29

Fuck him and his bad driving

♡   ↻   ♡ 1

Luke's Girl @lukesgirl · Apr 29

I agree with your premise but no need to swear.

♡   ↻   ♡ 6

Lydia @lydia3649 · Apr 29

Not surprising really, Daddy probably paid someone to make it go away #teamluke #andersonarmy

♡   ↻   ♡ 9

Luke's Girl @lukesgirl · Apr 29

YES! #teamluke #andersonarmy

♡   ↻   ♡

Mrs Finley @f1girl1245673 · Apr 29

It's spelt #teamtyler

♡   ↻   ♡ 1

Baz @bazracingfan · Apr 29

WTF are team luke and tyler?

♡ 1   ↻   ♡

Aaron Zoom @Brambifan · Apr 29

Go home Baz, you're drunk.

♡   ↻   ♡ 1

Love in the Fast Lane

Petra Vogel ✓ @petraRTL · Apr 29

Update from the steward's office: no penalty for Finley of Wilson Racing for the incident involving Lewandowski.

💬 589   🔁 356   ♡ 1.6K

Man of ur dreamz @britboyf1 · Apr 29

Such utter bollocks. You however are fit.

Man of ur dreamz @britboyf1 · Apr 29

You're fit.

Man of ur dreamz @britboyf1 · Apr 29

Oi, Petra you're fit.

Aaron Zoom @Brambifan · Apr 29

Think she got that you think she's fit mate

♡ 1

Mrs Finley @f1girl1245673 · Apr 29

#teamtyler

♡ 36

Man of ur dreamz @Britboyf1 · Apr 29

Piss off with your teams, this aint some 2009 vampire diaries shit

Mrs Finley @f1girl1245673 · Apr 29

You're right, it's not. But also, #teamdamon

♡ 12

Aaron Zoom @Brambifan · Apr 29

Can we get back to the F1 now.

79

Sophie E. Mills

Ferrari ✓ @Ferrari · Apr 29

We are disappointed with the decision of the stewards and will be appealing.

💬 1.4K　　⇄ 354　　♡ 4.6K

Aaron Zoooom @Brambifan · Apr 29

Ooooh it's not over yet.

💬　　⇄　　♡

San @andersan48062 · Apr 29

Luke should have won.

💬　　⇄　　♡ 5

Man of ur dreamz @britboyf1 · Apr 29

He should, he's the best driver on the whole grid

💬　　⇄ 1　　♡

Tyler's Number 1 @Finleyfaaaan1456 · Apr 29

Lukey boy must have been pissed hahahahahahahahahahahaha

💬　　⇄　　♡

Luke's Girl @lukesgirl · Apr 29

Mature.

💬　　⇄　　♡

Love in the Fast Lane

Aaron Zoooom @Brambifan · Apr 29

Is anyone else not buying the whole "they're best friends" thing the team is trying to sell?

💬 13   🔁   ♡ 5

Luke's Girl @lukesgirl · Apr 29

Nope, no way. Finley is so arrogant, Luke wouldn't be friends with someone like that.

San @andersan48062 · Apr 29

Agree, there's just no way.

Mrs Finley @f1girl1245673 · Apr 29

Eurgh these #teamluke peeps are annoying me. Like their golden boy wouldn't do everything he could to win too. Does no one remember Austin 2017? I sure do *grumpy face*

💬   🔁   ♡ 11

Finley's Number 1 @Finleyfaaaan1456 · Apr 29

Exactly! Thank you! Plus Tyler had. The. Line. Lewandowski should have backed out.

Luke's Girl @lukesgirl · Apr 29

#teamluke #andersonarmy

Nine

Spanish Grand Prix – Circuit de Barcelona-Catalunya - Montmeló
May 12th

Luke watched Tyler yawn, check his phone and roll his eyes in the middle of the team debrief. The conceited bastard couldn't even sit through one meeting without making it about him. Luke shifted in his seat with frustration.

'Overall it was a fantastic result for the team. Well done everyone, and Luke, Tyler good job on a nice clean race,' Martin said from the top of the table. His lips moved without any sound as the delay through the headphones put it out of sync. 'Luke, congratulations on the win, great performance,' he added before wrapping up the meeting.

Luke smiled to himself, giving himself the grace of being proud of what he had achieved out there. Second win in the bag and this one had felt a little easier, more like the wins from last year. With that promise to himself, he had kept Finley at a good distance behind him and the rookie had been unable to match his pace, battling away with Lewandowski for most of the race instead.

It suited Luke, the further away Tyler Finley was from him, the better he could concentrate.

'Okay, team photo, out front in ten,' Clark said this time to the room, laying his headphones on the desk. Tyler slunk out first, desperate to end the torture of being reminded he had come second, but Luke didn't have time to think too hard about it before he was engulfed in a hug. Dash pulled back, his face alight with the cheesiest of smiles.

'Dude, you were brilliant out there,' he said keeping his hands on Luke's biceps. 'I know you know that, but I just thought I'd say.'

'It was great teamwork,' Luke replied, following his race engineer out of the room and back into the garage. And it had been teamwork. After Azerbaijan, Luke had gone out of his way to include Tyler's mechanics in everything outside of racing, forcing them to sit with them at breakfast, bantering with them in the corridors and putting on the charm offensive. He wasn't sure it had convinced them but it had secured him another win so he must have been on the right track. The problem was, that getting the team on side was easy compared to having to pretend that he was friends with Tyler. He bristled whenever he saw him and dislike stung him like he was walking through a colony of bees. His breathing did this strange thing where it hitched when Luke laid eyes on him but he found it hard to look away.

The team gathered out the front of the garage, getting ready for the traditional winner's photo. The sea of press, cameras at the ready, formed a wall opposite them as Luke waited in the wings.

'Let's give them a show eh?' Emma whispered as she walked past. She glanced at Tyler and then the waiting press when Luke questioned her with a look.

He set his jaw, tensing and hardening his gaze somewhere off in the distance. He gritted his teeth, ready to give the best performance of his life.

Luke felt him before he saw him saunter up beside him and wait like he was. When the team had finished scuffling and found their places, Luke stepped out of the garage first, his media smile dancing on his lips as he clapped hands with all the team members he walked past on his way to the centre of the assembled group. Tyler followed, his eyes glued to the back of Luke's head.

The team cheered and whistled, celebrating the team's one-two finish. Luke clapped them right back, grinning, trying to enjoy the moment but his mind was already dreading what he knew he had to do.

He turned and his body felt heavy with defiance. They were a metre apart and the fire roared inside of him as he set eyes on his teammate. Luke hoped he was managing to hide his feelings better than Tyler was. He held out his hand and Finley looked at it for a moment.

'Great job, mate,' Luke said but it came out strangled. He could feel all eyes on him. From the press, from the team and Emma, all assessing his performance.

After what felt like an eternity, Tyler took the extended hand and shook it once before Luke let it go. It wasn't distrust that seared up his arm or dislike that coursed through him. Tyler's hand was warm and smooth, and Luke pretended the heat he'd felt creep up his neck was what he always felt when he looked at Tyler.

Luke didn't let it affect him in the moment. He smiled but turned his gaze away, then settled himself on the floor beside the huge first-place trophy and Dash, who grabbed his shoulder and shook him with pure elation.

This time the smile on Luke's lips was real as he gazed up at the cameras, the flashes going off one after the other like a raging lightning storm.

'Are you coming?' Vicki said as she continued to pack up the garage with the rest of the lads a while later. Luke jolted out of his thoughts as he coiled up a thick cable.

'What? Where?'

'You know you don't have to help,' Jamie said from behind him.

'He's a good team player,' Vicki said nudging Luke.

'You mean he had nothing better to do.' Jamie laughed with a mischievous glint playing in his eyes.

'The way I see it, the more people who pitch in, the quicker everyone gets to go home,' Luke said shrugging. Across the garage his eyes found his teammate, laughing with his crew, not lifting a single finger and if anything, slowing them down.

'Always so selfless,' Emma quipped as she entered the garage.

'Are you coming then?' Vicki asked again and everyone seemed to know what she was talking about except for him.

'Where?'

'Some of the lads met a couple of local birds…'

'Girls,' Emma interrupted but it didn't stop Jamie talking, he just raised an eyebrow.

'…and they have invited us down to the beach for a fire or something.'

'Team celebration,' Vicki said, trying to coax him into agreeing. 'Come on, it'll be fun. I'll buy you a beer.'

'Or you could bring that bottle of champagne,' Emma interjected.

'It's called a magnum, so uncouth,' Jamie joked nudging

her.

'I'm supposed to be on a flight,' Luke said, thinking over the idea in his head. Then, he saw an opportunity. 'Are those guys going?' He nodded to the other side of the garage and Jamie smiled.

'They sure are.'

'What time's your flight? I could delay it?' Emma offered. She smiled like she knew he was about to crack.

Johan appeared behind him, having heard the tail end of the conversation, he raised an eyebrow. He wasn't convinced this was the way to play it.

'We'll be there,' Luke said, not giving Johan a moment to contradict him. Tyler's head snapped up as he heard Luke's answer. His blue eyes trained on Luke's face, the stare so intense Luke had to look away again. He didn't want to like the way Tyler looked at him, so he buried the feeling.

The fire crackled and the laughter got lost in the black night as the waves lapped against the shore.

Luke sat on the warm sand, his elbows resting on his knees, a beer bottle swinging between them in his hands. He focused on the white spot of the moon's reflection on the dark water, his mind blank.

He felt a wave of exhaustion curl over him as he heard Vicki squeal. Jamie and some of the other mechanics had picked her up and were running towards the water, her arms and legs flailing as she tried to untangle herself but they were too strong. Johan's angular profile glowed by the firelight as he stood watching with the rest of the team a good ten metres away.

'They'll pay for that in the morning.'

Luke looked up but he didn't need to to recognise the deep tones of Tyler Finley's voice. He stood beside Luke, looking out over the ocean too, as the guys dumped Vicki in the water. Tyler swayed and chuckled as she screamed profanities after them. Luke noted the designer polo Tyler wore and the expensive waft of his aftershave, a wave of distrust coursed through him.

Tyler sat down unsteadily and pulled his legs up into the same position. Stunned, Luke watched Emma help Vicki out of the water and Jamie, who felt bad, give her his fleece.

'Well done for today,' Tyler said filling the silence Luke was leaving. 'It was a great drive.'

Luke had no idea what to say so he stayed quiet. He'd spent the last two hours buttering up the whole team whilst avoiding Tyler. The air around them fizzled with awkwardness as the silence expanded. Tyler cleared his throat, like he was about to say something, but thought better of it. He took a swig from his bottle and then dug it into the sand.

'I know you don't rate me,' he started, a slight waver in his usual confidence. He left gaps between the words as his mouth caught up with his brain. 'I know you think I bribed my way here. But I care about this. Sure, my dad's money helps but it's still my dream, I've worked hard for this.'

'I don't doubt it.' Luke finally spoke but contrary to what he had said, there was doubt written all over his words.

'You do,' Tyler rebuked, spurred on by the fact that Luke had spoken to him. He glared at Luke with dilated pupils. 'You don't like me. That's fine, we don't have to be friends.'

They lapsed into silence again, Luke not denying how he felt about Tyler. There was no need to pretend. There was no love lost there. There were no cameras, no one to pretend to, they weren't at work anymore and given half a chance Luke wouldn't even be having this conversation. Tyler Finley would be as far away from him as humanly possible but he needed Tyler's team on his side too.

'I'm sorry I shouted at you in Australia,' Tyler said, his

voice a whisper but the feelings were there. 'There was no excuse, I was upset.'

Tyler took a deep breath and downed the rest of his beer, wiping his mouth with the back of his hand. He swayed again like the ground was moving beneath him.

'Part of me would love to not have my dad there you know.' His words were slurred and his tone changed, it was huskier and fuelled with emotion and Luke could tell he was about to be let into something few people knew. 'Have you ever met him? He's like a bulldog. He won't give up, on anything, and he expects the fucking world from everyone. Including me. It's suffocating. I let the pressure get the better of me in Australia. He'd been banging on all winter about me winning the first race. It was like anything less wouldn't be good enough. And I'm telling you this because I'm pissed as a fart and we both know I won't remember this in the morning. Also, I nervous talk around you, it's like verbal diarrhoea I can't stop it. And now I've said diarrhoea, please don't ever remind me of this conversation.'

Luke couldn't help the small smile that spread over his lips, he took a sip of beer to hide it and the flaming anger he felt inside him dissipated, spreading out from the ball of rage to a warmth that expanded through his chest, down his legs and arms.

'Has anyone ever told you you talk too much?' he said to cover his unease at this new feeling. He stole a glance at Tyler, his dilated pupils giving away how much he'd had to drink already.

'Yeah, pretty much everyone. In fact, you're the only person who can silence me with one look.'

Luke turned, quirking his eyebrow up, probing with his brown eyes like he was trying to uncover his deepest, darkest secrets.

'Yep, that's the one, right there.' Tyler smiled and Luke felt something flutter inside his chest, as fast as it arrived it disappeared and he couldn't be sure he hadn't imagined it. 'Do you always smoulder?'

'I don't smoulder,' Luke shot back, turning away from him and staring back out to the ocean to calm the extra beating of his heart.

'Yes, you do.'

Tyler's words hung in the silence. He cleared his throat again, his toe digging into the sand. 'That was a great move on Nabiyev by the way.'

'You mean when he leapt out the way because of the blue flags?' Luke almost enjoyed the sound of Tyler's voice and he squashed the thought. Tyler was trouble and he needed to keep him at arm's length.

'Yeah, that's the one.' Tyler chuckled. 'Martin was delighted with our little performance earlier. Jessie though, pretty sure she didn't buy it.'

'I'm not a very good actor,' Luke said staring out to the water, where Jamie was swimming.

'You're doing pretty well now, you should save it for the cameras,' Tyler said, tipping his bottle to him.

'Who says I'm acting?' Luke turned to Tyler and assessed him with his gaze. There was something about him that drew Luke in, even with his heels dug into the sand. In the distance, Johan approached.

'Luke, we've got to go. Flight is in an hour.'

Luke stood up and dusted the sand off of his trousers. Looking down at Tyler sat there, staring straight ahead, he didn't know what to make of what had happened.

He lifted his hand and gave a half-hearted wave, lost for words.

'See you in Monaco,' he said and then followed Johan to say goodbye to the rest of the team.

As he lay there, the early hours of the morning slipping away, the day getting closer to dawning, Luke's eyes were wide open, replaying his conversation with Tyler. His parents were the complete opposite, they were happy whether he was winning championships or putting his plate in the dishwasher. They loved him unconditionally. He couldn't imagine anything different.

Maybe Luke had been unfairly harsh on him, maybe he'd misunderstood the outbursts. Maybe that's how Tyler got through the day, how he dealt with the huge amount of pressure he felt daily from his billionaire father. The outburst in Australia, the arrogance of thinking he was the best.

A shot of empathy ran through him as Tyler's words, laced with emotion, ran through his mind again. The blue of his eyes flaring with frustration and anger as he'd said how suffocated he felt, how nothing was ever good enough in his father's eyes.

He wondered if Tyler would have any recollection of their conversation in the morning. Thankfully, Luke had only had one beer, he was already thinking about the race ahead. Still leading the championship and with this win in Barcelona under his belt he'd built a bit of a gap up to Tyler in second and over Lewandowski now in third.

Maybe having Tyler as his gunner wouldn't be such a bad thing, but he needed to make sure he was still ahead going into the summer break so that the team backed his campaign for champion and not the other way around.

For a fleeting moment, he wondered how that would play out, what with Martin Clark being buddies with Joseph Finley, whose money, as Tyler had admitted himself, spoke volumes about what happened within that team.

Ten

Monaco Grand Prix – Monte Carlo – Monaco
May 24th

'This is stupid.' Luke fiddled with his shirt collar as he tried to straighten it in the mirror. His brow furrowed in annoyance, as he stared back at himself. His hair was clean and glossy under the light of his bedroom, and he was clad in an expensive navy suit that Emma had delivered to him that morning. He didn't look too bad if he did say so himself.

'Yes, such a chore spending the afternoon and evening with some of the most beautiful people in the world, whilst you drink free champagne and eat free food. Such hard work.' Luke had spent enough time with Johan to note the sarcasm even if his voice remained as flat as ever.

'How about you go for me then?' Luke bit back as he came around the corner into the lounge where Johan was reclined on the sofa in his loungewear, flicking through the TV channels.

'Sadly my friend, I'm not the one the people want.' He put his hand on his heart like he was wounded by that statement and Luke smiled, his shoulders falling at the release of tension.

'I'm going to murder Emma and Jessie,' Luke said. He didn't mean it but he had done such a good job of avoiding these types of events over the years. Overindulgent, excessive and not his style at all. It turned out his new title and the fact that his new team principal wanted his two drivers to be seen together, meant that Luke had to go. Luke, however, had no interest in parading around pretending to be something he wasn't.

'My car's here.' Luke sighed, resigned to the fact that he had to do this. He felt a dash of nerves course through his system as his polished black shoes clicked on the tiled flooring. 'I guess I'll catch you later.'

'Don't forget to bring me back some numbers from the models!' Johan shouted from the living room.

Luke tutted and shut the door behind him.

Out on the road, a sleek black Mercedes waited for him with Emma stashed inside. She looked exquisite in a navy jumpsuit, gold high heels and jewellery and he didn't hesitate in telling her so. She blushed but only for a moment before she brushed him off and resumed her professional composure.

'I'm not happy with you for this,' Luke said across the back seat. 'You're supposed to be the gatekeeper, to keep me from these terrible ideas.' He was teasing but the underlying tone was clear. Don't do this again.

'Luke, you know as well as I that I work for the team. And Martin was insistent that you be at this event,' she said, scrolling through her e-mails.

'But a fashion show? Really? It could not be any less me,' he grumbled, not ready to give it up.

'And you know, that aside from the race, the Amber Lounge event is the place to be this weekend. Since you're already upset with me, I'm going to tell you now, then hopefully you'll be over it by the time we get there but you and Tyler are doing a photo op and interview together beforehand. Smile that winning smile and suck it up. You can do it. I believe in you.' She didn't sound like she did, or she was too distracted by her phone to care.

'Oh for god's sake. Anything else?'

'Yes, you're wearing Armani,' she turned and grinned, her gold hoop earrings swinging either side of her head. 'Photo op, interview, make up, show, home. Not too hard.'

'Great,' he muttered and turned to look out of the window. The high rises of Monaco passed by a lot slower than they did when he was in the WR19. He couldn't wait to race on Sunday, he loved this track and he also loved that he could walk home from the paddock afterwards and straight into his bed. It was such a test of skill and precision, hitting all the right braking points, all the corners with accuracy and most importantly, avoiding all of the barriers.

The car pulled up outside the Méridien Beach Plaza, a sandy-coloured building with an infinite amount of reflective glass. Photographers swarmed out the front, waiting to pounce on all the celebrities due to attend. Luke got out first and ran around to open the door for Emma, her heel wobbling on the pavement as she found her footing. He held out his arm which she took and the camera flashes started, his name being called as they walked up the carpet together.

'Bet you wish you'd bought a date now,' she said as they crossed the threshold. He could imagine how that would have gone down, Martin no doubt would have been delighted if he'd brought a woman, but a man, he wasn't so sure.

Press lined one wall of the conference room, whilst the other had a white backdrop with the Amber Lounge logo on it. Sonia, the founder of the event, stood to one side, in a deep-cut white dress, overseeing the proceedings. The presenter talked animatedly to Matteo Brambilla and Kyle Kelly, both clad in suits. Kelly's a vibrant shade of pink with a floral shirt and Brambilla, more reserved, in a grey two-piece with a white t-shirt underneath. They laughed and chatted as the press took photos and recorded the interview, the red light on the cameras flashing.

Still holding on to Emma, Luke spotted Jessie, her nose in her phone, dressed up to the nine's too and Martin behind a velvet rope talking with his head close with Tyler's. Luke stopped as he took in his teammate. The black suit fitted him perfectly with little flecks of colour through it and the black t-shirt underneath brought out the blue of his eyes. He looked handsome and the heat inside Luke's chest bloomed for a second before he stamped it out.

Emma tugged at his arm and reluctantly, he walked over to the rest of his group.

'Ah Luke, looking good,' Martin said as Tyler's eyes landed on him, skirting up and down, taking all of him in. Luke ignored him, not willing to give in and not wanting to challenge him with his own stare. He remembered their conversation on the beach in Barcelona even if Tyler didn't.

Brambilla and Kelly moved on and the presenter looked over to them. Luke pulled his suit jacket down and adjusted the button as Tyler strolled up to her.

'Remember, you like each other,' Emma hissed before Luke took a step. He spun to stare at her and she gave him a sheepish smile and two thumbs up. He shook his head but it had worked, he smiled to himself and when he reached Tyler and the presenter, he was in a better mood.

'Well if it isn't the two best-looking teammates on the grid,' she said, beaming at the cameras. 'Please don't tell anyone else I said that,' she stage-whispered and for the small smile Luke gave her, Tyler gave her a big bright one.

'And if the press is to be believed, the biggest rivals as well?' She winked and Tyler grinned again, this time he reached round and put a hand on Luke's back, pulling him closer, enough that Luke breathed in the deep musky scent of his aftershave and he felt that fire flower again. This time he knew it wasn't anger but he didn't want to admit what he thought it was.

'It's great to be here,' Luke said, clearing his throat. 'The Monaco Grand Prix is iconic and it's incredible to have such a fantastic event to run alongside it.'

'Sonia and the team have done a wonderful job.' Tyler winked at her, in a way that made her cheeks turn a deep shade of pink. Luke had no doubt that that wink and that look had made many a woman do whatever he wanted. 'And to be raising money for such a wonderful cause as well, we're excited to be here.'

'You're both doing the fashion show later,' she continued, relishing the attention from Tyler.

'I can't speak for Luke, but let's hope I don't trip over my own feet.'

'I'm sure you'll both be wonderful,' she said with a smile. 'Can you talk me through what you're wearing?'

'I'm glad you asked,' Tyler said. 'My suit is by an up-and-coming British Designer, Ben Dawson, a good friend of mine. This is the Finley, a slim fit, single-breasted three-piece suit designed and created specifically for this event.'

The presenter nodded, impressed.

'I love the fabric, a wool blend, in charcoal with flecks of red, blue and white,' he finished, tugging on the lapels. 'We'll be auctioning it off after the event with all proceeds going to tonight's charity.'

'That's fantastic, and you, Luke?' The presenter turned to him but he was staring at Tyler.

'Armani.' He repeated what Emma had told him in the car, the single word seeming insufficient after Tyler's speech. Tyler gave him a small smile, amusement dancing in his eyes.

Shortly after, the two men were carted off to another room which was full to the brim of models clad in little more than swimwear, chairs and makeup strewed across every surface. Hairdressers fluffed, gelled and combed wisps into place. Luke was careered off to one side of the room and Tyler to another to be briefed and made up, and to ensure they were as perfect as they appeared to be.

Through the whole ordeal, Luke's eyes wandered over the crowd, catching Tyler flirting with the Victoria's Secret models that were hanging around. He saw him laughing with some celebrities he was sure he'd seen before somewhere and at one point, Tyler was flattering Petra, who was dressed in a sunflower yellow ball gown, as she was presenting the evening show.

It wasn't until Luke nervously waited backstage for the fashion show to start that he saw Tyler walk over to him, his eyes down to the ground like he wasn't sure of what he was doing.

'Hey,' Tyler said as he approached Luke to stand beside him, away from everyone else. 'Still doing the strong silent type thing then?' Tyler joked but the smile slipped from his face when Luke didn't answer. The muscle in Luke's jaw twitched as he tried to hold in the smile. 'Damn I've never been this nervous, not even before my first race, this is so far out of my comfort zone.'

'Really?' The word slipped out of Luke's mouth before he had a chance to think it through. Tyler looked up and their eyes locked, searching. The intensity was too much, and Luke settled his gaze somewhere off in the distance.

'Do I look like I do fashion shows on the weekend?'

'You looked pretty comfortable back there with all the models, forgive me for thinking this used to be your day-to-day before you got dragged into driving a car on Sundays instead.' Tyler's face didn't change as he absorbed Luke's words. 'I'm nervous too.' Luke dropped his guard for a moment, needing reassurance that he wasn't alone in this and without Johan to give him a pep talk, or Emma who hadn't been allowed to hang out backstage, he was stuck with Tyler.

'You don't need to be nervous, you look very handsome in that suit.' Tyler said, no hint of a joke in his voice, forcing Luke to turn to look at him again. Luke searched his face for the angle he was playing but couldn't see anything malicious. Whenever Tyler was around, he felt like he was walking on a tightrope. He could slip at any second and he had no idea how to keep the balance.

'I take it you don't do these things very often?' Tyler asked.

Luke shook his head.

'No, I'd much rather be down at the local pub having a cold beer. I grew up in a semi in Buckinghamshire, my parents had to work two jobs so I could race and even then sometimes it wasn't enough. I'm still not used to all this. There's too much champagne, too many people pretending to be something they're not.'

'Are you? Pretending to be something you're not?' Tyler stared at Luke and Luke felt heat rise up his neck.

'With this suit on I am. I can't remember the last time I wore one.'

'The FIA prize giving last year?'

Luke laughed.

'Highly likely.' He tugged at his jacket, trying to loosen it around his shoulders. 'With David it was all about the racing, it was low-key, easy. I'm not into the glitz and glamour

Martin wants Wilson racing to be part of.'

'I get it,' Tyler said as someone pushed past him. He took a step towards Luke, Tyler's body heat radiating against him. 'You're like a fish out of water. You've taken a step into my world, like I came crashing into yours. Maybe we're more similar than we think, both needing to be in control of the situation.' Their eyes met, stilling as their gazes locked onto one another. Tyler's dipped down to Luke's neck, where he could feel the searing heat scorching his veins.

Tyler reached up and adjusted Luke's collar, untucking it from the lapels as Luke stood stock still, his mind blank. Tyler's hand brushed the underside of Luke's chin as he pulled back. The skin Tyler had touched rippled with goosebumps as they both realised what he had done. The air turned thick around them and Luke struggled to swallow.

'Luke, you're up,' came a voice that felt so far in the distance it didn't penetrate the fog in which Luke found himself.

'Luke,' Tyler said, taking a step back. Luke shook his head, clearing it of whatever he was thinking. The good thing was that it distracted him enough to walk down the catwalk that hovered above the pool, the water glinting in the late afternoon sun. He didn't even register the thousands of eyes that watched him put one foot in front of the other on the white gloss floor because his thoughts were still backstage. He turned where he was told to and walked down a side wing where he waited for Tyler to follow in his footsteps, then Kelly, Brambilla, Lewandowski and Nabiyev. The drivers lined up on each wing and waited as the Victoria's Secrets models paraded down the catwalk and came to stand beside a driver before they all went backstage again to rapturous applause.

Luke stepped off the stage and Petra appeared beside him, fluttering her lashes like she had something in her eye.

'Well don't you look handsome,' she said, sidling up to him as much as her meringue dress would let her.

'Thanks, Petra, you look very…sunny in that dress.' He wasn't sure if it was a compliment but she took it as one as she giggled, feigning modesty.

'Are you staying for the dinner? I will be hosting the evening so maybe you could save me a dance?' she continued and he felt terrible that she didn't get the hint.

'I won't be I'm afraid, big day tomorrow and I need my beauty rest,' he said trying to move aside and end the conversation but she stepped in front of him, blocking the route.

'You don't need any more beauty rest, you're already as beautiful as possible,' she smiled and he strained one back, wondering how he was going to leave.

'Isn't he just?' Tyler's smooth voice came from somewhere behind his right shoulder. 'I'm so sorry Petra, I'm going to have to steal Luke away, team business,' he added and although she looked disappointed, she, like everyone else, couldn't deny the charm of Tyler Finley.

She stepped aside and Tyler guided Luke towards the exit.

'Thanks,' he said. He couldn't understand why words evaded him when he was in conversation with Tyler. He could sit and talk to journalists for hours, even minutes after a race he could process his thoughts and articulate them but with Tyler, his mind was blank. He struggled to have a normal conversation, he didn't even want anything clever to say, just something. Now that the harsh contempt he had felt for him had waned, he was left tongue-tied and looking like a monosyllabic idiot.

It turned out, it was Tyler who could silence him with one look these days, not the other way around.

'You're welcome, now if you could let me win tomorrow.' Tyler grinned, and Luke burst out laughing. A proper laugh, a real one, because he couldn't help himself.

'If I win tomorrow,' Luke said. 'I want a suit like that.' He pointed to what Tyler was wearing, feeling warmth flood his cheeks.

The door swung open and on the other side, Emma stood waiting, looking nervous. But she relaxed when she saw Luke's smile and the two of them chatting.

'Not so bad then?'

'It was awful, can I go home now?' he smiled and she slipped her hand through his arm.

TYLER FINLEY: THE BEST ROOKIE IN FORMULA ONE HISTORY?
How is the newest member of the grid consistently this good?

By Sara Holdsworth

Date published: June 1st

Tyler Finley of Wilson Racing has certainly made a splash in the big boy pool so far this season. The Rookie, who had never competed in Formula One before, signed with championship-winning team Wilson Racing last October and has since competed in arguably the fastest car on the grid.

Son of billionaire business tycoon Joseph Finley, Tyler has silenced the critics who claimed he was only in the sport due to his father's money. After another win at the historical circuit of Monte Carlo at the weekend, Finley has a total of three wins out of the first six races, landing him in second place in the world championship, twenty-six points behind current championship leader and Finley's teammate, Luke Anderson.

Is Tyler Finley the best rookie Formula One has ever seen? The stats speak for themselves. Very few drivers have achieved podiums let alone wins on their debut in Formula One, yet Finley has taken it all in his stride, finishing in first place three times, and second place twice. Some have compared him to the great Sir Lewis Hamilton who succeeded in winning two races in his first year at McLaren back in 2006.

Martin Clark, team principal of Wilson Racing said: "Finley is fast, he has proven that fairly consistently since the beginning of the season. If anyone is questioning whether he deserves his seat still, then they aren't paying attention." Clark's close relationship with Joseph Finley has often been rumoured to be the reason Tyler got his seat in Formula One but it would seem, no matter the team, Finley would have put on a show.

Current World Champion and championship leader Luke Anderson is being schooled in how to succeed in your rookie season. In his first year in Formula One, he stacked up one third place and finished the championship in seventh place. "I want the best result for the team," Anderson said, "and if Finley can help us achieve another constructor's championship then great."

The two drivers were part of many who participated in the Amber Lounge fashion show last Friday, wearing designer suits as they paraded down the catwalk with models, a far cry from the overalls they usually wear. "It was great fun, I've never done anything like this before and I'm so pleased I got to share the experience with some of the other guys on the grid," Matteo Brambilla gushed about the event before qualifying on Saturday. "We raised a lot of money for charity as well, so win-win."

Finley is modest about his achievements and when questioned about his ability to win he attributed the work to his team. "They do such a great job, at the track and back at the factory, they work hard and none of this would happen without them. We've got a great team around us and we want to win. I want to win." He was coy when asked about the championship and his prospects of winning it.

"The season is long, we've had six races and things can still change. Luke [Anderson] is a very fast driver and he will not give it up easily. We'll see how it all pans out."

With the next race in Canada looming, time will tell if Tyler Finley is the best rookie F1 has ever seen and who will come out on top at the end of this season.

Eleven

Canadian Grand Prix - Circuit Gilles Villeneuve – Montréal
June 9th

The helicopter circled above the circuit on the Ile Notre Dame in the middle of the St Lawrence River. The man-made island was packed under the Sunday morning sunshine, perfect conditions for race day.

'It's time,' Emma said from the doorway.

'Do I have to?' Luke groaned. The huge grin on Johan's face didn't go unnoticed. He and Luke had been warming up with some stretches, getting ready for the race start, still a few hours away.

'Yep, come on, get up,' Emma said, holding her hand out like she was helping a toddler. With a hunch to his shoulders, Luke stood and followed Emma out into the corridor, sighing with resignation. Tyler's door was open and the room was empty. His race suit hung on the front of the cupboard, the little British flag on the belt beside his surname. Luke's eyes lingered on it longer than necessary, and he caught himself wondering if his race suit smelt like the expensive aftershave he'd worn on the beach in Barcelona.

'Do I have to act surprised?' Luke asked as they walked through the quiet motorhome. It had buzzed with activity all morning, throngs of fans, celebrities, and sponsors filling the café, the hospitality areas, and everywhere in between.

'You can if you want.' She shrugged. 'You could at least try and look happy about it.' Luke grimaced, baring his teeth.

'Yeah, don't do that,' Johan said.

They stepped out of the motorhome into the paddock and the water lapped up against the wall behind them. The Gilles Villeneuve circuit was built on the disused island after the Expo 67, the track was tight and twisty with long straights. It was hard on the brakes but popular with the teams and Luke could already hear the fans beyond the pits.

He pulled his sunglasses down over his eyes and followed Emma into the back of the brand-new paddock facility. It had been built with the Grand Prix in mind and it was beautiful. Replacing the temporary structures that were used during the race weekend, the concrete, glass, and wooden building was a true reflection of modern architecture and green innovation. Luke had been lucky enough to get a tour led by the designers at the beginning of the week as part of a sponsorship event.

Inside though, it looked exactly like every other race venue, the temporary walls the team brought with them were up, creating rooms and storage. His race number was bold in purple against the white surfaces.

The minute Luke stepped over the threshold he saw some of the team lined up down the corridor. As he approached they clapped and cheered.

Luke refused to let his discomfort show as he walked between them, shaking hands with some as he did so. Like an estuary, they opened out as he reached the main garage, Martin standing front and centre with Dash, Jessie, and Vicki. Luke mimicked their smiles as he approached and laid eyes on the huge cake between them. The camera crews were there and the crowd outside cheered.

'Happy Birthday Luke,' Martin said, presenting him with the cake. It was a large slab, covered in white icing with the words "Happy birthday" scrolled on it in purple. The rest of the team echoed Martin's words.

The clapping died down and Luke stuck the knife Jessie handed him into the cake.

'Right back to work everyone, we have a race to win,' Martin said then someone shouted: 'Wait!'

The crowd quietened and Luke spun to see who had spoken. He noticed the cheeky grin on Jamie's face and groaned. 'We haven't sung Happy Birthday yet.'

'How could I forget, are we ready?' Martin laughed.

The whole team launched into the song and the crowd outside joined in. Luke glanced at all the faces staring back at him and landed on Tyler in the corner, hiding behind his mechanics, his lips barely moving. Tyler's face was impassive but his eyes locked on Luke, sending a spear of electricity through him.

Beside him, Tyler's Dad stood with his arms crossed, looking over the celebration with furrowed brows. He was clad in a pale pink shirt pulled tight over his bulging stomach and black slacks. He looked like the businessman that he was, and like Tyler's unofficial bodyguard. Luke noticed the tension in Tyler's shoulders as he stood straight, mimicking his father's posture. His jaw twitched as he locked it shut once the singing had stopped and sympathy flooded Luke as he imagined being under that much pressure.

Luke looked down at the cake he was still holding, then around for somewhere to put it. When he looked back up Tyler and his dad had vanished.

'I'll take it,' Jamie said still grinning. He carried it over to the team who hacked into it and Emma sidled up to him.

'Last thing and then I'll leave you alone,' she said walking to the back of the garage. 'VIP meet and greet.'

Luke followed her, walking past Johan who had a large slice of cake in his hand already.

They headed upstairs to the open-air level which was decked out with comfy armchairs, high-top tables and stools, and potted plants. The bar over the back was packed with guests and some had even taken their seats ready for the race start on the balcony looking over the pit lane and finish line.

The group they were meeting wasn't hard to spot. Three middle-aged men stood with Martin and Joseph Finley. They all wore variations of the same pressed shirt with slacks, holding beers, their cheeks a shade of dark pink from the alcohol. Their laughter dominated the area as they slapped each other on the shoulders.

As they approached, Luke heard Joseph Finley boasting.

'He will win, there's no other option. Tyler is the best driver on the grid, no doubt about it, isn't that true Martin?' He nudged Martin who wore an expression Luke couldn't decipher and Emma cleared her throat.

'Ah Luke, the birthday boy,' Martin said trying to hide his embarrassment behind a fake smile. These men were his friends, but Luke was his driver.

'The famous Luke Anderson,' one of them said, his hair so thin Luke could see his scalp beneath the poor attempt at a combover.

'Gentlemen.' Luke nodded at each of them in turn, making sure to keep eye contact as he did so.

'How do you think it'll go then today? Tough championship for you this year,' said another, nudging Joseph Finley with a grin that made him look like a toad.

'We'll give it our best,' Luke replied.

'That's the media answer, son, give us the real answer. Do you think you're fast enough to beat our young lad Tyler?' combover man asked.

Luke quirked an eyebrow but didn't reply, prompting Martin to intervene.

'Leave the poor boy alone.' Martin tried to laugh it off but Luke was annoyed.

'I have a bone to pick with you Martin actually,' Toad man said. 'Where's all the fanny? With two strapping young lads in your team, you'd think you could pull in a bit more talent than this.' The guy roared as he looked around the group of VIPs and took another huge gulp of his drink.

'Yeah, we didn't come all this way to stare at the same stuff we see across the boardroom.'

'We run a racing team, not a brothel.' Martin tried to keep his tone light but Luke bristled.

Emma glared at Martin who turned a shade of red as one of the men said: 'You've got to tell them who's boss buddy, or maybe the media's right.'

Martin strained a smile, his eyes flitting between Luke and his friends but he didn't say a word.

'Enjoy the race gentlemen,' Luke said, turning to leave. He'd heard enough but he knew better than to speak his mind.

'Aren't you going to sign anything for us?' the last one asked with a smirk.

'What would you like me to sign?' Luke asked, his face deadpan.

'Don't offer to sign John's pecs whatever you do, no one needs to see that at this time of the morning,' thinning hair guy said, like he was the funniest man in the room.

'Or any other time of day,' Toad Man added.

'That'll be all Luke, thanks,' Martin said and Luke took his leave, not wanting to be subjected to any more of this poor excuse for banter.

'Spoilsport Mart, thank goodness the better driver is on his way...' he might have lowered his voice but it wasn't enough for Luke to not overhear.

'Arseholes,' Luke muttered as they got to the stairs. Emma pulled the door open as Tyler jumped up the last few steps. The two men stood face to face and Luke glared at him before sidestepping and walking away.

'You go get ready,' Emma said as they reached the bottom. 'Like Martin said, you've got a race to win.'

There was no birthday luck for Luke and the race was another to forget. After the shambles of Monaco where he'd started on the front row and finished third on what should have easily been another Wilson one-two.

He had no idea why he lacked so much pace. It felt like he was driving his dad's lawnmower around the Canadian circuit. He couldn't keep up with Tyler and spent most of the race with Lewandowski stuck to his rear end.

Behind the visor, he felt his frustration increase with every missed apex, every second he was late on the pedal, every time he had to check his mirrors for Lewandowski.

The only saving grace was that he finished in second, but the twenty seconds between himself and Finley felt like he was down in tenth. The result may have looked good but the performance wasn't there and he could feel it.

The team was pleased with the one-two but Luke found himself stuck beneath a black cloud. The frustrations of the last few races had turned his mood sour.

'Are you coming out back for the team celebrations?' Emma asked as she walked him to the motorhome after his post-race press duties. 'It's going to be hilarious. Martin made a bet with Tyler that if he won, he had to jump into the river.' Emma chuckled at the prospect. Luke had zero inclination to join in with the fun. It had been the worst birthday ever and that was saying something for someone who never celebrated it.

'I might pass.'

'Luke come on, it's your birthday. Are you going out later to celebrate?'

'No, I'm going home.'

'On your birthday?' she asked, her eyebrows flying up to her hairline.

'Not a big birthday fan,' he said and she looked at him like he was crazy.

As he sat on his bench, he heard the team cheer and the splash of Tyler jumping into the river. A few moments later there was another splash and another. He peered out of the window and saw Martin, and Tyler's race engineer bobbing up and down in the water beside him.

Luke packed the few belongings he had in his bag and wheeled his suitcase out of the motorhome to the paddock gates.

He headed for the airport and wasted time in the business class lounge, staring off into the distance, the race replaying in his mind.

Once settled in his seat, he put his headphones on and tuned the world out. The plane took off and the pressure pushed down on his shoulders as it left the Canadian tarmac. The sky outside darkened the further the plane rose and Luke closed his eyes.

He knew the rest of the crew were way back at the other end of the plane, the travel team having booked their seats all at once. If he had it his way, Luke would have the whole crew up here with him because one: it would reduce the number of people who gawked at him whenever he needed a piss, and two: they deserved it as much as he did. They worked just as hard, if not harder over the race weekend.

A soft tap on the shoulder woke him from his slumber. When Luke looked up, an air attendant smiled down at him, holding a bottle of champagne. He pulled his headphones off.

'Hi, I'm sorry to disturb you, I have a gift for you.'

Luke's eyebrows quirked up as she handed him the bottle. He turned it over in his hand. It was a nineteen fifty-nine Dom Perignon. Luke didn't know much about champagne but he knew it was expensive. Round the neck, a little card hung from gold thread. He picked it up and opened it with his thumb and finger, reading the scrawl.

Happy Birthday Luke, and I'm sorry for whatever my
dad may or may not have said – Tyler

Warmth spread through his limbs, a settling sense of calm after the rubbish weekend as Luke re-read the card. He undid the knot in the gold thread and slipped the card into his bag before putting the bottle on the floor. He pulled his earphones back on and closed his eyes.

He felt a pang of loneliness as the plane jolted in the turbulence. After a few minutes, the feeling not dissipating, he pulled out his phone and scrolled through his messages. He found the thread he was looking for and typed out a message to his sister. He hadn't seen her since before Barcelona when he'd popped in after a day at the factory and he missed her.

Not finding the sleep he was looking for, he turned on the screen in front of him and scrolled through the movie selection. *Brave* came up but one look at Merida and he couldn't shake Sara Holdsworth from his mind so settled on *Gnomeo and Juliet*.

Twelve

Monte Carlo - Monaco
June 12th

Luke pulled hard on the resistance band. His bicep contracted then released. He pulled again. This time harder. He let out a grunt, guttural and feral. His eyebrows pulled together as he narrowed his stare until he was focusing on a link connecting the metal poles that formed the barrier on the edge of the cliff.

He switched arms and pulled again, sweat beading on his forehead with the effort and the blazing mid-morning Mediterranean sun.

'Okay, you can stop now,' Johan said from a little further away where he was videoing the workout both for Instagram (under Emma's instruction to post more) and so they could review it at a later date and see the progress.

Luke did another ten on each arm to prove a point.

He was frustrated and the resistant bands, being strangled in his strong fists, were taking the brunt of it.

Everything was falling apart.

He'd never had a lack of performance without understanding where it came from. For some reason, Finley was managing to do things with the car that he couldn't and Luke was aggravated by his poor results.

He let go of the resistance bands and went straight into some squat jumps. Johan sighed, knowing better than to try and stop him, and sat down on the immaculate paving of the Promenade of Champions.

Luke's legs bent, thighs bulging against his shorts, sweat giving his skin a sheen as he pressed out of the squat into a high jump, his feet leaving at least a foot's gap between themselves and the pavement. He landed with a thud and went again.

'How long are we going to be out here? My fair Finnish skin cannot survive this for much longer.' Johan squinted up to the sky, hiding his eyes behind his hand as he stared at Luke.

'You can go home if you want,' Luke puffed between movements. He did two more jumps, then fell to the ground and started doing some push-ups.

'You know your problem isn't with your fitness,' Johan said with a lazy drawl. 'You're the fittest you've ever been. Your problem is up here.' He tapped the side of his head with his finger. Luke paused for a moment to look up before resuming his push-ups.

'I don't know how to control this.' He tapped the side of his head too. 'This, however,' he waved his hand around his body, 'I do.'

He lunged, this time wilder, uncontrolled.

'Okay, stop. You're going to hurt yourself.' Johan pulled

him out of the lunge and put his hands on either side of his shoulders. 'What's going on?'

'I want to win and I'm not winning.'

'This is not the first time you've not been winning. What else is going on?' Johan let go of him and Luke walked over to the barrier and leant up against it. His arms locked straight, his head bent over and his eyes closed.

He didn't know how to voice what he was feeling. He didn't even know what he was feeling. All he knew was that he couldn't focus, everything seemed hazy, fleeting thoughts and feelings swirled around inside him and he was struggling to keep it all in. It felt like he was hovering an inch above the ground at all times, like the oxygen wasn't quite making it to his brain so he could concentrate on what he wanted to.

He was distracted and he didn't know why.

Nothing had changed. The team was the same and the car was better. Was he, Luke Anderson usually impermeable to pressure, finally feeling the weight of it? Was the expectation of defending his World Championship too much? Was this what was going to break him?

He breathed out through his mouth. He didn't know what to tell Johan.

'You're still leading the championship,' Johan started.

'Just...'

'But you're still first. You're the only person stopping you from winning these races. The car's fine, your strength and stamina are incredible. It's you, standing in your way.' There was a slight edge of frustration to Johan's calm and monotone voice which seemed to snap Luke out of his current trance.

'I'd argue that Tyler Finley's stopping me from winning.'

'I would argue you're letting him,' Johan snapped back, as he tidied away the equipment. 'Go for a run. I will see you back at the flat for lunch.'

Johan walked off and left Luke staring out to the sea.

He took a deep breath and filled his lungs with the salty air, letting Johan's words sit with him for a moment. If he was standing in his own way he didn't know how or why. He didn't know how to stop it or how to regain control of whatever was happening. He was weary and they'd only done a third of the season. How was he supposed to claw it back from here?

'Nice day for it.' Luke stiffened at the familiar voice behind him, not daring to turn around. The warmth from a body met Luke's arm as the person leant up against the railings too.

'I didn't know you lived here.' The words escaped Luke's lips, like dribble on his pillow at night, without him being able to control it.

'I don't. I was down this way, you know, so thought I'd pop in and see what the fuss was about.'

'And you happened to find me here?' Luke turned his head and stared at Tyler's profile. The slope of his nose, the curve of his lips, his eyes reflecting the brilliant sun not unlike the water that spread out in front of them.

'Ah, well...' Tyler ran a hand through his thick black hair, pushing it off his face, and turned to Luke looking a little sheepish. 'If I'm perfectly honest, I saw on your Instagram that you were here and I thought, hey why not? It doesn't seem like the best idea now, but you know, here we are.'

'I bloody told Johan not to post it live,' Luke grumbled, shifting his weight from one foot to another. Tyler's lips pulled back to reveal his straight, white teeth and Luke mimicked him.

'That's true, you never know, some crazy fan might come and find you here or stalk you without you knowing.'

'Is that what you are? A crazy fan?'

'Wohwoh, I'm not sure I would go that far. I'd expect you to be nicer to me if I was.'

'I'm nice to you,' Luke countered.

'That's debatable.' Tyler was gaining confidence, leaning one elbow on the railing and turning his body towards Luke, amusement dancing in his eyes. The photo Luke's sister had shown him all those months ago flashed through his mind and he wondered if Tyler looked like that under the designer blue t-shirt he was wearing. He caught himself staring before Tyler noticed.

'Thanks for the champagne.' Luke ran his hand through his hair and then pulled his heel up to his bum to stretch out his quad which was cooling down and seizing up. Tyler eyed him and nodded before Luke said, 'I was about to go for a run. I guess I'll see you at the weekend.'

'Or I could come with you?' Tyler offered, shrugging his shoulders like it was no big deal. Luke thought it over a moment.

'Don't you get enough pleasure beating me on track? Do you feel the need to best me in my workouts too?'

Tyler laughed and tapped him on the arm with the back of his hand before saying: 'Come on then buddy, let's see what you've got.' He skipped into the first step and was a few metres up the road before Luke turned to stare after him. He shook his head and sprinted to catch up.

'How are you feeling about the weekend?' Luke asked as they fell into step with each other, with the same stride length and natural pace.

'I guess the question would be, how do you feel about it?'

Was he expecting Tyler to tell him his secrets on how to get the car to work for him? Probably not. Johan was right, Luke's issues had nothing to do with the car and all to do with his mindset. A future champion thinks like he's already a champion and Luke was already a champion.

He knew, hands down, that he had it in him to do this again. He needed to forget about the guy who pounded the pavement with him, who had sought him out in the whole of Monaco to what? Chat with him? Go for a run? Maybe Tyler was playing an angle after all, trying to get more info out of Luke since he avoided him most of the time at the race track.

Luke shook the thoughts from his head. Maybe Tyler was trying to keep the peace, keep both sides of the garage working together like Luke had. They wanted to win. It made sense, maybe Luke should have tried harder, after all, Tyler had apologised in Barcelona for the whole Australia fiasco and he'd sent him champagne for his birthday.

Luke felt Tyler's body heat close beside him, their arms fluttering together when one had to move for a pedestrian. The heat inside his stomach swelled each time they touched and Luke was pretty sure it was no longer anger that was causing that fire to ignite.

Trying to break free from the current he found himself in, Luke accelerated and left Tyler behind. It took less than a second for Tyler's lightning reactions and competitive nature to push him to catch up. When he did, Tyler shoved him and they both laughed.

'Trying to lose me already?' Tyler said and Luke smiled too even if his eyes were full of confusion. They ran past the hotel they'd both been at a few weeks before, walking down the runway of the Amber Lounge, and continued out of the city.

They sprinted for a bit then slowed to a jog, not stopping until they'd been going for half an hour, the sound of the waves, the traffic, and their heavy breathing keeping them company.

Luke arrived at the Pointe du Cap Martin first, Tyler a second behind him, both breathing hard, their chests rising and falling fast after the exertion.

'That's the result I'm expecting on Sunday,' Luke said, his hands on his hips walking around in a circle at the edge of the rocky cliff. A lonely man sat with his fishing rod in the sea, he didn't even bother to see who had spoken, lost in his own world.

'Not if I can help it.' Tyler grinned and Luke felt his eyes drawn to Tyler's lips, snagging on the parted curves. He turned away, shaking his head, willing his heart to slow down so he could catch his breath.

'Why are you here?' Luke demanded, losing the smile, narrowing his eyes again, looking for answers on Tyler's face. Tyler shuffled, turning his back on Luke and walking away, trying to find an answer.

'Jessie's quite persistent that we need to be presenting a united front for the press and I thought, that maybe if we spent some time together away from the cameras you might…warm to me a bit more. I know I messed up in Australia, I'm really sorry about that.'

'You've already apologised.'

'I have?' Tyler looked startled, searching through his mind for when he'd done that, and when he drew a blank his face creased up.

'In Barcelona, on the beach?'

'I don't remember that.' Tyler ran a hand over the back of his neck. 'Okay, now it's even more awkward.'

'It's fine,' Luke said, keeping his eyes on the horizon and not looking at Tyler.

'We're very different. I think everyone can see that, but surely, we can find some common ground on something. What's your favourite colour?' he said.

'Black.'

'That's not a colour.'

'Yes, it is.'

'What's your favourite drink?'

'Water.'

'Of course, it is,' Tyler rolled his eyes and Luke tried hard to keep the smirk inside. 'Sports team?'

'Wilson Racing'

'Apart from ours…'

'I don't follow any teams, I like solo sports like snowboarding or running. Does Team GB count as a team?'

'I'm going to say yes because then we can agree that at the Olympics, Team GB is the superior team.' He grinned and Luke felt the heat again which irritated him beyond belief. He wanted to feel nothing when it came to Tyler, neither good nor bad. He wanted to feel neutral, that was what he needed to aim for to sort his head out.

'What else? Favourite race track?'

'This is stupid,' Luke said getting ready to head back towards the city.

'Favourite track?'

'Austria.'

'Did you make that up?' Tyler fell into step with him as they took the route in reverse. 'I thought you were more of a Spa kinda guy, you know fearless. Actually, maybe Mexico, I bet you love that stadium section when they all cheer for you.' Luke gave him the look, the one Tyler had accused him of using to silence him back on the beach.

'Okay, maybe not,' Tyler faltered. 'Look, I'm a nice guy, I promise. We've got that press day coming up and I want it to go well otherwise Jessie may have my balls on a block at the end of it.'

Luke winced but his lips curved up. He'd love to see that. He wanted it to go well too because no one wanted to upset Jessie and right now he couldn't see how it could go wrong. He liked this Tyler, the one who laughed, who spoke without thinking and let his mouth run wild. The one whose perfect lips curled up at the corner, letting a shadow of a dimple graze his cheek.

Liking his teammate was good to a point but they were

still competitors, they were still fighting for the same thing out there on track and he needed to focus on that. He couldn't let whatever was happening inside himself distract from it any longer.

Thirteen

**French Grand Prix – Circuit Paul Ricard – Le Castellet
June 23rd**

The garage was packed with bodies, the front wing was being put on the car, and the drinks bag fitted behind the seat. Lots of people bustling around getting the cooling fans and the tyre warmers onto the grid trolleys, polishing the purple and black car until it gleamed under the fluorescence. The VIP area at the back was filling up with friends, family, and celebrities and it took Luke a moment before he laid eyes on the person he was looking for.

Nick waved when she saw him, pushing through the small group to the front of the pod to hug her brother over the half wall separating them from the working area. Her hair was loose and sweat beaded on her forehead. It was a hot day in the south of France, a stone's throw from Marseille.

Luke and Johan had driven the gifted Wilson sports car he'd received after winning the championship along the southern coastline, taking the scenic route past Cannes and Saint Tropez, soaking in the glorious sunshine.

After his run with Tyler, Luke felt more in control and had managed to get his head back in the right place before the race. He hadn't avoided him on Thursday doing press, instead, they exchanged pleasantries and as Luke dodged Petra, who seemed intent on catching him alone, Tyler helped him escape. The atmosphere in the garage was different, more harmonious and fun. Luke couldn't tell if his efforts were paying off or whether it was because the summer break was looming, but he felt like the elastic had pinged between the two drivers and it had released everyone else to feel less on edge too.

It was race day and Luke had been chilling in his room with Johan and his sister but he'd been pulled off into a last-minute interview leaving Nick to fend for herself for an hour. Although she was in more than capable hands with the hospitality team, she seemed pleased to see him again, even briefly. He dumped his helmet and balaclava on his seat, his overalls hanging down from the waist, and smiled.

'I'm glad you could make it,' he said above the noise.

'Me too.' It wasn't her first time at a Grand Prix weekend but it had become few and far between when she and his parents could make it out to watch him race in person. They were all busy with work, projects, and their own lives. After so many years of sacrifice to support him and his career, his passion, he didn't mind that they were taking some time back. They'd been at under half of the races last year and that had been nice but he understood why they weren't there as much this year.

He was World Champion, he'd achieved what he set out to back when he first started racing competitively. But it was nice to have Nick there at the French Grand Prix. A short flight and she'd be home by tea time. It was one of the best things about being back in Europe. That and being able to drive to this race rather than getting on another plane.

Luke's eyes found Tyler as he and Vicki entered the garage, his arm around her shoulders, Vicki blushing at something he'd said and Luke's stomach turned.

Nick followed his gaze and almost fell over the half wall in excitement as she grabbed hold of Luke's shirt.

'Please introduce me,' she said in an excited whisper and he saw a flash of teenage Nicola, screaming and bouncing on the balls of her feet at a One Direction concert. He smirked which seemed to catch Tyler's eye as he looked over to them right when Nick stared at him. Her cheeks flushed a deep red and she flicked her eyes back to Luke.

'Oh my god, he saw us.' Her hands flew to her mouth as she tried not to watch but Luke could sense he was coming their way.

'Get a grip woman.' He laughed when Tyler reached them.

'Hey,' Tyler said, his own helmet on his arm, his overalls hanging off his hips. The sight did something to Luke's insides that he couldn't ignore. He'd seen plenty of drivers with their overalls clinging to their hips but none of them made his pulse accelerate quite like Tyler did.

'Tyler,' Luke was sure he saw Nick bob up and down, 'this is my sister, Nicola.'

Luke watched the exchange, half amused half surprised as his composed and strong-willed sister lost all sense of herself in front of Tyler Finley. She grinned, blushed, and forgot to say anything when he asked her how she was.

'I can see who got all the looks in the family,' Tyler said holding onto her hand for longer than was necessary. 'Luke, you could have told me your sister was this good looking.'

Something fizzed and popped inside of Luke that didn't

make him feel great but it was fleeting because Vicki touched his shoulder to get his attention. It was time.

'Are you hanging about afterwards?' Tyler asked Nick, 'I'd love to get to know you more.' She nodded so hard her head almost fell off and he walked to his side of the garage waving at her, that gorgeous smile on his lips again.

'Pinch me,' she said sighing, 'did that just happen?'

'Good god,' Luke breathed, wedging his earplugs in and pulling his balaclava on. 'I'll catch you later.'

In a split second, she switched back into his sister as she said: 'Good luck! Go beat that son of a...' The last word got lost in the layers of his helmet as he pulled it on but he smiled all the same.

The Wilson-branded headphones she'd been given were a vibrant purple, she slid them on, tucking her long hair behind her ears, and rested on the ledge, ready to watch him race.

He completed an out lap, assessing the track and the conditions to see if anything had changed from the day before. He attuned his senses to the car to see how it felt and if he needed to make any adjustments. Once parked on the grid, Jamie helped him out of the car and took his helmet as Luke found shade beneath the umbrella Johan held up.

With his back to the crowd and the grandstands, Luke sat by the side wall and watched the grid from afar, trying to keep cool under the sunshade. He returned Lorenzo Nunez's wave, a Porsche Supercup driver, who'd been around the paddock for over a decade. The thirty-five year old was a talented driver but had never quite managed to get his name in the history books. A shame considering the promise he'd held at the beginning of his career.

Headphones on and head down, he closed his eyes and ran through the lap in his mind again. Corner one, sweeping into two, braking for three...

He was starting on pole but that was no guarantee with

Tyler right beside him on the front row and Lewandowski lined up behind him. The car had felt good yesterday when he'd been slinging it around the lap and managed to stick it at the top of the timing boards and he was quietly confident about their chances today. The sun was out, the heat worked well for the WR19 and there were no signs of rain anywhere nearby. But with fifty-three laps to complete, Luke kept his expectations in check.

The media circled, angling for an interview but he refused to meet their probing stares. He didn't want to be disturbed, he was zoned into the race, running through the plan, the track, and the corners. Blocking out the sound of the crowd, the helicopters overhead, the music from the entertainment.

Johan tapped him on the shoulder when it was time to head to the front for the national anthem and the End Racism display that was rolled out at the start of each race. Luke loved the message, but he didn't love that it only seemed to matter when the cameras were rolling.

He stood beside the other drivers, his eyes finding Tyler in the line-up, as an opera singer belted out La Marseillaise. The crowd joined in filling the air with music and when it stopped the horns blared from the stands, and the smoke flares lit up and covered the track with blue, red, and white smoke for Moreau, the local man who was lining up in fifth.

Then it was time to get in the car and Luke allowed himself one last look over to Tyler on the opposite bank before pulling his overalls up, plugging his earphones in, and sliding his balaclava down.

Once the helmet was on and he was in the car, the rest of the world melted away.

'Radio check.' Dash's voice came straight into his ears so Luke heard him clear as day despite the angry growl of the engine behind him.

'Check.' Luke replied, determination taking up all of his

energy as he prepared himself to start the formation lap.

He weaved from side to side, warming up his tyres as he went around the track, squeezing the accelerator, and keeping one eye on his tiny side mirror and Tyler behind him. He backed the train up and Tyler pulled right up beside him as he rounded the last corner, Luke wanted to make sure he wouldn't be sat too long at the front of the grid letting his tyres cool down.

Luke slotted into the first grid spot and Tyler into the second and he had to trust everyone else was doing the same. When the first red light came on, he forced himself to forget about everything. Everything that had plagued him for the last month or so melted into the ground and out of that cockpit where he felt fresh and clear-headed for the first time in a while.

The fifth red light came on and although it was seconds, it felt like longer until they all went out. Quick as a flash, his reaction time one of the fastest on the grid, Luke released the clutch and the car bolted forwards, pushing him into his seat with force. He shifted through the gears, finding speed as he launched down to the first corner, which was more of a slight kink. He checked his mirrors and saw Tyler getting bogged down halfway down the straight and Lewandowski ploughing past him into that first corner.

Luke got a great exit and hit the accelerator hard, leaving his rival in the dirty air as he headed for the tight sequence of turns three, four, five, six, and seven. When he hit the next straight, there was enough air between him and Lewandowski for him to stop thinking about what was behind and focus on pushing forwards.

'Great first lap mate, let's settle in and go for Plan A,' Dash said as Luke headed down the main straight again to complete his first lap.

'How far back is Mik?' he asked, trying to build a picture

in his head of what was happening behind him.

'You're one and a half seconds clear of the Ferrari,' Dash answered straight away. 'Your teammate is a further second behind him.'

Luke focused his gaze on the black tarmac that stretched out in front of him that stopped at the white line and red and white curbs. Further out, the blue striped run-off areas weren't visible in his peripheral vision as he zoned into his lead.

He kept pumping out the lap times, hitting the delta on the screen, and turning each sector green with personal bests. There was no one around him and Dash was quiet on the radio, so Luke worked hard to not let his mind stray too far from the job at hand.

He continued to focus on the next upshift, the next braking point, the next corner. Never letting anything else cross his mind as the engine roared behind him, pushing him onwards and towards that finish line. He remembered the elation of winning a race, the adrenaline that flushed through his body as he put his whole self behind every turn of the wheel, willing the car on.

'You have a ten second lead over Lewandowski, give it all you've got for the next two laps,' Dash said from the pit wall, where he watched Luke's every move, analysed the data, and liaised with the strategists. Luke could imagine him, hunched over his desk, scribbling notes, and his sister in the back of the garage holding her breath, waiting for the next moment she could squeeze him.

'Copy,' Luke said not a trace of the effort he was putting in audible in his voice. He took Dash's comment seriously and put his foot down, pumping out a few qualifying-type laps and using up all the rubber on his tyres before Dash said: 'box, box' and Luke peeled off the track down the pit lane. Punching the limiter as he reached the white line, he pootled down to his box. The team waited, guns up as he hit his marks, and as slick as ever, they completed the tyre change in less than two seconds.

With the back end kicking out, Luke scooted down the pitlane and accelerated back onto the track, the team having found him a nice gap to keep pushing.

'Where's Tyler?' he asked, telling himself he cared because of the race and the championship and for no other reason.

'He isn't a threat to us, he's battling the Ferrari. You still have an eleven second lead over Mik.'

Luke let that sit for a moment and then pushed Tyler from his mind. If that was what he needed to do to get the wins then that was what he was going to do. There was no space for distractions, for a wandering mind, or for doubt in this championship. Tyler was making sure of that, as were the Ferraris.

He rounded the last corner for the last time, the chequered flag waving up ahead high above the pit wall. The crowd beside him cheered and he pelted down the straight to cross the line, winner of the French Grand Prix.

'Phenomenal weekend everyone,' he said over the radio, feeling that familiar buzz that came with winning. 'Incredible, I'm so proud of everyone and all the hard work you've all put in. Thank you so much.'

'Well done mate, incredible drive. Good to have you back on top,' Dash replied before Martin Clark cut in: 'Well done Luke, great job.' He sounded out of breath like he was the one who had raced for over an hour and a half going an average of one hundred and eighty miles per hour under the beating sun.

When Luke pulled into the pits, he jumped out of the car and launched himself at his team who hugged him tight, slapping his helmet in congratulations, and out the corner of his eye, he saw Tyler get out of his purple car behind the number three. Something pinched inside Luke's chest but he tried not to let it dull the spark he'd lit inside himself.

He knew he could do it and he felt like he'd found the key to quietening the voices inside his head long enough to be able to keep winning.

The Internet – Twitter
June 30th

FIA @fia · Jun 30

#F1 – Luke Anderson wins the Austrian Grand Prix at the Red Bull Ring in Spielberg

💬 832   🔁 478   ♡ 4.6K

Luke's Girl @lukesgirl · Jun 30

Your reply here!

Luke's Girl
@lukesgirl

YEEEES! Get in there #teamluke #andersonarmy

4:34 PM · Jun 30, 2019

5 Likes

Love in the Fast Lane

Lydia @lydia3649 · Jun 30
OMG I'm sooooo HAPPY #teamluke #andersonarmy
💬 6   🔁 1   ♡ 7

Luke's Girl @lukesgirl · Jun 30
I knew he had it in him, he's just the GOAT
💬   🔁   ♡ 2

Mrs Finley @f1girl1245673 · Jun 30
Really the GOAT? Are you kidding 🤦 #teamtyler
💬   🔁   ♡

Man of ur dreamz @britboyf1 · Jun 30
Right, if Finley hadn't had that damage he would've won, hands down.
💬   🔁   ♡

Lydia @lydia3649 · Jun 30
He should've been more careful and not crashed into Nabiyev.
💬   🔁   ♡ 1

Man of ur dreamz @britboyf1 · Jun 30
If we're talking GOAT, why are you not talking about how Finley came back from 18th to finish 5th huh?
💬   🔁   ♡

Lydia @lydia3649 · Jun 30
Like he's the first driver to ever have done that 🙄
💬   🔁   ♡ 2

Baz @bazracingfan · Jun 30
What's a goat got to do with F1?

Aaron Zoooom @Brambifan · Jun 30
Greatest Of All Time

Baz @bazracingfan · Jun 30
Aww thanks bro.

Aaron Zoooom @Brambifan · Jun 30
No that's what GOAT is, Greatest of All Time.

Baz @bazracingfan · Jun 30
Ok I get it, you like goat's, you weirdo.

Josh @joshlovesf1 · Jun 30
Can't believe how close the championship is now! Can't wait to be at Silverstone in a few weeks cheering on Anderson with all my #teamluke peeps 🐐 #andersonarmy

Lydia @lydia3649 · Jun 30
Ohmigod are you coming? We DEF need to meet up!

Love in the Fast Lane

Aaron Zoooom @Brambifan · Jun 30

Who are we thinking is going to win this year? Anderson? Tyler' Lewandowski?

♡ 6

Tyler's Number 1 @Finleyfaaaan1456 · Jun 30

Mate, Lewandowski is TRAILING

San @andersan48062 · Jun 30

He's only 71 points down, he's hardly out of it.

♡ 2

Aaron Zoooom @Brambifan · Jun 30

Exactly, my money is on him. Anderson has been a bit all over the show to be honest and Finley, well....

Ice Ice Baby @iceman17 · Jun 30

Well what? Finley's second and can you imagine him winning a championship in his first season 💀

♡ 7

Lydia @lydia3649 · Jun 30

It won't happen Luke's got this. #andersonarmy

Ice Ice Baby @iceman17 · Jun 30

Let's see eh? How about you come on a date with me if Finley wins.

Lydia @lydia3649 · Jun 30

Gross.

Bruno @brunof1 · Jun 30

So who's coming to party when Tyler Finley beats boring Luke Anderson to the title this year?

♡ 1

Luke's Girl @lukesgirl · Jun 30

Dream on. He's not that good. #teamluke #andersonarmy

♡ 1

Aaron Zoooom @Brambifan · Jun 30

Silverstone's going to be fun. I hope they've got separate grandstands for the #teamluke and #teamtyler or they'll need extra security @SilverstoneUK

♡ 13

Luke's Girl @lukesgirl · Jun 30

We're not savages. Well #teamluke aren't, I can't speak for those Finley fans

♡ 1

Cal @F1dramallama · Jun 30

We're not savages either but don't come for my boy or I'll come for you

Love in the Fast Lane

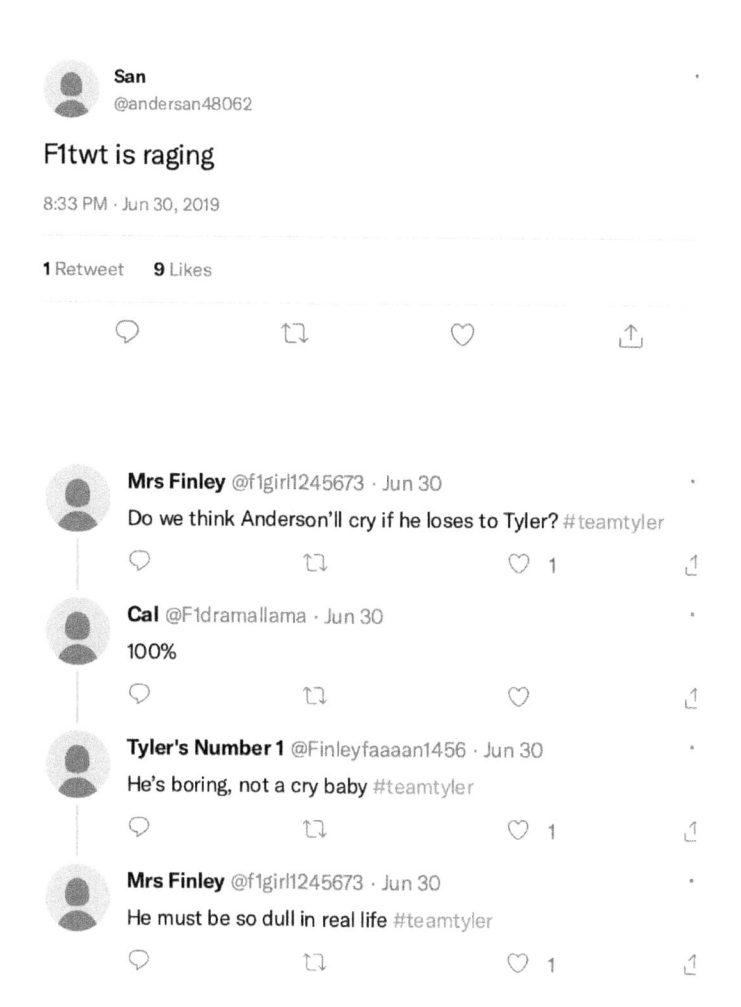

San
@andersan48062

F1twt is raging

8:33 PM · Jun 30, 2019

1 Retweet   **9** Likes

Mrs Finley @f1girl1245673 · Jun 30
Do we think Anderson'll cry if he loses to Tyler? #teamtyler
♡ 1

Cal @F1dramallama · Jun 30
100%

Tyler's Number 1 @Finleyfaaaan1456 · Jun 30
He's boring, not a cry baby #teamtyler
♡ 1

Mrs Finley @f1girl1245673 · Jun 30
He must be so dull in real life #teamtyler
♡ 1

Lulu @LulunNabi · Jun 30
Hi everyone, I'm Lulu and new to F1twitter, what's going on? I'm a Firas Nabiyev fan.

♡ 27

Baz @bazracingfan · Jun 30
Why? He's not very fast is he.

Aaron Zoooom @Brambifan · Jun 30
Not everyone's a glory hunter Baz.

♡ 3

Baz @bazracingfan · Jun 30
What's that?

Luke's Girl @lukesgirl · Jun 30
Welcome Lulu! F1 twitter's very divided at the moment, you may want to pick a side.

♡ 2

Lulu @LulunNabi · Jun 30
Hi! I like both, they seem cool.

♡ 1

Aaron Zoooom @Brambifan · Jun 30
Quickest way to get ostracised Lulu. I would know.

Luke's Girl @lukesgirl · Jun 30
Aww Aaron we love you! It's not your fault Brambilla's a little on the mouldy side. He's just been left out too long in the sun, he needs a good rest.

♡ 1

Aaron Zoooom @Brambifan · Jun 30
Matteo Brambilla for life

💬 1   ♡ 1

Luke's Girl @lukesgirl · Jun 30
I'm sure he's grateful for the support. He's gotta have someone to love him.

💬 1   ♡ 1

Aaron Zoooom @Brambifan · Jun 30
Love is love 🏳️‍🌈

♡ 31

Fourteen

British Grand Prix Press Day – Silverstone Circuit - Northamptonshire
July 10th

Emma waited as Luke stepped out of his Mercedes in a car park somewhere in the middle of the Silverstone race track. They weren't at the Hamilton straight, where all the team lorries were setting up and getting ready for the race but outside of the offices near the old pits. Her hair was pulled back into a small ponytail and she wore the team's purple waterproof over black trousers, collar pulled up high against the wind on the airfield.

'Good morning,' she said with enough bounce to put Tigger to shame and gave him a swift hug.

Luke knew they were the stars of this weekend. Two Brits in world championship-winning cars, battling it out at the front of the field, it was all about them. There was no avoiding the attention, not from the fans and not from the press. He knew it would be busy with a whole press day today ahead of the official weekend even starting. They were scheduled to do the official press conference tomorrow and then appearances on the fan stage and, of course, in the VIP areas.

He fell into step with Emma, a good half a foot shorter than him, as they walked towards the back end of the old garages.

'Bloody cold,' Luke grumbled as he scanned the car park for signs of life.

'It's a busy one today, I take it you got the schedule?' She shoved her hands deep into her pockets too. 'We're meeting Jessie and Tyler upstairs first for a briefing and then it's straight into the first activity.'

'Do you girls enjoy putting us through all this?' Luke remembered the schedule that included a driving Q&A, a foot race down the Hamilton straight, two sit-down interviews inside a hangar, and a "surprise activity" by the Sky Sports F1 crew.

'Count yourself lucky, there was a suggestion of taking you to the Snozone to go skiing.' She raised an eyebrow at him.

'Okay, fine, that definitely would've been worse.'

They reached the back of the garage and headed up the stairs to the meeting room. The metal stairs clanked underfoot, the building the same shade of grey as the sky.

Emma opened the door for him and he strolled in, his eyes always searching, the fluttering inside his chest starting up like the wind whipping into a tornado. Jessie sat at the desk, the office freezing like someone had forgotten to put the heating on.

'We better hope the weather cheers up for the race,' Emma

said into the cavernous space, making Jessie jerk her head up to greet the new arrivals but Luke's eyes were on the back corner of the room where Tyler stood in the same purple overcoat, chatting to Martin and Louise from the events team.

Luke realised he'd stopped walking when Emma turned to stare at him. He tore his eyes away from Tyler and sat down opposite Jessie.

'Right, we're all here, morning team.' Jessie shuffled her papers, ready for the briefing.

Luke nodded along as he skimmed through the schedule again. He felt Tyler's eyes on him from across the room but he didn't allow himself to look up. He'd be spending enough time with him throughout the day, he could afford to ignore him and whatever was happening inside his chest for a little while longer.

Jessie wrapped it up and they headed down the metal steps to the freezing pit lane. The wind howled down between the pit wall and the garages as they walked towards the huddle of press waiting up the other end. Jessie and Emma rushed ahead to greet them.

'I feel like our conversation from the other week may come in handy,' Tyler said as he fell into step with Luke, who kept his eyes straight ahead, not trusting himself to look around. 'Although you might want to change your favourite track answer to Silverstone. You know, just a thought.'

'Thanks,' he muttered, his smile audible in his voice.

'Anyway, it'll be a good opportunity to get to know each other, it's not like we're halfway through the year or anything.'

'Would you like me to call my sister instead? The preferred sibling,' Luke said with a hint of humour.

Jessie and Emma chatted ahead to the interviewers and cameramen, looking at the sports car that sat waiting for the two drivers, who were taking their time in making it up the pit lane.

'Is that a trace of jealousy I hear from the stoic Luke Anderson?' Tyler laughed, enjoying every moment of this conversation and the uncomfortable situation Luke had got himself in. Luke tensed, wondering if he had given himself away but before he could decide, they reached the rest of the team.

They couldn't catch a breath before the cameras rolled, straight into the first of many press activities for the day.

Luke climbed into the driver's seat first, trying to relax into it. Tyler was tasked with asking him fan-submitted questions as Luke drove around the circuit as fast as he could whilst answering them. Easy in principle but as drivers, they were almost always in control of the car, and being a passenger was not something either of them would enjoy. Luke volunteered to drive first, to get a feel for the car and the speed before he was thrown into the passenger seat for role reversal.

Cameras covered the dash, pointing at all angles, eyes always on them. The special edition Wilson Honda was a vibrant purple, so low to the ground Luke felt like he was sitting on the floor like when he climbed into his race car.

Helmets on, Tyler checked himself in the mirror.

'These chinless helmets are so unflattering. My cheeks are all squished up.' He jabbed himself in the face and Luke couldn't help but smile at the pout on Tyler's face.

'Are you ready?' Luke said switching on the car to a huge roar of the engine, he pushed the accelerator and the noise reverberated around the empty walls of the pit lane.

'Oh God, please don't kill me.' Tyler grabbed hold of the overhead handle and gritted his teeth and Luke burst out laughing. It broke out of him like sunlight through a dark cloud, brilliant and illuminating. Tyler scowled but a smile danced on his lips and something played in his eyes that

Luke couldn't quite decipher.

'I'll try my best,' he said as he slammed his foot down onto the pedal and the car jerked forwards going from zero to sixty in two seconds. Ploughing out of the pit lane and onto the track, Tyler swore loudly beside him as he was thrown around the car at each corner despite wearing a seatbelt.

'Are you going to ask me those questions?' Luke said, hands gripping the steering wheel, in complete control as he hit the curb around Becketts.

'Oh my God, can you slow down?' Tyler replied, not concerned at all about the cards he was holding, fear dancing in his eyes.

'I thought the point was to drive as fast as possible...' Luke grinned because for once he was comfortable and Tyler wasn't. He was so used to being on the back foot with him, never sure what he might say or do next but this time, he was in the driver's seat, quite literally, and Tyler couldn't do anything about it.

'Okay, right. I can do this.' He pulled out the first card and tried to read it as they bumped down the Hangar Straight. 'Who do you like better, Finley or Vasquez?'

Luke's head spun round and he must have been giving Tyler the look again because his smile dropped before he said: 'Okay bad joke, it doesn't say that. Would you rather jump from an aeroplane or fly a fighter jet?'

'Fly a fighter jet,' Luke replied without hesitating.

'If you could swap out your teammate for anyone else on the grid, who would it be?'

'Probably Kyle Kelly, he's a good laugh.'

'And I'm not?' Luke didn't want to get into any more trouble so he remained tight-lipped. 'You've got a one-way ticket to the moon, who do you give it to?'

'You.' Luke grinned wickedly and Tyler feigned hurt. Luke's insides turned to liquid, and he gave himself a mental berating. He needed to get a grip and stop acting like his sister.

'Well, that's rude. I thought we were friends.' It was Luke's turn to quirk an eyebrow. He looked back to the road, pushing the car to its limits and feeling the thrill of adrenaline as the grandstands and trees flashed past them.

'Next question?'

Tyler shuffled through the cards and Luke let go of the steering wheel to stop him from sifting through them.

'Oi, don't cheat.' He laughed, grabbing the cards from Tyler's hand.

'Don't let go of the steering wheel!' Tyler almost squealed as their hands touched on the cards. Luke felt a pulse of electricity course between them and he pulled his hand back like he had been scorched. They locked eyes for a split second before Luke's returned to the road and his hand to the wheel.

'What's the most disgusting thing you've ever eaten?' Tyler read as Luke guided the car back into the pits.

'I don't know, raw egg is pretty rank or mushy peas.'

'Mushy peas? Are you kidding? Are you even British? I'm offended by that comment.'

It felt good to laugh with Tyler but the way he was making Luke feel was not something he could deal with right now. He needed to remember who Tyler was and why that could never happen.

Luke pulled the car back in front of the garage where the camera crew, Jessie, and Emma were waiting for them.

'Right, let's switch,' Jessie said.

Luke was delighted that he didn't find Tyler's driving as scary as he had his. He managed to ask all the questions which Tyler answered in good humour and Luke spent a great deal of the drive laughing, forgetting that there were cameras in there recording them.

After the foot race and a couple of interviews, they sat

down with Petra from RTL who for once made no attempt to flirt with Luke. Instead, she focused all of her attention on Tyler who revelled in it, leaving Luke to be himself and not worry too much about what she might say next. Whether she was doing it to make him jealous or whether she had taken a fancy to Tyler, Luke didn't know.

'Do you think it'll be as amazing as everyone says it will on Sunday?' Tyler asked as they ate their lunch in a back office somewhere away from everyone else. Jessie was off sorting out the details with Sky and Emma had vanished. Tyler and Luke were alone in the white-walled room, sat on old grey sofas that seemed to have been brought there to die.

'Silverstone's pretty incredible on race day,' Luke conceded as he ate another McCoy's crisp from the packet they'd been given. 'It's like a festival, the fans are so noisy and supportive. It's…I don't know. It's different than some of the other races. Maybe because it's home and I've been coming here for so long. In Italy, it's all about Ferrari and the Tifosi, and here, it's all about Wilson and well…'

'You.' Tyler smiled, looking at Luke out of the corner of his eye as he did so. That same undecipherable look swirling around in it.

'Not this year though, I guess I'll have to share that with you.'

'We're the stars of the show,' Tyler said, pretending to be a celebrity which had Luke laughing so hard his cheeks hurt.

Teammates were never friends when competing at the top. The stakes were too high to be swayed by friendship. But somehow, he couldn't help himself. There was something magnetic about Tyler that kept pulling him in. The irritation faded and transformed into something new now that he was getting to know him. It was akin to a feeling he'd had a long time ago and had forgotten about.

Luke looked at him from under hooded lids. The slope of

Tyler's nose, down to the curve of his lips, the stubble poking through the pores of his golden skin. Luke wanted to reach up and touch the skin right beneath Tyler's ear. He liked the way it made him feel when Tyler laughed at one of his jokes and the way Tyler couldn't stop the stream of words coming out of his mouth when he was nervous. Even though he knew he couldn't feel that way.

'I need to make sure I don't let my Dad down.' Tyler huffed out a laugh but it was hollow as he kept his eyes on his lap. 'It's a big weekend for him, bringing all of his associates. It wouldn't do to have his son not win when he's told everyone I will.' Even though neither of them had moved, it felt like Tyler was right beside him. Luke could see each follicle of stubble on his chin and the tinge of purple beneath his eyes like he hadn't been sleeping.

'You could never let anyone down,' Luke whispered. The blue eyes Luke had come to know so well turned to look at him beneath thick lashes. Tyler's head tilted upwards as he gazed back at Luke. Luke's lips parted as his eyes flicked down to Tyler's mouth.

'Are you two ready?' Jessie popped her head around the side of the door.

They left the rest of their lunch as they followed her out, Luke slipping his coat on because it was still raining. Tyler huddled close to protect himself from the onslaught of rain, his body shielded by Luke's larger one.

Luke's hand shook, nothing to do with the temperature outside and everything to do with what he might have done if Jessie hadn't walked in.

'What do you think they'll have us doing?' Tyler seemed unfazed.

Luke didn't get a chance to answer as they crossed the road and saw the huge metal frame on the grass, standing tall in the drizzle. The two Sky presenters were huddled beneath a large golf umbrella and two cameramen were doing the same not far off.

Jessie walked them over and said: 'Don't say anything stupid, don't fall off and I'll bring you a coffee once I've warmed up.' With that she was gone, leaving Luke and Tyler staring at the aerial apparatus, the trapezist hanging upside down from the horizontal bar.

'I think you should give me your phone so I can call your sister when you inevitably fall off and break your neck,' Tyler said.

'I can't believe the team signed off on this.' Luke looked up as the second artist swung and grabbed hold of the first, his legs leaving the other trapeze to fly back. 'This has got bad news written all over it.'

Fifteen

British Grand Prix – Silverstone Circuit – Northamptonshire
July 14th

Four days later, Luke sat in his driver's room, the roar of the crowd a distant, constant rumble outside the door. He stared down at his phone. At Tyler staring back at him. He'd looked at the photo more times than he could remember over the last few days. Tyler had taken a selfie whilst Luke swung uncontrollably on a trapeze behind him, his smile lighting up the grey day and his blue eyes like orbs of the Mediterranean piercing through the screen.

'Fifteen-minute countdown,' Johan said from the desk, snapping Luke's attention away from his phone. He needed to focus.

It was still miserable outside, the rain having not stopped

all weekend and it was set to be a very wet race. Not good for the Wilson team whose car did not like the water one little bit. He hadn't done well in qualifying the day before and was starting down in fourth and Tyler down in eighth. They had a lot of work to do and needed to beat the Ferraris to keep the margin in the championship.

A soft knock on the door pulled him back to the present and brown eyes looked back at him through the crack. His mum pushed it open as his dad hovered behind, not able to follow her in.

'We wanted to wish you good luck,' she said with a nervous smile. She'd never liked the career path he'd chosen but over the years she had come to accept it. It didn't mean the all-consuming nerves she'd always felt had disappeared, but she was more adept at hiding them. The slight tremble of her hand gave her away as Luke stood to hug her.

'Thanks, Mum.' Her shoulder-length hair was impeccable as always and for a split second, he could see why everyone said he looked like her. Apart from the worry lines around her eyes and forehead, they had the same straight nose, the same round brown eyes, and the same sandy mane.

His dad shook his hand with a wide smile.

'We'll be upstairs watching, your sister has chosen the back of the garage again I think,' he said.

Luke nodded and watched them retreat down the corridor as Tyler's door opened. The two men locked eyes and Tyler looked poised to say something, his mouth dropping open, the whir of his brain showing in his eyes.

'Right let's go,' Johan said from behind Luke and Tyler closed his mouth, nodded once, and headed down the corridor in Luke's parents' wake.

'You've got this,' Johan said as he handed Luke his helmet at the back of the garage. 'The only one who can tell you 'you can't win' is you and you don't have to listen.'

'Nice. Who said that?'

'Jessica Ennis-Hill,' Johan said with a smile.

His sister gave him the thumbs up from the VIP box and Vicki nodded in his direction, her face set and stern, ready for battle. He glanced over to the other side of the garage and watched Tyler slip off his coat, his overalls already done up to his neck to keep the cold out.

Then it was visor down.

The race was shocking, worse than he thought it would be.

He tangled with Tanaka going into Village on the first lap, the Japanese driver unable to keep his car from sliding into the back side of Luke's, tapping him into a spin. He got going again but he was down in thirteenth behind his teammate with some damage to the floor.

It was a lonely first stint. With no one within fighting distance and having to battle the car to keep it on the black stuff, it was hard going and frustrating with no progress being made.

He watched as Nabiyev skidded and bumped across the gravel and went back first into the barriers.

He gained a few places in the pits, and a number of other cars slid off into the barriers too. There were safety cars and yellow flags flying all afternoon as the drizzle didn't stop.

'It's undrivable,' Luke told Dash over the radio as he fought to keep his purple machine on the track around Stowe three-quarters of the way through the race. He wanted to park up and be done with it but unless they red-flagged the race, there were still some points to be had and he needed all the help he could get in the championship.

'Copy, not much we can do I'm afraid,' Dash replied which exasperated Luke further. After his comeback at the last two races the last thing he wanted was to lose his momentum before the summer break.

The fans, as dedicated as ever, packed the grandstands and

the hills, the purple of team Wilson the dominant colour flying on the flags, the caps, and the t-shirts. The other thing that had been noticeable the whole weekend was the huge divide between Team Luke and Team Tyler.

As much as they had tried to present a united front, it seemed the press and the fans had decided otherwise; forcing them to be enemies and competitors above everything else.

Luke and Tyler fought tooth and nail the whole race against the rest of the field, but even the uplift of the crowd couldn't get them higher up the grid and couldn't change Luke's mood when he was allowed to guide the car into the pits after the chequered flag.

He yanked the headrest out and the steering wheel, exhausted from the effort of fighting against the eight hundred kilo machine in the rain.

He was soaked through to the bone and cold, and he didn't bother taking his helmet off as he walked into the empty room to be weighed on his way to the paddock. He filled his lungs until it hurt and felt weary at the idea of doing press; there was something deep in him that was pulling at him, tugging him towards something else but he couldn't quite figure out what it was that he wanted.

Emma greeted him with an umbrella and a branded cap, then walked him to the interview pen where his eyes were drawn straight to Petra. Her yellow umbrella and mac made her stand out amongst the grey and black of everyone else. Emma guided him straight over to the lady from Sky, who he'd hung out with at the trapeze a few days ago. He smiled grimly, trying hard to shake the mood that had settled over him throughout the race.

'Ah Luke, not what you or the fans had hoped for today?' she said mimicking his expression.

'Yeah, not ideal.' He ran his hand through his sweaty wet hair and sighed. 'We've got a lot of work to do to get the car working in the rain. Unless you can do an anti-rain chant for us for the rest of the season?' He gave her his media smile; an automatic reflex and he couldn't have been more grateful for the endless practice he'd had over the years as she lapped it up.

'I mean, I can try but I can't promise anything. The Ferraris were strong today, and Lewandowski has closed the championship gap, how do you feel about that?'

'They've worked hard on improving the car, but we'll need to come back fighting in Germany and hope we can improve as well.'

'I'm sorry it wasn't the home race you guys wanted, the team must be as disappointed as the fans?'

'Of course. The fans have been brilliant this weekend, they've been sat out in that every day and they're still cheering. They're incredible. The team's worked so hard this weekend to get this result but it's a shame we couldn't be on the podium for them.'

'Thanks, Luke,' she finished. He nodded and moved away to the next one, guided by Emma who held up her own recording device. He gave variations of the same answers for a further twenty minutes until Emma released him to get changed before the team debrief.

Johan left him in peace, sensing the dark cloud still hanging over his head as he showered and warmed himself up. He grabbed a tea on his way out of the motorhome and dashed under a brolly, cradling the takeaway cup in his other hand.

When he walked into the meeting room, computers and headsets were all set up, and most of the team was already there. Martin at the head, Vicki, Dash, and Tyler. Luke couldn't bring himself to even look at the latter but something inside of him settled down, the pulling gone. He took his seat and zoned into the data coming up on the screen, his headphones wedged over his ears as he listened to the debrief.

Zoned out, his thoughts trailed back to the race, replaying it through his mind to see if there was anything he could have changed but there wasn't. He knew that. He'd driven that car with everything he had. Despite the damage, despite the rain, he had done everything he could. Seventh was the result he would have to live with. He was disappointed for everyone, including the fans, he would have loved to have stood on the podium and lapped up the atmosphere. It was a feeling like no other, that surge of support, a wave of energy that made him feel like he was flying. It was the only feeling that made sense to him, the only thing he could cling to in those darker days, knowing he would feel it again. Maybe not today, maybe not next time, but he would be back on top soon.

He felt a sharp tap against his foot under the table and when he looked up Tyler was staring at him, his eyebrow quirked up. Luke struggled to rearrange his features from the impassive gaze he'd worn since he got out of the car so he flicked his eyes back down to the screen showing yet another graph, leaving Tyler to stare at his forehead instead.

At the end of the meeting, he escaped back to the motorhome to pack up. He wanted to put the whole weekend behind him, a tie-dye swirl of feelings inside making it hard to focus on anything.

'I'll catch you back in Monaco,' Johan said as the two men left the driver's room for the last time that weekend. Johan headed for the door and Luke to the lift to go up to the rooftop hospitality area to collect his family. Wilson Racing was one of the only motorhomes in the paddock to have a lift and as he was too tired to take the stairs, he waited for the small metal cabin to come down to the ground floor.

There were still some VIPs milling around, some team

members finishing up their work on laptops, and mechanics packing up the garage opposite.

The doors opened with a slow grind and he got in alone, pressing the close door button more times than was necessary. He leant up against the back wall, expelling all the air from his lungs, feeling the tension in his shoulders, the frustration in his bones.

As the doors closed, a hand stopped them, pinging them open again. Luke looked up in time to see Tyler slip into the lift and mimic his actions by jabbing the button with the two arrows facing inward.

'Hey,' Luke said running a hand through his hair and Tyler gave him a sad sort of smile. The lift clanked and the doors closed.

'Today sucked huh?' he replied, crossing his arms in front of his chest.

'Yep,' Luke nodded. He felt Tyler shift closer to him, his body heat a welcome relief from the cold outside that seemed to have settled into Luke's bones despite the hot shower and the sweatshirt he was wearing. He felt the lift stutter as it tried to get going.

'Look,' Tyler turned so he faced him, wearing an expression Luke had never seen on his self-confident face. It betrayed uncertainty and a little awkwardness like he didn't know what he was going to say. He chewed on the inside of his cheek and then sucked his bottom lip into his mouth.

Luke didn't let him start.

With no self-control and a well of feelings he had been suppressing bubbling over, he moved the half a metre between them and put his hand on Tyler's cheek, searching his face for an indication that he should stop.

He didn't find one.

He leant in before reason could stop him and hovered for a second before he touched his lips to Tyler's.

The air crackled and something burst inside of him, fed up of being stuffed away in a corner to be forgotten about. Lost in the sweet taste of his mouth and the feel of Tyler's cheek under his fingertips, he wasn't aware of anything else. With the soft touch of Tyler's lips against his, everything made sense.

Everything that had been brewing inside of him from the moment he'd found out that Tyler Finley would be joining the team. All those hours he'd spent watching him race, watching his interviews, scanning his social media channels, something he'd never done with any other teammate, it all came together and painted a very precise picture. He pulled away, his eyes still closed, savouring the taste of Tyler's mouth until reason took over.

He yanked his hands away like Tyler's skin was lava and panic surged through him.

What had he done?

He took a huge step back, as far back as he could inside the tiny box, and turned to look straight ahead, as the doors opened to reveal a guest pressing the call lift button.

Luke cleared his throat and walked out, leaving Tyler behind without a backwards glance. He felt the shame bubble up in him as he tried to make sense of what had happened. Without Tyler's face so close to his, nothing made sense anymore. He was back to being Luke, the Formula One driver with a well of unfocused and confusing feelings.

He walked over to where his parents sat waiting for him with his sister and her boyfriend. His mum pulled him into a hug and he felt numb.

'Good drive buddy' his dad said, clapping him on the back.

'You can't say that dad, he finished seventh, hardly groundbreaking.' Nick smirked and that familiar view relaxed his shoulders enough to let him smile back.

His mum threaded her arm through his, guiding him towards the stairs as she said: 'Shall we go home?'

Sixteen

**Chipping Norton – Oxfordshire
July 15th**

Luke stared at the ceiling of his parents' spare room, the magnolia walls looked drab against the bright white of it.

The detached house sat in the middle of a three-acre patch of land on the border of the Cotswolds, with a private driveway and a main gate separating them from the small country road that lay beyond the dry-stone wall. Luke had bought it for them a few years back, a thank you for all the sacrifices they had made for him.

As he lay there, he wondered if he should have put some conditions on the purchase, like how under no circumstances could they paint the walls magnolia.

He heard the shower switch on and assumed it was Nick or Dan who were sharing the other spare room, the one with the en-suite. They'd swindled it by arguing that there were two of them, whereas Luke could use the main bathroom that was opposite his room.

Luke didn't care.

He hadn't been able to focus on dinner the night before, the whole family at one table for the first time since Christmas. He'd pushed the potatoes around his plate, only a tiny bit of the beef making it past his lips. The same lips he had used to kiss Tyler merely hours before.

He felt sick to his stomach. The churning of bile, like a balloon expanding in his abdomen, squashing his lungs against his rib cage. What had he done?

He rolled onto his side. The pale pink curtains were see-through and the rain from the day before had made way for a glorious summer's day. The sun streamed through and blinded him. The birds, in full swing outside his window, had taken up position on the huge walnut tree to start their chorus from as early as half past five.

It's not as if they had woken him up, he hadn't slept. His mind replaying that exact moment on loop. Why on earth had he felt the need to kiss him? There was nothing that had indicated he wanted it, nothing to make Luke think that Tyler liked men, in fact, quite the opposite. Had Tyler not spent the first half of the season flirting with every single woman he had laid eyes on? He had even flirted with Luke's sister.

Luke groaned and pulled the pillow over his head, trying to block out the world and erase the last twenty-four hours from his mind.

He had no idea how he was going to be able to turn up to the next race and face him. At best Tyler would pretend it had never happened and they could go back to being what they were at the beginning of the season, nothing more than colleagues who didn't speak. At worst, it was sexual harassment in the workplace.

Luke squeezed his eyes shut, the light from outside drowning in the darkness of his eyelids before Tyler's face appeared in his mind's eye.

'FUCK!' he swore into the pillow. He'd made a bad situation worse and there was no recovering from that. Tyler knew who he was.

Everything that had been fighting to escape him since the start of the season lay bare in front of him and he didn't know how he was going to stuff it all back in.

He'd learnt a long time ago that there was no place for distractions when you wanted to be on top. And Tyler was a huge distraction.

Deciding that nothing good could come from lying in bed all day feeling sorry for himself, even though that's what he wanted to do, Luke pulled back the flowery duvet and put his feet on the cold original floorboards. He shrugged on a hoodie and matching joggers before opening the door out onto the landing.

The house wasn't small but it wasn't a mansion either, the landing as big as his entire flat back in Monaco. It felt different, very British with the exposed beams and more magnolia walls. His parents' bedroom door was open with no one inside. His sister's, however, was still shut, the shower going strong behind the wall.

He walked down the stairs, trying to flatten his bed hair, his bare feet feeling each knot, lump, and nail in the wooden floor.

'Morning.' His dad smiled from the kitchen table, a steaming mug of coffee in front of the newspaper he was reading. His mum was by the stove with her back to him. She was cooking away, her blonde hair pulled into a messy bun. The familiar sight brought him comfort.

The smell of bacon, which would usually make him take a seat opposite his father in anticipation, made his stomach turn. Lynn cracked an egg into the frying pan as the toast popped out of the toaster and Luke felt the bile rise up his throat again.

'I'm going for a run,' he announced before dashing back up the stairs to change. He didn't see the odd look his father gave him or his mother's raised eyebrow.

He changed faster than a pit stop and headed out of the front door without another word. He didn't know how he was going to make it through the day, let alone the rest of the season. He was on edge, waiting for his phone to go off, for Tyler to call him or HR. Or worse, the press.

He heard Martin's warning echo around his head from their first meeting back in January. No scandals. This couldn't get out. What if someone had seen them? This would be the biggest scandal of all, teammates, hooking up, a gay man at the pinnacle of motorsport. He groaned again, the reality of what he'd done too much to deal with.

His feet pounded the road, the green hedges rising on either side like a blanket protecting him from the outside world. He sped up wanting to run away from whatever the hell was happening and making him lose grip.

He remembered when he was fifteen and competing in the KF1 championship, the highest level of karting before heading into real race car domain, the turning point in his career. The moment he revisited in his nightmares when he threw away a whole year's worth of racing, of working towards his career because he let a relationship get the better of him.

He remembered the look in his parent's eyes as they told him that it was fine, that it didn't matter, but it had mattered.

He'd stopped competing for a whole year, which was a lifetime in the motorsport world and all of the accolades, press attention, and waves he had made by being the fastest, most impressive driver of his class died down. He'd not known whether he would ever make a comeback after that but he'd learnt from it and he'd worked his arse off to get back on top, putting away all of the distractions that would make him lose.

He was throwing it all away again and for what?

He shook his head wishing Johan was here with some words of wisdom to get him back on track but he wasn't sure Johan could help him now.

When he came back through the front door, Nick and Dan were at the kitchen table, tucking into the bacon and eggs, his mother washing up the dirty plates.

'Hi sweetie,' Lynn said smiling. 'Can I get you anything?' He felt Nick's eyes drawn to him, narrowing as they scrutinised him and he knew she could tell something was off.

Luke shook his head, still not able to face food.

'Maybe when I've had a shower,' he replied before dashing back up the stairs to his room.

He checked his phone but there was still nothing, then he did something Emma would be proud of and opened up Instagram. He went straight for the search bar and found Tyler Finley with the blue tick next to his name. Despite Luke being the World Champion, Tyler had about two hundred thousand more followers than he did but they were both in the millions. The blue button beneath his profile picture said "follow back" but Luke ignored it and scrolled down to Tyler's latest post.

The photo, taken in the paddock, was posted this morning. It showed Tyler under a bright purple umbrella held by Jessie who was blurred in the background, a Sky F1 microphone in front of his face. He was smiling and Luke's stomach did a little jump to the bottom of his throat.

The caption was about the race and their bad luck, no clues at all about what had happened in the lift afterwards but why he expected Tyler to plaster it on social media he had no idea. Reason had left him the second Tyler had walked into that lift.

Luke then looked at his two stories, one a repost from the Wilson Racing account about the race result, the other a mid-flight shot of Tyler by the plane window, looking out over the mountains.

He wasn't in England anymore. Luke's heart deflated.

Tyler seemed to be continuing his life as normal. Maybe Luke had made the whole thing up in his head. He could have believed that if he didn't still feel the softness of Tyler's lips against his.

Once showered, his hair damp and flopping over his forehead, he made his way back downstairs. The kitchen was empty, not a sound coming from the lounge or the dining room. He wondered if his sister had returned to her room until he saw them lounging outside in the back garden, watching his father sat atop a ride-on lawnmower.

Luke strolled out to join the rest of his family and saw his mother in the vegetable patch, straw hat on, bent over the tomatoes, inspecting them.

He perched on the second chair beside his sister but his dad noticed him.

'Nope,' he shouted over the noise of the mower before he cut the engine. 'I know you had a rubbish day yesterday but that does not excuse you from chores,' his dad said, climbing off the machine and patting the seat. Luke grinned and made his way over, taking a seat on the mower.

'Remember it's not a race car,' he added as Luke turned it back on and zoomed off, grinning his head off. His dad laughed and shook his head.

The noise of the engine almost drowned out his thoughts as he drove the mower up and down the lawn, turning in perfect circles at each end before going back the other way.

He watched from afar as his sister, her boyfriend, and his parents chatted and laughed together and it made him happy watching them. He did miss them when he was away, which was a lot but he always made sure to come back for a week after the British Grand Prix, it was his mini staycation, a break from all the flights and travel. The factory wasn't far away so he'd pop in to do some simulator work in the next few days before heading back to Monaco, then on to Germany.

The travelling circus.

But for now, he contented himself with enjoying the moment, even if his stomach twisted into a million knots, tightening each time he thought about that moment.

It was starting to blur around the edges, like memories do, and it had been so fleeting he couldn't discern the details. Had Tyler pushed him away or had he, Luke, pulled back? Had Tyler kissed him too, had he even given him the chance or did he force him into it?

Everything was such a muddle in his mind, that he couldn't tell what was real and what was a figment of his imagination.

He didn't even know if he wanted Tyler to have kissed him back.

He was still brooding over it when his mum called him over to the patio for lunch, the table set with flowers cut from the garden, the floral plates Nick had given her for Christmas on each placemat.

When he walked over Nick gave him a look. She knew something was wrong, whether she had guessed what it was, he didn't know but he'd never been able to lie to her.

Always clued into the minuscule changes in his behaviour, in his body language, in his tone, or his reaction, she always seemed to know when something was up. She stared up at him, her brown eyes searching his face like she was reading the lines of an encyclopedia looking for an answer.

'Are you okay? You seem a bit off today?' she said, bringing her hand up to his arm and giving it a little squeeze.

He tried to find the words to explain but they failed him. He stared ahead, out to the garden that was more a field but with pristine lines in the dark green grass from his morning's work. He opened his mouth and then closed it again. Nick waited but when nothing came out, she resigned herself.

'I'm here, whenever you feel like you might want to talk about it.'

He nodded, swallowing the lump in his throat.

He lay back under the floral duvet after an evening of pretending all was fine. His mum and Nicola though, seeing straight through it. It was still daylight outside despite the late hour and he knew he wouldn't sleep again tonight even with the tired ache he felt in his muscles. His eyes drooped but his mind refused to switch off.

Luke pulled out his phone and scrolled through Instagram again, under Tyler's name it said: "Active Now". He closed the app before opening it again. Indecision plaguing him. His fingers hovered over the keyboard on the blank message as he wracked his brain for what he wanted to say. He didn't even know how he felt so trying to articulate that was complicated. What could he even say, "I'm sorry I assaulted your mouth with mine"? "I don't know if you noticed but I kissed you yesterday and I'm sorry"?

He closed the app again with a frustrated growl and threw his phone across the room. It hit the wall with a sickening crunch. He didn't bother to get up, he was too tired.

He closed his eyes and decided that if he couldn't banish Tyler from his mind, then he would sit and stare at his face on the back of his eyelids instead.

He didn't know what was worse. Tyler being an arse or Tyler being nice. For a fleeting moment he wished Tyler

Finley had never come into his life and before the thought took hold, his heart squashed the idea and he knew he had lost.

Seventeen

**German Grand Prix – Hockenheimring – Hockenheim
July 28th**

The fog rolled over the Rhine valley, coating the race track in a thick, impenetrable white cloud. The trees around the circuit were barely visible from the paddock where Luke walked with determination towards the Wilson Racing motorhome. It was already busy with VIPs and mechanics, the smell of coffee drifting over them as the machine gurgled in the background.

The lift goaded him as he walked past it, a flash of shame and regret coursed through him as he went straight into his driver's room where he slammed the door, blocking out the world.

He had managed to avoid his teammate since he had arrived on Thursday, only seeing him for meetings but never making eye contact and never being alone with him. He couldn't trust himself around him, his body having a mind of its own whenever they were in close proximity.

For the last week, Luke had managed to erase the Silverstone incident from his mind, pushing it aside and locking it inside a box he buried in the deepest part of his subconscious. That was until Tyler had walked into the motorhome on Thursday morning and Luke had felt his presence. A pull to go to him, the ghost of a kiss still lingering on his lips as he watched him from the other side of the room, greeting his team with an easy smile. After that, it took a Herculean effort for Luke to pretend like he didn't exist.

The light tap on the door sent Luke's heart hammering again, waiting for Tyler to seek him out for an explanation, but it calmed when Johan peered round the side of the door.

'You good? Look like you've seen a ghost. Stop being so jumpy,' his trainer said, closing the door behind him and dropping his backpack on the floor by the desk.

Luke picked up the stress ball and threw it against the wall, watched it bounce back and left it till the last moment to stretch out his arm and catch it, like a frog catching a fly, with sharp and precise movements.

'D'you reckon this fog will clear?' Johan continued, getting his laptop out and setting himself up in his usual spot, oblivious to Luke's turmoil.

'I bloody hope so, can't race if you can't see.' Luke shrugged.

He had qualified in first, ahead of Lewandowski and Tyler. He wanted redemption for Silverstone.

Nothing, not even the lingering thoughts and embarrassment from what he had done was going to stop him from getting his car to the finish line first.

He was desperate to get in it, to feel the power behind him as it propelled him forwards. The feeling of being weightless, as the car hurtled round the track, but at the same time being pushed down into the ground with the downforce, sticking to the tarmac like chewing gum to a shoe. The need to be in control of something so much bigger than himself.

Then he could get out of here and away from Tyler for a few days, so he could draw in air again and breathe without his recent mistake hanging over him like the fog on this track.

By the start of the race, the fog had retreated to the trees leaving the track free for them to compete. Luke left it until the last minute to head to the grid, knowing Tyler would already be in the car when he got there. Not needing the constant reminder of how he had messed everything up.

Out of the entire grid, he was the last driver to hop into his car, the mechanics pulling away minutes later and then Luke was leading them all around the formation lap, the high-speed track unfurling in front of him.

The minute his visor had snapped shut, his focus was solely on the job.

He drove his arse off, hitting each corner with precision, the car gripping on the front end giving him great traction on the way out of each corner. He followed the team's direction and Amanda's strategy, which left everyone else in the dust.

It must have been boring for the fans because it was a parade, the top six all finished where they started but Luke didn't care. He'd redeemed himself from the last race and finished top of the podium.

When he walked into the winner's room, after celebrating with his team in the pit lane, he realised Tyler had finished third and would be there too. His heart jumped into his throat as he rubbed his face in frustration. It was hard to avoid someone he spent the whole time with and who seemed to pull on his thoughts with the force of gravity.

It took every ounce of the energy he had left to ignore him, the cameras probing and watching, broadcasting the whole thing to the wider world.

Everything Jessie and Emma had been working on these last few months, was about to disappear in one moment. The press didn't care for the whole picture, they only cared about what sold stories, and Luke and Tyler's rivalry sold stories.

It wouldn't matter that they had spent months presenting a united front, showing up as a team, laughing together to show how they got on. This one moment would be the one they would cling to.

Despite knowing all of this, Luke couldn't bring himself to even so much as look in Tyler's direction. He couldn't bear to see rejection in his eyes, or worse, them reciprocating what Luke felt. His heart soared at the possibility, but he squashed it, knowing Tyler couldn't have felt the same. And even if he did, there was no world in which they could ever be.

The atmosphere in the room was tense, a cold wind blowing through them like the trees that surrounded the track.

Luke turned his back on Tyler to drink his water, determined to hold it together and ignore whatever he would see in Tyler's eyes.

Luke felt a slight tap on his shoulder and on reflex turned, coming face to face with him. His whole body tensed up, each muscle, down to the ones in his fingers scrunched on high alert. The one muscle he couldn't control started hammering at its own speed in his chest as Luke's eyes grazed down the clean line of Tyler's jaw. Sweat trickled down the side of Tyler's face and Luke squeezed his hands tighter at his sides so he didn't reach out and wipe it away.

'Congratulations,' Tyler said, his voice flat, devoid of any emotion, and Luke felt the cracking inside his rib cage, like the earth during a drought.

Tyler stretched out his hand, his palm open and Luke swallowed hard. He couldn't make his body work, the fog from that morning having descended on his mind instead. Luke looked up but didn't make eye contact, he looked somewhere past Tyler's right ear to the large TV screen on the wall displaying tweets about him. Fans celebrating his win online. Keeping his face impassive, Luke gave a curt nod and then turned to the other man in the room, leaving a good few metres between himself and Tyler, letting his breathing return to normal.

'Great job,' Luke said to Lewandowski, desperate to engage the Pole into conversation so Tyler would move away and he could think clearly again.

'Not as quick as you,' Lewandowski replied with a sheepish grin. They talked about the race to fill the time until they headed to the podium but Luke was acutely aware of Tyler's gaze.

A cheer erupted from the fans and his team below as he walked onto the podium first. It was easier to ignore him up there, the sea of red and purple cheering, screaming, waving flags, moving as one as they celebrated their favourite drivers. Lewandowski followed him on, taking his place on the lower step, and finally Tyler, on his other side, on the lowest step.

The Chairman of the German Motor Sport Federation handed Luke his trophy as the crowd roared. It was hard to enjoy the celebration when he couldn't shake the thought of Tyler that seemed to have embedded itself into his core. It was like a seed had planted itself inside his chest and no matter how much he didn't water it, it kept growing and growing.

He still had media to do and a whole debrief to get through before he was free to leave the track and head home back to Monaco. Thankfully, they wouldn't be doing media together because he didn't know how much longer he could keep it together.

As he walked out of the motorhome, changed into his Wilson polo neck and jeans, he headed for the pits and the final hurdle before he could head home. Relief washed over him that he'd made it through a whole weekend.

Maybe he could do this. Maybe they could forget about it and pretend like nothing had happened.

Emma came storming out of the motorhome after him and grabbed him by the back of the t-shirt, too short to reach his shoulders.

'What the hell was that?' She hissed.

'What the hell was what?' He asked, the relief he'd felt a second ago deflating as he took in her creased forehead, her narrowed eyes, and the danger that flashed in them.

'Are you kidding me?' she continued in hushed tones, her eyes darting around to see who was in the vicinity. 'We've worked so hard to improve the image of the team and you go and ruin it in one single moment. Why? What happened? You guys were getting on great at Silverstone. He didn't crash into you today, he was nowhere near you. What was all that in the winner's room?'

Luke shrugged, trying to hide the guilt he felt. He hated disappointing Emma. She was like the mum of the team and she and Jessie worked so hard all the time. He felt awful for doing that to her. To them.

'You better goddamn hope that no one noticed. Who am I kidding, it was artic in that room. It oozed through the damn screen. For god sake.'

'I'm sorry,' he managed to say, not knowing how else to explain to her that just being in Tyler's presence was causing him such utter discomfort and confusion, that bringing himself to talk to him, after what he'd done, was unimaginable.

She must have seen the anguish in his eyes because her face softened, her head tilting to the side as she stared at him for a moment.

Emma pulled him into a hug.

'It's fine, we'll sort it, but don't let it happen again,' she warned. Luke nodded before going into the back of the garage.

The debrief was quick. Not a single glance was thrown Tyler's way for the whole hour and he was free.

He was free to go and leave Germany and Tyler behind. With a slight skip in his step, he went to grab his stuff from his room but Johan had already packed it up and taken it to the car, ready to head to the airport.

Luke waved goodbye to the staff clearing out the motorhome and headed for the paddock gate and the car park.

It was right there, straight ahead of him. A few minutes' walk and he'd be free.

'Can I talk to you?'

He hadn't noticed Tyler lurking beside the Ferrari motorhome, out of sight. The sinking sun cast shadows over the lines of his face.

'Now?' Luke said, filled with all the dread he'd let free ten minutes ago thinking he'd made it through the weekend unscathed. Tyler nodded and jerked his head to the side. Luke hesitated.

'It's not a great time,' he said, casting his eyes around for both someone to save him and in case anyone was watching. Tyler arched an eyebrow, his face serious and devastatingly handsome. The dark curl of his overgrown hair kissed his forehead and the red of his lips was as inviting as strawberries in summer. Luke sighed and followed him down the side of the motorhome, lingering near the exit for a quick escape.

'What's up?' he said, trying to keep his voice level, not wanting to betray what he was feeling. Which was a mix of confusion, apprehension, and the urgent need to kiss him again. He stuffed his hands deep in his pockets, rocking on the balls of his feet, not sure what to do with his body as he kept the distance between them.

'What's up? Are you kidding?' Tyler reeled taking a step towards him, his expression still unreadable. When were people going to stop asking him that today? 'You've been avoiding me all weekend to start with.'

'No, I haven't,' Luke lied, looking anywhere but at Tyler. Heat crept up his neck.

'Yes you have, don't bullshit me. Let's not even get started on what happened at Silverstone.'

Luke felt the full intensity of Tyler's stare as it bore into him, trying to see his soul. He couldn't figure out what he was seeing in Tyler's eyes. Trying to read him was like trying to understand a book in a foreign language.

'Then let's not talk about it,' Luke said shifting. 'It was a mistake. Let's forget about it and move on. I need to go anyway, Johan is waiting for me in the car. I've got a flight to catch.' The crushing feeling of his lungs contracting made him raise his hand in an awkward wave, before spinning on his heels and walking away.

'Is that it?' Tyler said louder and betrayed a trace of frustration in his tone. Luke shrugged, the pressure inside increasing. What else was there to say? Either way, it could never be.

Tyler looked like he was about to say something and Luke cut him off.

'See you around,' he said and resumed his walk to the paddock gates. His hands shook as he pushed through the turnstile and he couldn't catch his breath. It was suffocating him, getting stuck in his nose and throat, not making it down to his lungs. He felt the walls of his mind closing in on him and his heart rate accelerate like it wanted to jump out of his chest. His skin felt on fire and his stomach churned.

The harder he tried to suck air into his lungs the more they refused to co-operate and he felt like he was having a heart attack, right there, outside the paddock gates. He bent over, his hands on his knees as he tried to breathe through it.

It sent him straight back to that day.

The day that had detoured him from the course he was on. The day that had pulled him away from the one thing he had loved the most: racing.

Lost in his memory, still trying to breathe, he didn't hear the car pull up or Johan climb out. His best friend grabbed hold of him.

'Luke? Luke, can you hear me? Luke.' He heard Johan's voice in the distance like he was shouting at him from the other end of a stadium, then it grew stronger, louder and as if someone had pulled the cork out of an over-pressurised bottle of champagne, his lungs popped and the air flooded into them.

Luke gasped, sucking in the fresh cool air.

'Deep breaths,' Johan said as people stared.

'I'm fine, I'm fine,' Luke said trying to stand up, his limbs still shaking. He drew his six-foot frame up to full height.

Luke walked to the car and climbed in, ignoring the people that had been milling around, watching the World Champion break down outside the paddock gates.

'Take me home,' Luke said and Johan nodded, getting into the driver's seat beside him.

WILSON RACING: A TEAM ON THE BRINK OF COLLAPSE

How Martin Clark is ruining one of the most iconic brands of all time.

By Sara Holdsworth

Date published: July 31st

The Formula One World Championship race is heating up after the last round at the Hockenheimring in Germany. Anderson took the victory, with closest rivals, Tyler Finley and Mikolaj Lewandowski taking third and second respectively.

The German Grand Prix marked the eleventh race of the season and the halfway point in the jam-packed twenty-one race calendar which is due to finish on the first of December in Sao Paulo, Brazil.

With only fifty-nine points separating Anderson, currently first in the championship, and Lewandowski in third, it's all to play for. "It's definitely an exciting season," Anderson said after his race at Silverstone, UK, where the Wilson Racing cars finished inside the top ten, "but this result hasn't helped us. The Ferraris are strong in the wet and proved today how competitive they can be."

With two drivers in the top three, Wilson Racing is in a great position to take away another constructor's championship ahead of Ferrari and Lotus, which would be the best result possible for new team principal Martin Clark. "For sure, the guys and girls are doing their absolute best to try and get another constructors championship under their belts. They've come a long way from the days when tenth was a stretch. But there's still a long way to go." Like the driver's championship, it will be a race to the finish with Ferrari only trailing by a few wins.

It's a shame that the Wilson Racing team can't keep the drama to the track. Since his appointment back in December last year, Martin Clark seems to have done the exact opposite of what he wanted with the team's brand. Pledging to bring the traditional image of Wilson Racing up to date and into the twenty-first century, so far all he has managed is to ensure the team graces the front pages of gossip magazines.

Unable to keep a hold on his drivers, the team is reportedly being divided straight down the middle, it's a family feud gone wrong. An insider said: "The atmosphere in the team is awful at the moment. Martin is never around and both sides of the garage feel neglected. The drivers are running riot and the press team are herding cats.'

It hasn't gone unnoticed how the team is trying to pull the wool over our eyes about the internal goings-on at Wilson Racing. With a lack of management, feuding drivers, fake narratives, and friendships, it's the Press team that deserves a trophy.

No other team has ever appeared so chaotic under new management and it's a surprise they are still able to achieve the results they are. It begs the question, how much longer will owner Albert Wilson put up with Martin Clark's poor handling of his legacy?

With one more race until the summer break, the teams are desperate for a rest but also, crucially, the chance to work on the car with all the data they have collected so far. "The summer break is a tricky one, the drivers get to reset and recharge but the teams are still working hard on improving the car. We're hopeful we can make some progress in getting the car to work better in the wet conditions. Especially as the more traditionally wet races, like the USA, Belgium and Japan are coming up. We need to get it sorted." Dave "Dash" Marx, Anderson's Race Engineer, explained.

The next round will take place at the Hungaroring in Hungary, a circuit in the small traditional village of Mogyoród. "I love Hungaroring, it's great fun to drive with a configuration of short bursts of speed along with slower corners and the one straight. It's got a great mix and always makes for a fun race." It's no surprise that Lewandowski is a fan of the track having won the last three races at the circuit.

Anderson has had much less luck when it comes to the Hungarian Grand Prix, finishing eighth in the previous year, the first time he has finished the race since starting his career in Formula One. "Yeah, I don't have a great relationship with that track. I don't believe in curses and omens but if anything would make me, it would be that track," Anderson said keeping his humour despite the string of bad results there. "Let's hope this year is a bit different. I can't afford any more bad results if I want to keep the lead in the championship"

The rivalry between the two Wilson Racing drivers is going strong. Despite the camaraderie we've seen at recent races, the atmosphere inside the winner's room after the race in Germany was artic between the two Brits. Neither one commented on their teammate as they spent the weekend ignoring one another. Whatever Wilson Racing is selling us, we're not buying it.

Time will tell who will come away from this year as World Champion but let us know who your money is on below in the comments.

Eighteen

**Hungarian Grand Prix – Hungaroring – Mogyoród
August 4th**

The good thing was that Luke's panic attack in Germany hadn't made the newspapers. The bad news was that Jessie was fuming.

Luke had winced when Johan had shown him Sara's most recent article, her words scathing and for the most part, untrue.

It turned out Luke was avoiding Emma, Jessie, and Tyler in the paddock on Thursday which was impossible because his first meeting of the day was a press briefing with those exact three people and Martin Clark to boot.

He dragged his feet getting to the track and he dragged his feet going up to the meeting room on the first floor. Not feeling anywhere near ready to face the consequences of his actions. He'd never been on anyone's bad side and it was an unfamiliar feeling that didn't sit well with him.

The weather outside was glorious and if nothing else the weekend promised great conditions for racing.

As planned, he was the last to arrive and four pairs of eyes bore into him as he took his seat. He avoided eye contact with everyone and felt himself shrink under their gazes. He'd created this mess and he had no idea how to fix it.

'We all know why we're here,' Jessie started, giving Luke a pointed look.

'Can I chip in,' Martin said and Luke's stomach tried to find the ground. Jessie spread her hand out and moved it across the table, a gesture to give Martin the floor.

'Lads, please don't make me regret taking you both on. We're being accused of fabricating a relationship between you two and that's not what we want. I don't give a shit how you feel about one another but I want 100% pure professionalism from you both going forwards. The press is slating us, did you even hear me at the beginning of the season? No scandals? I want you on your best behaviour, last warning. Understood?'

Luke nodded, he knew this was all on him. He'd messed it up the first time when he couldn't bear to be in the same room as Tyler and he'd messed it up now by speeding to the other end of the scale. What was happening to him? His hands shook under the table as he kept his gaze down.

He couldn't wait for the weekend to be over so he could switch off for a while over the summer. So he didn't have to worry about awkward conversations and being on his best behaviour.

He could sense Tyler looking at him and he did everything he could to avoid glancing in his direction but his stomach jolted and twisted, the few days apart having done nothing to squelch the feelings he was trying to push away.

He'd have to be professional in public spaces but that was it. He needed, for his sanity, to keep his distance everywhere else even if deep down that was the last thing he wanted to do.

'Like I said at the beginning of the year, we don't care if you don't like each other,' Jessie took over. Luke hoped to God that the heat he felt inside his chest wasn't showing up on his cheeks too. 'But out there,' she jabbed her finger at the window. 'You two are best friends. Got it?'

'Got it,' Tyler said as Luke stayed silent.

'To squash the rumours, today you two are going to be doing press together. Every interview. The FIA has requested you both be in the official press conference too. I want to see your best acting skills on display and one whiff of something being off and I will hound you,' Jessie said this with a smile but they all knew she wasn't joking. 'Please stop making my life hard.' Luke chuckled at the irony.

Jessie had no idea how hard she was making his life. A whole day, stuck to Tyler like glue and having to pretend that nothing was wrong was going to be agony, like a million little knives pricking into him. He had no idea how he was going to survive it but he had no choice, Martin and Jessie had made that very clear.

'One last thing, I'm not sure if you guys are aware but there've been some controversial decisions in Hungary around LGBT rights. I've heard from other teams that some of the drivers are planning on making a stand, some kind of gesture, not sure what at the moment but please don't get involved. I know that's a tough ask but we need to keep a low profile this weekend. Let's not add fuel to the fire, okay?' Jessie looked over to Martin who gave her an approving nod. 'Right, first interview in twenty.'

'Game face on,' Martin shouted a little too loudly for how close he was beside Luke and then clapped him hard on the back.

It was excruciating sitting so close to Tyler. Luke could smell his aftershave and feel every slight movement he made. His nerve endings tingled with every inhale and contact between them. It was also scary how good Tyler was at pretending everything was fine.

He flirted with all the women, switching his charm on, so much so that even the men were eating out of the palm of his hand. He engaged Luke in conversation, giving him opportunities to chip in and making sure it seemed like the atmosphere around them was warm. Luke tried not to stare as he admired his ability to befriend everyone and anyone in the vicinity.

They played a game with the Sky F1 presenters that involved finding out how well they knew each other. Their backs an inch away from each other throughout, making Luke sweat as he resisted the urge to lean back into him. It turned out they didn't know each other that well either and after each interview, Tyler disappeared with Jessie and reappeared right before the next one. Each time it felt like the sun had gone behind a cloud, drawing the heat away with it. Jessie and Emma chaperoned them the entire day, neither letting them out of their sight even for a moment whenever they were outside the motorhome, and thankfully, that meant they didn't get a minute alone either.

Luke had his lunch in his room with Johan, but he put his headphones on and retreated inside his mind, not wanting to talk more than he had to.

After lunch, Emma came to walk him to the official FIA press conference. He sipped on his water, through a longer than necessary straw, the water bottle branded with the Wilson racing logo and also that of the water provider that sponsored the team.

The air temperature soared into the thirties by early afternoon and Luke thought maybe, just maybe he could turn his luck around when it came to the Hungarian Grand Prix.

'Good luck mate,' Lorenzo Nunez said as they walked past. 'I'd ask for tips but with your track record here, not such a good idea.' He laughed, his lined face lighting up with a cocky smile.

'Should I say congratulations on your retirement?' Luke said trying to inject some enthusiasm into his voice.

'Definitely, I can't wait to spend more time with the kids,' he said with a wide grin.

They walked in silence until they reached the conference room and then Emma turned to Luke. She put her hands on either side of his arms.

'Last one,' she said giving him a small smile. She could tell how hard today had been on him and she cared. She patted his arms and then moved away so he could head into the room.

Tyler sat behind the table in the middle beside Kyle Kelly and Manuel De Leon, his jaw clenched, a muscle twitching below the smooth surface of his skin. His blue eyes stared at the carpet in front of the table, his mind elsewhere.

Luke spotted the rainbow pin on Kelly's chest but ignored it, heeding Jessie's warning. A young lad wearing an FIA branded t-shirt came and miked him up before pointing to the seat beside Tyler.

Luke cleared his throat, and glanced at Emma who nodded, and Jessie who glared at him. He took his seat and stared straight ahead at the sea of journalists sat on black plastic chairs, microphones poised and ready, the camera in the middle, red light flashing.

In the second row on the left-hand side, Luke spotted Sara Holdsworth, her curly red hair like a beacon amongst the crowd. She analysed the two men and Luke shifted in his seat.

Firas Nabiyev came running in five minutes later and then they were underway. There were the usual questions about the race, what they were expecting, the track, and racing in general. Luke's eyes glazed over as the others talked, joining in but mostly keeping to himself.

'Hi, Sara from CultRacing.'

So far, they had avoided any question about their relationship or the idea of a manufactured friendship but by the look on Sara's face, they were about to get it now.

'Tyler, would you say that you have a good relationship with your teammate?' Sara said, her eyes narrowing, boring into them like she was searching his soul.

'I think so, yeah. There's a lot of respect between us and he's a funny guy you know.' Tyler ran his hand through his thick hair, no trace of the nerves that were jiggling Luke's leg beneath the table.

'How do you feel about the rumours that your friendship is manufactured, a show if you will, that the team has asked you to put on?'

Tyler sat back and dropped his hands to his side as he replied: 'I don't concern myself with what anyone has to say. We race hard and we work together to get the best result for the team, that's all that matters.'

A moment later, Luke felt the warmth of Tyler's palm on his thigh as it stilled his shaking leg. The sudden contact drowned out the room and Luke swallowed the lump in his throat, not realising that Sara was looking at him.

'Luke? Would you agree with that statement?' she continued, pressing on like she was the only journalist in the room. Luke didn't dare look in Tyler's direction, instead, he searched for the FIA guy running the conference to persuade him with a stare to move on from Sara. The atmosphere in the room was uncomfortable, the other drivers were fascinated by their fingers, the table cloth, or the white painted walls but the young lad was deep in conversation with another official.

'Sure,' he said in the end. 'Tyler's a fast driver and brings a lot of skill and knowledge to the team. We're doing our best to get the best result for the team.'

'But personally,' she pushed, 'would you say you're good friends, acquaintances? Would you hang out on the weekend? The fans want to know,' she added with a sadistic smile. Luke's gaze flicked to Petra who rolled her eyes with a clear show of irritation on her face.

Tyler, who had been so calm and collected through the entire day, tensed, his energy changing, bubbling with anger at the continued line of questioning. Sara had a way about her, a way of saying things that pushed all the buttons you didn't want her to push.

'I mean, do we hang out on the weekend, no,' Luke said and Tyler took his hand away from his thigh, leaving the spot feeling cold and bare but Luke continued, 'Will we ever be best friends? Probably not, but he's a nice guy and we get on well enough to work together. We're not sworn enemies like the media would like you to believe. We're co-workers.'

Luke finished up as Emma and Jessie nodded in approval. When Luke thought he'd made it, Sara asked one last question, which seemed to be a question too much for Tyler, whose whole body was as tense as a washboard beside him.

'Tyler, would you agree?'

Tyler stood up, the chair falling backwards with the force of it.

'These questions are bullshit,' he said pulling off his microphone, anger flashing in his eyes as he dumped it on the table. 'We're here to race, not chat about emotions and feelings.'

With one blazing look at Luke, he stormed out of the room, Jessie running after him. Emma closed her eyes with a hand to her forehead.

They'd failed at the last hurdle.

Sara looked delighted as the FIA official wrapped up the press conference and even though Luke should have been pleased it wasn't him that had messed up this time, he felt empty and flat.

As he walked back to his driver's room, he saw Tyler's door ajar. Through the gap, Tyler paced back and forth, one hand on his hip, the other pulling at this hair. The muscles in his shoulders bunched beneath his shirt.

Luke hesitated, his breath catching, his mind blank. He touched the door and pushed it open, checking the corridor before slipping in. Tyler swung round, nostrils flaring, eyes ablaze, like a bull cornered in the arena. Luke felt the full force of his hatred and wanted to turn and run but he didn't. Something kept him glued to the ground.

'Are you okay?' he said, searching Tyler's face for a sign that he should stay. But the look he found there was not unlike the one Tyler had given him all those months ago in Australia, the unbridled rage building up under his skin as he struggled to contain it. 'Hey, it's okay.' Luke took a step forward and reached out, placing his hand on Tyler's arm. He struggled to ignore the heat that gathered where their skin touched and wondered if Tyler could feel it too. Tyler's face relaxed and his shoulders slumped, his nostrils regaining their perfect form. His lips parted, poised to say what was on his mind when footsteps beyond the door grabbed their attention. Luke dropped his hand and took two steps back, extending the distance between them.

'Luke?' Johan's voice was bodiless until he pushed the door open.

'Coming,' he said his eyes still trained on Tyler's face. Tyler gave a slight nod and Luke left the room.

He didn't see Tyler for the rest of the weekend. Through

the practice sessions and qualifying they were back to being two separate sides of a team. They skirted around one another in private and made sure they were never in the same place in public at the same time.

Despite the perfect conditions for the race, it was abysmal for Team Wilson.

Luke was rear-ended into the first corner by a back marker out of place and with his less than ideal qualifying slot there was nothing he could have done. He had damage to the floor and the rear wing and despite the team's best efforts, he retired from the race on lap thirty, upholding his terrible record at the Hungaroring.

Tyler didn't fare any better. As he overlapped a different back marker on lap fifty, they tangled, sending Tyler into the wall and missing out on a solid second place finish. Lewandowski went on to win and left Wilson Racing licking their wounds.

The debrief was short, the press even shorter and Luke was back in his motorhome before the race had even finished. The luxury RV, his home away from home at the European races, was nothing like the team's one. This one had a kitchen, a lounge, a bedroom, a bathroom, and even a garage.

Luke sat on the cream leather sofa, the TV on, broadcasting the support race that was happening right outside his doors. Nunez led the train and had for most of the race. Luke could hear the sound of the engines through the soundproofing.

He picked up his beer and took a slug, wiping his hand over his mouth.

He was tired.

It had been a long first half of the season and he was glad he could head home and hibernate for a while. Figure some things out, try and forget about some other things.

He wasn't one of those flashy drivers who headed off to exotic islands for the summer, he was a homeboy and he was looking forward to waking up in the small flat he'd paid a fortune for and enjoying the peace and quiet.

Johan was on his way home to Finland for a few weeks too, so he'd have the place to himself.

There was a soft knock on the door which jerked him out of his brooding. It was too early for the car to take him to the airport and Johan had left before the debrief, taking the rental with him so he could fly home and surprise his sister and nephew.

Luke walked the two feet to the front door and swung it open.

Tyler stood on the tarmac at the bottom of the steps, his hair messy from being inside the helmet, his face red with effort. He glanced around but their area of the paddock was empty.

'Can I come in?' he asked, his teeth clenched and hands balled up at his side. He'd changed out of his team kit and was wearing a white polo, which highlighted his tan and faded blue jeans.

Luke hesitated, his heart fighting with his brain for a moment before he stepped aside.

'You don't look happy.' Luke's mind reached for the first thing it could find as the door of the motorhome swung shut behind them.

'That's because I'm not,' Tyler snapped. 'I lost second place because some bozo couldn't keep his car in a straight line.'

Tyler walked over to the table but Luke stayed planted, the furthest distance away he could get in the small space. His mind raced and his palms sweated as he tried to keep his breathing in check. It was the first time they had been alone since Tyler had cornered him after the German Grand Prix. Luke knew he needed to apologise for everything that had happened since Silverstone but the words wouldn't come out. Instead, he said: 'I'm glad I wasn't the bozo.' A slight grin spread over his lips as he tried to lighten Tyler's mood.

Tyler spun, his blue eyes darker somehow and blazing with heat as they roamed over Luke's face, searching, probing. He didn't find the humour in Luke's comment.

'Fuck!' Tyler swore, burying his hands in his hair and grabbing fistfuls.

Before Luke realised what was happening, Tyler's legs had eaten up the space between them. He grabbed Luke's face with both hands and pulled Luke's lips to his.

The soft heat engulfed Luke's mouth as his mind tried to catch up with what was happening. There was a soothing blankness in his head that he had been reaching for ever since that moment in the lift. Relief and peace washed over him as he relaxed into Tyler's body. His own mouth found momentum against Tyler's and the small, delicious pecks, led to tongues melting together as Luke wrapped his arms around Tyler's waist, pulling him closer. His whole body ached to touch and be touched by Tyler, who stroked his thumb over Luke's jawline, reassuring and hungry for more.

Desire pooled in the pit of his torso, wanting and needing him. Tyler was strong and sturdy beneath Luke's hands and as his walls fell, Luke grabbed at him with fervour. He ran his hands through his dark hair, pulling his head towards him so that the kiss was deepened, that sweet taste he'd dreamt about filling him.

Tyler's hands travelled down Luke's shoulders to his chest and he found the bottom of Luke's t-shirt, pulling it up and sliding his hands under it. The shock of skin on skin sent ripples of pleasure through Luke's entire body and he was sure somewhere on the opposite side of the world, volcanos were exploding and tidal waves were crashing.

They clawed at each other, pulling and tugging at their clothes trying to get closer to one another until they ran out of breath. Luke wasn't sure who pulled back first, but with chests heaving they stilled, foreheads touching, eyes closed, and catching their breath.

Nineteen

Monte Carlo – Monaco
August 22nd

The air was still for Monaco, the wind either came in from the sea or down from the mountains but rarely was it this calm. Luke sat out on the balcony of his tiny flat, the morning sun beating down in the clear blue sky and the heat warming him through to his core.

His coffee cup sat on the small wicker table, curls of steam coming off the surface that shone like smoky glass. Beside it, a newspaper, untouched but poised to be opened on the sports page.

Luke's hair was damp from the shower he'd taken after his morning run, his muscles tingling after the exertion. Exceptionally, he'd driven out to the mountains and ran up a trail instead of along the seafront, gagging for endorphins and to work out his long legs.

He wasn't wealthy enough to afford a flat with a sea view, instead, his balcony looked out over the back end of Monaco, where the buildings rose up as the slope climbed towards the hills, a sliver of the greenery visible through the gaps in between the skyscrapers.

He picked up his coffee and took a sip. And like a constant itch he needed to scratch, he also picked up his phone and opened Instagram. He scrolled through until he found Tyler's profile then he clicked on it like he had done almost every hour for the last eighteen days.

How had it been over two weeks since he and Tyler had made out inside his motorhome in Hungary? Two weeks with not even one phone call or text from him.

Luke had no idea where they stood; despite the intimacy of their actions they hadn't managed to say a word to one another as a knock on the door had made them jump apart. It was Emma letting him know that his car was there, ready to take him to the airport. Curiosity flooded her eyes as they travelled between them but she hadn't uttered a word.

She also hadn't left, waiting for Luke to gather his things and walking him out of the paddock. He'd left Tyler in his wake and now he was more confused than ever.

He thought Tyler might have called him, or even texted to say something but no. Nothing.

It was a two-way street but Luke was reluctant to go down it, so he hadn't made the first move either. He flip-flopped between wanting to find out what it all meant and not wanting it to go any further.

He took another sip of his coffee, some birds swooped down overhead and off towards the hills beyond. The sound of the traffic was loud, horns hooting as they scrambled around the tight streets of the Principality. When he retired, he wanted to live somewhere calmer, with more greenery and not so far off the ground. He imagined living in a house like his parents in the Oxfordshire countryside with a family. Close enough to his sister so she could look after his kids sometimes and his parents so he could look after them.

He clicked on Tyler's stories which showed new content and Luke's stomach dropped as he watched Tyler in his swimwear, hanging out by the crystal-clear seas of either the Caribbean or the Maldives with some very attractive women. He was beautiful beneath the sun, his eyes the same shade as the sky above him. Luke's heart contracted, a lump forming in his throat as one gorgeous brunette got into the shot and wrapped her arms around his shoulders then kissed him on the cheek, lingering longer than was appropriate if they were just friends. Worst of all, Tyler didn't seem to mind. He looked happy and relaxed, soaking in the sun and making the most of the summer break.

Luke couldn't bear it. He closed the app, turned his phone off, and slammed it down face-first onto the table. He picked up the newspaper and tried to read something to distract himself but even though his eyes read the words, his brain wasn't taking them in.

There were so many unanswered questions. Was Tyler gay? Was he confused? Was he, Luke, an experiment? Was he bisexual? Was Tyler leading him on? So many thoughts curled round his head to the point where he was giving himself a headache.

Luke knew who he was. He always had.

He knew he was gay before he even knew he wanted to be a race car driver. It never held him back, it never changed who he was. He kept his personal life, personal. Out of the limelight, away from prying eyes.

He had no interest in coming out to anyone or labelling himself for other people's comfort.

He was Luke Anderson and to him and all those he loved,

that's all that mattered.

He'd had a few fleeting hookups over the years but racing and winning had always been more important. There was never a question of them or his career because it was always his career, hands down, no debate.

But no one had gotten under his skin like Tyler Finley had and as much as he'd told himself that kissing him was a mistake and that Tyler wasn't interested, what had happened in the motorhome had changed that.

But with no word from him, Luke felt lost. Swallowed up in a Katy Perry song, hot and cold. He didn't want to feel the sting of rejection or the complications of a relationship with Tyler.

He didn't do commitment. He didn't do complicated. So he did nothing.

He couldn't talk to anyone about it, not even his sister who had sensed things were off when she'd visited the weekend before, probing him with questions he didn't want or know how to answer. The one thing he could do to distract himself was train.

Johan had left specific orders that Luke was to rest for the first two weeks of the summer break. His body was tired and needed care, not punishment. Light exercise only which in Johan's book included short walks and yoga. Luke had done neither since being back in Monaco, he had pounded the pavements every day, racking up miles upon miles. He'd been out cycling in the mountains and trail running too. He even spent two hours in the gym every evening and swimming lengths in the building pool.

It was the one thing that got him off to sleep at night, instead of staring at the ceiling thinking about Tyler.

He closed the newspaper admitting defeat and grabbed his swim shorts and towel from the airer in the lounge. He padded down the hallway to the lift and punched the button to the basement.

It was empty apart from one lady he'd seen before running on the treadmill with more grace than if she were on a runway. He turned left and headed for the pool changing rooms. It was quiet, no one else in the water as he dived in, head first, and held his breath for as long as he could before surfacing and front crawling to the other end of the Olympic-sized pool.

He linked up the laps, letting the momentum of his stroke pull him along the water, his mind focused on improving his technique with every arch of his arm. He inhaled through his nose each time he turned his head and then blew out the air through his mouth into the clear water. When his arms tired, he pushed himself further until his whole body screamed at him to stop.

He had no idea what the time was when he pulled himself out of the water and sat on the edge dangling his feet in. The old gentleman that lived upstairs had appeared at some point and he glided up and down the pool like he had nowhere else to be.

Luke took his leave and headed back to his flat.

As he came out of the lift, he checked down the corridor to his left, away from his flat and it was empty but as he looked the other way, a dark shadow blocked the light from the window at the opposite end.

Luke took slow steps towards his flat, one eye on the shadow. It wasn't often that people lingered in the hallways of these buildings. They either lived there and were on their way home or like a lot of the flats, they were empty most of the year, their owners having them for tax purposes.

As he approached, he noticed the person was outside his flat. Pacing with their head bent low, then looking up at the door before pacing again.

'Can I help you?' Luke said, trying to focus on their face,

the backlight of the window keeping them shadowed. They startled at the sound of his voice and when they looked up, Luke would have recognised those blue eyes anywhere.

Tyler looked out of place in the corridor. They stood meters apart, neither attempting to close the gap between them.

'Hey,' Tyler said staring at his feet, his hand rubbing the back of his neck.

'Hey,' Luke replied. Tyler took a step back as Luke approached his front door and unlocked it. 'How long have you been stood here?'

'Longer than what's respectable no doubt. I'm surprised your neighbours haven't called the police.' He laughed, running his hand through his hair and Luke's heart fluttered in response.

'I don't think anyone's home on this floor,' Luke said shrugging and walking into his flat. 'Why are you here?'

'Aren't you going to invite me in?'

Luke wasn't one hundred per cent sure he wanted Tyler to come in. He was taken aback by his sudden appearance after watching him gallivanting on the other side of the world hours ago but he left the door open as he went further into the flat. He dropped his bag on the hall floor and carried on into the lounge.

'Nice place,' Tyler called from the hall as the door clicked shut behind him. He followed Luke but they stood at opposite ends of the small room, not making eye contact.

'This is a lot more awkward than I'd imagined it,' Tyler said with a small laugh, making Luke look up at him. His eyes stood out against the deeper tan of his skin. It was like someone had taken each perfect curve, line, and colour and rolled them into one being.

'How did you imagine this going?' Luke said, keeping his voice even despite feeling anything but inside.

Seeing Tyler in his flat made everything from the past few weeks real. Silverstone wasn't a mistake, it was born of feelings he hadn't felt creeping up on him. It was a subconscious decision to admit to himself that there was more going on there than he wanted to concede. The hatred he had tried so hard to maintain was a cover for the fact that the man standing in front of him was flawless and everything Luke wanted, even though he knew he could never have it.

'I thought you'd invite me in for starters, but maybe that's something I've got to get used to,' he said but when Luke didn't return the smile he added, 'I also thought you'd be happy to see me.' Tyler gave a little shrug.

Luke felt trapped in his own body, in his own mind. He wanted to go to him but he didn't know how. He wanted something concrete to go off of, it written in black and white. The clear path of their future laid out for him to assess before he decided.

'Come on Luke, I've had your tongue inside my mouth, can you say something?'

'I don't know what to say.'

'That's very apparent.' Tyler pushed off the doorframe and took a step into the room and Luke stepped back.

'I saw you on Instagram, with those…girls.' Luke managed to choke out and the second the words passed his lips he hated himself for the reproachful edge to his voice.

Tyler frowned, then his face cleared, realisation seeping into him. He chuckled which irritated Luke more.

'Is that the problem here? You think…in fact, I don't know what you think. Your face is constantly impassive and I haven't a clue what to believe half the time. How about you bloody tell me what you're thinking? Would be a hell of a lot easier than me trying to guess.' Tyler strolled into the room with confidence, stopping a metre away from Luke, the smell of his skin engulfed Luke's senses.

Luke stared, words failing him, his heart thumping his rib cage.

'Or we can stay silent, I mean whatever. But so you know, I'm not leaving until you've talked to me. You can't kiss me in a lift then ignore me, then let me kiss you…it's messing with my head man.'

Messing with his head? Was he joking? Luke's brain was soup when it came to Tyler but they appeared to be as confused as each other.

'I know you like to be all strong and silent but please, I need you to say something right now. Should I leave?'

'No,' Luke said and they locked eyes. The intensity in that one stare created enough vibration in the universe that a string could have been created from the energy coursing between them. 'Don't leave' He stepped closer to Tyler. His breath caught in his throat as his heartbeat accelerated again, pounding faster than when he was hammering the trails, in the centre of his chest. His clammy hands betrayed his nerves but he didn't know what he wanted more: to pull Tyler to him and risk everything or to stay in the safety of his old ways, leaving the door closed.

'Okay, I won't,' Tyler said in a whisper. They were stuck in this push and pull, neither of them able to take a step forward, the intensity too much to bear.

When they collided in the middle, neither of them knew who had made the first move.

Their mouths crashed together, limbs tangling as they grabbed for clothing, frenzied and urgent. Luke palmed Tyler's strong, broad back and drew him closer. Breathing in the smell of his skin, the taste of his mouth, and the feel of his muscles beneath his fingers. Revelling in the moment, not wanting it to end.

'Luke,' Tyler breathed between kisses. Luke halted, pulling back an inch, his fingers still entwined in Tyler's hair. He questioned him with a look. 'What are we doing?' he breathed, his word laboured like he didn't want to be asking.

'I thought it was pretty obvious,' Luke replied, silencing Tyler with another kiss. Tyler melted against him and Luke's stomach pooled with warmth. He felt himself grow inside his joggers and for a split second, he thought about pulling away. What were they doing? But Tyler's fingers trailed around the waistband of his trousers and instead, Luke leaned into it. Wanting it more than he would ever care to admit, he pulled Tyler's t-shirt over his head and stared at the flawless expanse of muscle. The tightness in his lower belly increased as he pushed his hardness against Tyler. Grabbing, kissing, and undressing as they found the sofa.

Tyler pushed him down, his hands soft and commanding on his chest, and climbed on top. His hands followed the small trail of light blonde hair down Luke's stomach to beneath his waistband and found what he was looking for. Luke closed his eyes and arched his back against the pressure that was building between his hips. Nothing else mattered but the feeling of Tyler's hand wrapped around him.

Twenty

Monte Carlo – Monaco
Summer Break

'I know this might seem like a silly question, considering what we've just done but, are you gay?' Tyler said.

Luke draped his arm over Tyler's shoulder and Tyler snuggled into Luke's chest. It turned out Tyler's chest was as chiselled as the photo his sister had shown him in the pub but it was even better in person.

Luke laughed, a full non-censored laugh that made his stomach bounce up and down.

'Definitely,' he replied, stroking Tyler's thick, dark hair. He didn't think he'd ever get over how soft it was. 'You?'

'After that? I'm not so sure,' Tyler said into Luke's chest and Luke froze. Tyler looked up and grinned, a mischievous glint in his eye.

'You bastard.' Luke laughed.

'Had you going for a minute there, didn't I?' Luke jerked his hips upwards and tossed Tyler off the sofa and onto the floor. He rolled and landed on his front, his naked bottom up in the air, a few shades lighter than his arms.

'Well that wasn't kind,' Tyler said, pouting. He pushed himself up onto his elbows and scooted over to where Luke lay on the sofa. He tilted his head up and locked eyes with him.

Luke bent down and kissed him, not the frenzied kissing they had engaged in before but a slow, drawn-out kiss that made his fingers tingle. He cupped Tyler's face and pulled him into him.

'Can't believe you chose this over the Maldives,' Luke said when he pulled away, waving his hand at the small living room.

'I was in Turks and Caicos I'll have you know.'

'Of course, you were.' Luke laughed and rolled onto his back and propped his head up with his arm. He couldn't remember the last time he had felt so relaxed.

'It was alright, I got bored,' Tyler said and Luke didn't know whether he should be taking him seriously or not.

'Those girls not doing it for you?' Luke said remembering the brunette again. Tyler quirked an eyebrow.

'Have you been stalking me, Mr Anderson?'

'No...maybe. But come on, you'd have to be blind to not see you flirting with everyone and anyone.'

'I don't flirt with everyone and certainly not anyone,' he said, his shoulders tensing, taken aback.

'What about Vicki in Barcelona, Petra at Silverstone, or my sister in France?' He was enjoying the teasing and not being on the other end of it for once.

'I was being nice.'

'Nice?'

'You wouldn't know flirting if it hit you in the face,' Tyler said, inching closer to Luke. 'I could have stripped naked in front of you and you still wouldn't realise that I only had eyes for you.'

Luke looked down and Tyler's eyes were ablaze with lust. His stomach bottomed out and he turned away, not wanting to understand what Tyler was saying.

'You didn't fancy going on holiday?' Tyler said a moment later, the tension dissipated.

'I like being at home. We travel so much the rest of the year, I'm lucky if I get to spend more than three consecutive days here.'

'Do you not get lonely?' Tyler propped himself up onto his elbows.

'I like my own company and my sister came over last weekend.' Luke shrugged. His life might feel boring to a billionaire heir but it suited him just fine.

'I love how close you are with your family.' Tyler sighed, rolling over and yanking the blanket off of Luke to put over himself.

'Are you not with yours?'

'Maybe physically. My dad hovers over me like a hawk. I wouldn't say we were emotionally close, no. My mum died when I was a teenager and my brother went weird after that. I don't see much of him either. I think he'd like Dad's attention, which I'd be quite happy to give him, but Dad's not into microbiology so,' Tyler shrugged. 'He sends him a large donation every year and I think he considers that involvement enough.'

'That sucks for your brother,' Luke said as he stared at the ceiling trying to imagine what that must have been like growing up. Being your father's least favourite child, not having his support or him ever being there.

'Can I ask you something?' Tyler said and Luke knew it

was serious because Tyler looked to the floor, fiddling with the edge of the blanket.

'Sure.'

'The other week, in Germany.' His voice was the softest Luke had ever heard but the mention of Germany made him tense up. 'You know after you wouldn't talk to me. What happened?'

Luke didn't answer straight away, the idea of being vulnerable with Tyler scared him.

'I saw you leaving the paddock with Johan...' He let the words hang there in the silence. Luke took a deep breath, swinging between being honest and hiding the moment away like a dirty secret.

'I had a panic attack.' Tyler's head snapped up to stare at him. The infallible Luke Anderson was human after all. Tyler put his hand on Luke's arm and the warmth and comfort seeped into him but Luke couldn't take the sympathy.

'Was that because of me?'

'It was a lot of things.' Luke brushed Tyler's hand off and Tyler took the hint that he didn't want to talk about it anymore. He observed Luke for a moment before smiling and resuming his lazy laissez-faire attitude.

'Don't think I didn't notice the entire Pixar collection over there,' Tyler said with a smirk, pointing to the bookcase that lined the back wall of the lounge.

'It's not all Pixar, there's some DreamWorks in there too. *Shrek* for example.'

'You're such a nerd,' he said, his blue eyes wide and mocking. 'So which one's your favourite?'

'I'm not telling you.'

'Oh go on. Don't tell me, it's *Cars*.' Luke shook his head but his lips pulled up at the corners, Tyler looked sexy even when he was teasing him. His messed-up hair from having Luke's hands in them and the flush of his cheeks post-sex made him all the more gorgeous.

'Please don't say *Wall-E*.'

'Have you seen it?'

'God no, why would I torment myself with that?'

'It's sweet.' Luke shrugged.

'*Frozen*? You strike me as an Elsa.'

'I'm not talking about this if you're going to take the piss.'

'Aw okay, I'll stop. But I'm curious, tell me and I promise I won't laugh.' Luke thought it over a moment before he caved.

'*How to Train Your Dragon*.'

'Huh,' he said with a slight nod like he hadn't expected that answer. 'I've never seen it.'

'I used to quite like *Brave* but I can't watch it anymore because it reminds me of that journo, Sara Holdsworth.'

'Witch,' Tyler muttered with a scowl. 'You do know that you can get these movies on streaming services right? You don't need to own a bookcase of plastic cases.'

'I like having the physical copy. No one can take them away from me,' he grumbled. 'Anyway, you hungry?'

'Don't tell me you cook too? You really are the perfect man.' Tyler smirked. There was something about Tyler's jokiness that Luke could never quite figure out. Everything was veiled with humour and he kind of liked that it kept him guessing.

'Don't get too excited. Johan cooks, I've been living off pasta these last two weeks.' Luke pulled his boxer shorts and trousers back on and Tyler followed suit before heading to the kitchen too.

'You don't look like you have.' Tyler cast an appreciative eye over Luke's body which made him blush under the fluorescence of the kitchen.

The room was half the size of the lounge, with space for two people, a far cry from what everyone imagined Monaco flats to look like. There were no crystal chandeliers, or fur rugs, no expensive artwork or leather sofas. It wasn't homely, the cream walls, which were a shade or two lighter than his parents' magnolia house, were bare. There was nothing personal, no photos or ornaments, no soft furnishings, it was still a blank canvas. Luke was never there so he hadn't had time to turn it into a home. His mum said it would benefit from the female touch but he wouldn't let her near it. It was a convenience, somewhere to put his head down between races. It was temporary.

Standing there in the kitchen, their clothes back on and the harsh light above them, Luke had expected it to feel odd having Tyler in his flat but the truth was, it didn't.

Tyler had made himself comfortable on the bar stool Luke usually sat on and watched him.

'I see you've kept my champagne,' Tyler said reaching over the unit to the bottle.

'It looks too expensive to drink.'

'It's worth it though. I'll get you another and maybe we could share this one.'

Luke opened each cupboard praying he still had something left that he could pass off as presentable but most of them were bare. He rubbed the back of his neck, wracking his brains for what he could pull together.

'What did my dad say to you in Canada?' Tyler asked and it took Luke a moment to realise what Tyler was talking about. But then the memory came back to him. He wasn't sure he wanted to talk about it, it was his dad after all but there was a pleading look in Tyler's eyes that made Luke exhale.

'It doesn't matter,' Luke said turning back to the cupboards.

'Yes, it does. I want to know.'

'It wasn't him, more his guests.' He turned back around and leant on the unit in front of Tyler, their hands meeting across it, entangled. Tyler rolled his eyes.

'I should've guessed.'

'They weren't being very pleasant.' Luke thought over his assessment and changed his mind. 'Actually, they were being sexist pigs. All that male bravado.'

'Toxic masculinity you mean. I'm not surprised. I'm sorry you had to hear that.' Tyler looked it as well, his lips in a gentle pout, turned down, and wide eyes.

'I was in a bad mood anyway and they didn't help. I should be used to it by now though, there's a lot of it in the paddock.'

'I wish there wasn't,' Tyler said, rubbing a hand over his face.

'Me too.' He let go of Tyler and turned back to the cupboards, fingering a packet of crisps and wondering if that passed off as food.

He didn't hear Tyler come up behind him until his arms were around his waist, pulling him into his hard chest.

'I've changed my mind,' he said in a sultry tone, making the hairs on the back of Luke's neck stand up. 'I'm not hungry for food.'

Luke felt his stomach tense and turned to find Tyler devouring him with his eyes. He hoped this wouldn't be the last time he'd see that look in his eye because to know that he was the one who elicited it made him so hard.

Tyler dragged him to the bedroom this time, kissing him hungrily, banging into walls as they felt their way down the corridor, through the door, and onto the double bed.

He fell on top of Luke and growled, low and deep, and Luke forgot everything.

The morning sun hit the window at an angle, casting a diagonal stripe of light onto the wall opposite Luke's bed where he and Tyler lay. Luke was awake, on his side, watching Tyler's slow breathing, his back rising and falling with each breath. Luke stretched out his hand, let it hover an inch above Tyler's shoulder then dropped it back onto the bed.

Tyler stirred but fell back to sleep with a slight snort. A small smile crawled onto Luke's face as he rolled onto his back and stared up at the ceiling again.

It was surreal that he was here. The day before, Luke had been brooding out on the balcony as he watched Tyler jet ski with a gorgeous brunette in the Caribbean and now he was lying in his bed. Naked.

He felt himself stirring again and he couldn't help but reach out a hand and touch the bottom of Tyler's back, dark against the white sheets. He traced little circles through the patch of hair at the bottom of his spine, then trailed his fingers back up. Tyler shivered, stirring from his slumber. When he rolled over he brought his hands up and knotted his fingers into Luke's hair, tugging him towards him.

Their lips met as Luke pushed his hips into Tyler's back making his intention clear.

Lost in the hot taste of Tyler's mouth and the touch of his hard muscles, Luke didn't hear the door open.

'What the...?' Johan said from the doorway, staring at the melee of arms and legs intertwined on the bed.

'Get the fuck out,' Luke shouted, chucking his pillow at the door. Tyler burst out laughing as if he were sat at a comedy show rather than having been caught having sex with his teammate.

'Shit, shit, shit.' Luke said, not finding the funny side of it. He jumped out of bed and willed his penis to quit standing to attention, pulling on some trousers and a t-shirt.

'It's not funny,' he said to Tyler who howled under the covers.

'It's a little funny,' Tyler said, ignoring the scowl on Luke's face. Luke picked the pillow up from the floor and chucked it at Tyler.

He took a deep breath before walking into the hall, listening for a sound to give away Johan's location.

He found him on the balcony, looking out over the street and the mountains. His broad back was straight and his blonde hair neatly combed.

The door scraped as it slid open.

'I'm going to need some holy water to cleanse my eyes after that.' His accent removed all traces of the humour that danced in his eyes.

'Mate, I'm so sorry,' Luke started, his hands open in surrender and apology.

'It's fine, but you could have texted me.'

Luke ran his hand over the back of his neck, massaging away the stress and wondering what he could say to explain. He walked over to where Johan leant up against the railing and turned his back to the view.

'How long has this been going on?' Johan asked, blinking hard as if trying to eradicate the image of Tyler and Luke from his mind.

'Umm,' Luke hesitated. 'I guess when I kissed him in the lift at Silverstone.' He wasn't sure that was when it had started, maybe it had ingrained itself in his mind the first moment he'd watched Tyler in an interview at the end of last year or was it the moment he watched him flirt with all the girls in the garage, or even when they had shouted at each other across the paddock in Australia. He couldn't be sure.

'Oh.'

'You can't say a word,' Luke said when Johan's silence extended.

'Of course,' his friend replied and they lapsed into awkwardness. The implications for both their careers were heavy with the decision that Tyler and Luke had made the moment they had acted on whatever feelings they had.

'What exactly is going on?' Johan asked, his eyes probing, wondering how he had missed what was happening right under his nose this whole time.

'Nothing, it's just some fun,' Luke replied because he didn't know what else to say. They hadn't talked about it, not that he knew what he would say if they did. He didn't know what he wanted. Johan quirked an eyebrow but before he could question it, Tyler's voice came from somewhere inside the flat.

'I'm going to go...'

Luke spun around, wondering if he'd overheard or if Tyler was trying to sneak out now they had been caught. His chest tightened, not wanting the magical moments of the last sixteen hours to be over.

'I'll come with you,' Luke said into the void. Johan arched his eyebrow higher but Luke ignored him, going back to his bedroom to change instead.

He met Tyler back in the main corridor outside his flat. In silence, they took the lift down to the main lobby and then out onto the busy streets of Monaco as the late morning sun beat down on to the pavement.

'Was Johan okay?' Tyler said, keeping his distance from Luke as they walked down the street towards the sea.

'Yeah, he's fine. Don't worry he won't say anything,' Luke said. He hoped he'd reassured him, Johan was trustworthy and he'd never uttered a word about any of Luke's past relationships, there was no reason for him to now.

'Have you guys known each other long?' They fell into step and walked along the promenade like they had done all those months ago when Tyler had shown up for what had seemed like no reason. Luke wondered whether Tyler had felt that pull between them then.

'We have. We used to go to school together.'

It was a glorious day on the Mediterranean coast and the sun glinted off the surface of the deep blue sea like glitter. Luke imagined him and Tyler down at the beach, sipping cocktails and kissing beneath the straw umbrellas. But that could never happen.

'Isn't he Scandinavian?' Tyler asked confused.

'He is. He's from Finland. That's where he's been for the last two weeks. His family moved back a few years ago.'

'I see.' Tyler paused, his face screwed up into a frown as he decided whether to say what was on his mind. 'And you and him? Have you ever…?' Tyler let the question hang, not finishing his thought. Luke couldn't help the tug at the corner of his mouth, bringing a small smile to his face.

'Never. He likes women and only women. Also, he's not my type.'

The tension left Tyler's shoulders and Luke felt the need to pull him close and kiss him again.

'You have a type?' Tyler's eyebrow quirked up.

'Apparently so.' Luke laughed as he puffed the air out of his lungs. Luke moved closer to him, now that he'd been allowed to touch him, it was all he wanted to do.

They lapsed into silence again, the sound of the sea and birds keeping them company. Luke's fingers twitched knowing Tyler's were inches from his, but he didn't reach out. They were in public and no one could know what had happened inside the four walls of his flat, or all the things he wanted to do to Tyler now the light was green.

Tyler turned away from Luke to answer his phone, the distance growing between them. Luke wanted to pull him back, wrap him up in his arms, and kiss him until he was dizzy with lust but instead, they kept apart, the sea breeze blowing between them.

'I've got to go, the helicopter's on its way,' Tyler said, with a sad smile.

'Helicopter?'

'Yeah. I'll catch you next weekend in Belgium then,' Tyler said returning his phone to his pocket but he didn't move. His eyes locked on Luke, and flicked to his lips, lingering in the silence that expanded between them. Tyler stepped forwards, his hand reaching out for Luke's arm but he retracted.

'I'll walk with you,' Luke said but Tyler shook his head.

'No, it's fine. It's not far.' He paused, wanting to say more but he didn't. 'See you at Spa.'

Luke watched Tyler disappear around a corner, confusion clouding every thought in his mind.

Twenty-one

Belgian Grand Prix – Circuit de Spa-Francorchamps – Stavelot
August 29th

Luke's leg jiggled as he sat in the passenger seat of the Mercedes, Johan behind the wheel, the car crawling along the road into the circuit.

'Stop it,' Johan warned, hitting Luke's thigh. 'What's wrong with you?'

'Nothing's wrong,' Luke lied.

He was nervous. His palms turned slick with sweat whenever he thought about seeing Tyler. His heart pushed thick blood through his veins whenever the thought of Tyler kissing him crossed his mind. They hadn't been in touch since that day but he wanted to see him. He'd had a taste of Tyler and he wanted more. The heat crept up his neck at the thought.

He had no idea what Tyler thought and part of him was terrified that Tyler might kiss him in the middle of the paddock. He didn't want to avoid him but he knew at some point they would need to talk about it.

Luke and Johan had talked about it, once or twice, since Tyler had left. Johan had a bunch of questions Luke couldn't answer. All Luke knew was that whatever it was could never be more than stolen moments.

It would always have to be a secret.

The world of motorsport wasn't ready for openly gay men, let alone ones that were teammates. The brand itself was all about glamour and masculinity, fast cars and hot girls. Not that long ago they paid models to stand in front of the cars before the race, for show.

The world wasn't ready either. They visited so many countries that still viewed being gay as a crime, punishable by death in some, he couldn't jeopardise his career or his life for whatever this was.

He knew that. Tyler must have known that too.

It had to stay a secret.

On top of that, after Hungary, Lewandowski was closing in on the championship and Luke felt the pressure of getting a good result to keep the lead.

As they drove deeper into the Ardenne forest, Luke realised that Tyler was right, he was more of a Spa guy. He loved the circuit, with the change of elevation, the hairpin at La Source that threw you straight down to the bottom of Raidillon and Eau Rouge, with the steep incline and blind peak at full speed. Every lap was a leap of faith that you'd make it out the other side unscathed.

Johan pulled up outside the paddock turnstiles and Luke hopped out, his holdall in hand. He was staying in the motorhome for the weekend again, sharing with Johan, away from the crowds and the one hotel that would be full to the brim of fans. Not the best place to get a full night's sleep before a race that held such pressure.

The grey clouds rolled overhead but so far it had stayed dry. Luke nodded and waved at mechanics, other drivers, and team members as they crossed his path along the concrete highway of the paddock.

He wasn't in his room long before Johan let himself in, setting up shop at the desk. It was crazy that they left this room one weekend and found it exactly the same the week after in a different place in the world.

Luke had glanced at the lift on his way in, this time with a little smile playing on his lips at what had happened since.

'When is your boyfriend getting here?' Johan teased and Luke chucked his water bottle at him. He screwed his face up at the word, he didn't want a relationship. The word boyfriend wasn't part of his vocabulary.

The door flew open a second after Johan's comment and Luke's eyes grew wide as he waited to see who might have overheard them. Emma strolled in doing another balancing act with two steaming cups of coffee and her media schedule. She gave one of the cups to Luke who'd been so distracted that morning, he hadn't even thought about coffee.

'Thanks, Em,' he said, the curls of steam escaping the lid bringing with it the cosy smell of the brown liquid.

'You ready for the meet and greet?'

The nervous energy he'd been trying to control got the better of him as Emma tried to keep up with his long strides when they left the motorhome and made their way down the paddock. The sponsor event was in one of the conference rooms and Luke had hoped the first time he would see Tyler this weekend would be somewhere more private. He wanted to make sure they were good. That what had happened over the summer hadn't ruined their relationship as teammates, that it wasn't going to get in the way of the racing or get out and make ripples through the team and the press. That Tyler was okay.

He and Emma got to the side room first, he could hear the excited fans beyond the wall, chatting and laughing, the music not able to drown them out.

'Hello, hello,' Jessie said coming in next, her hair pulled into a tight ponytail, wearing the purple fleece of Team Wilson. 'Another week, another race,' she sing-songed. At least she was in a good mood, hopefully, they wouldn't mess it up for her this time. Luke's stomach knotted as he kept his eyes glued to the door.

'Where's Tyler?' Emma asked as she peered behind Jessie.

Jessie checked her watch and Luke copied her, the little numbers on his wrist ticking past the hour. Luke shrugged and tried to ignore the rock that had appeared in his stomach.

The idea that Tyler might not want to see him, that he may regret what had happened between them took hold of Luke. He'd tried to push those thoughts away over the last week, wanting to believe that by crossing that line they hadn't ruined everything. His legs moved by themselves making him pace.

Beyond the wall, he heard the music hush and the crowd quieten down as the MC greeted them. Luke's jaw twitched, his eyes back on the door, Jessie checking outside for her charge. From a door on the opposite side of the room, one of the event's team appeared.

'We're ready for you,' he said glancing around the room, his brows pulling together as he marked the noticeable absence of one of the drivers.

'Sorry I'm late,' Tyler said, breezing into the room. Luke's whole body relaxed at a secretive smile and glance in his direction. They walked into the event room, side by side. The music was loud, the crowd even louder. They erupted when they spotted the two drivers. Luke's relief was palpable, he'd almost convinced himself that Tyler would be mad at him and would ignore him the whole weekend but they were stood inches apart and Luke knew Tyler was holding back from bushing his fingers against his.

'I watched *How to Train Your Dragon*,' Tyler whispered as the presenter talked about the sponsors. 'Do I need to grow a beard? Is that what does it for you? Or is it the accent?' He winked before climbing the stairs onto the stage. Luke couldn't help but laugh, his eyes and smile wide as he watched Tyler wave to the crowd.

The sea of purple caps and t-shirts filled the whole conference room which had been turned into a nightclub. With a stage and a DJ, the main lights down low, the multicoloured spotlights swirled around like at the launch night event. They answered fan questions, and signed autographs on cards, caps, and even someone's arm all whilst keeping their distance. Luke found himself desperate to snatch a minute alone with him but once they came off stage, Jessie and Emma were right there.

'Have you seen this?' Jessie asked, snapping Luke's attention away from Tyler and back to her. She held out her phone and Luke tried to make sense of what he saw. It was the website for a trashy English newspaper and at the top there was a grainy photo. Luke squinted and realised it was a photo of him and Tyler out on the cliffs in Monaco. His pulse quickened, his breath shallow. He knew when it had been taken and he felt his hand shake as he handed it to Tyler.

Were they busted already? It couldn't be, nothing had happened, they'd talked. Luke wracked his brain for anything they did that would give them away.

'Well, you said you wanted us to act more like friends.' Tyler handed Jessie her phone back. 'Is that too much? Do we need to tone it down now?' His tone was mocking and a little sarcastic. His shoulders were still relaxed and nothing on his face gave him away. It was like, to him, nothing had happened between them and Luke hoped he was half the actor Tyler was.

'No, it's great. It's had a lot of buzz online, the twitterverse is confused and doesn't know what to think,' she said with a satisfied smile. Was this why she was in a good mood? Tyler and Luke being friends made her life easier. If only she knew.

'Keep up the good work,' she said, walking out into the paddock again. Luke tried to linger, wanting to catch Tyler alone but Jessie grabbed hold of him, running through his next media duties.

'You okay?' Emma said, falling into step with Luke as he watched Jessie and Tyler disappear down the paddock.

'Yeah,' he said feeling himself deflate. He didn't see much of Tyler for the rest of the day and part of him hoped he would appear at his motorhome door that evening but he didn't.

When Luke had given up on them having any contact that day, his phone pinged with a text.

Missed you today x

He wanted to tell him to come over but Johan was lounging on the sofa bench, watching and cackling at the TV, his feet up on the small table with a beer in one hand. It was also too risky, who knew whose prying eyes were hiding around corners? They'd been spotted in Monaco and they weren't the centre of attention there.

Luke struggled to contain how pleased Tyler's text had made him feel though. He sat down next to Johan and typed a reply.

'What's got you grinning like a monkey with a banana?'

'Oh shut up,' Luke snapped, thinking about what he could say to Tyler.

'It's not going to end well,' Johan continued, his eyes

flicking back to the TV. He'd mentioned this before when they'd talked about it and Luke hadn't wanted to hear it then and he didn't want to hear it now. 'You'd do better to forget about it before it goes any further.'

'Thank you for your input,' Luke snapped again, standing up and retreating to his bedroom.

Yeah, same.

He knew his reply sucked but he didn't know what else to say. He pulled his headphones on and drowned out the sound of the TV from next door.

The next day was business as usual. Luke, head down, got on with what he needed to do until qualifying. He stole a glance across the garage and exchanged a small smile with Tyler before he put his helmet on. There was no space for error here.

The Ferraris had been on top form through practice and somehow Luke needed to find extra time around the circuit if he wanted to challenge for pole.

He did two runs in the first qualifying session and topped the leaderboard ahead of Tyler but he had a feeling the Ferraris were sandbagging. It appeared he was right after the second session where Luke timed in in fifth and Tyler in fourth, the car sliding around beneath him.

'Dash, what's going on?' he said over the radio after his first run in the third and final qualifying session. 'This car feels completely different to this morning, I can barely keep it straight.'

The line stayed dead for a few minutes until Dash's voice came on.

'Box, box.'

Luke pulled into his pit box and the team wheeled him back into the garage. He watched the timing screens with one eye, the other casting a look over the data to see where he was losing time compared to Tyler. He had one more chance to sling it around the track and get as close to Lewandowski as he could because it seemed he wouldn't have enough pace to beat him.

With two minutes left, he pulled out of the garage and trundled down the pit lane, Tyler pulling out behind him. He warmed his tyres up as much as he could and charged up his battery before he slammed down on the accelerator and crossed the start line with seconds to spare to start his lap. He hoped Tyler had managed to as well but that thought vanished as he sped down to La Source. Then up the hill to Raidillon and Eau Rouge, named after the red river that crossed beneath the track, then down the Kemmel straight. His delta looked good, purples so far in each sector, the fastest time of all. He nailed the chicane at Les Combes and linked up the rest of the second sector.

As he turned around Stavelot, he saw the yellow flags waving and a McLaren beached in the gravel. He slowed the car as specified in the regulations, his lap ruined. He smacked the steering wheel in frustration.

'Dash, where does that leave us?' Luke asked, backing out of the lap and heading back for the pits.

'P8. Bad luck buddy.'

Tyler had managed to stay in sixth ready for tomorrow but with Lewandowski on pole it was looking like another damage limitation race. Lewandowski had regained second place in the championship after Hungary, overtaking Tyler and chasing down Luke with thirty-four points between. Mikolaj would take another chunk out of that in the race, so Luke needed to focus on getting as many points as possible.

After qualifying, his mind stuck on how he could gain as many places as he could in the race, Luke heard one of the worst sounds in motor racing rattle round the paddock. Somewhere in the distance, there was a squeal of tyres, rubber dragging across the track surface, the sickening crunch of metal on metal, and a collective gasp from the crowd.

Luke looked to Emma and they both knew it was nothing good.

The support race had started after qualifying had finished, they couldn't be that far through it but there was no doubt the racing had stopped. The dull sound of cars coming back into the pits could be heard and the crowd was silent. The whole atmosphere was subdued and the polar opposite of how it had been ten minutes before. It felt eerie in the silence.

Luke returned to the motorhome and there, he found most of the team huddled around a screen, no one speaking. He didn't register Tyler standing off to the side, his eyes drawn to the screen which wasn't showing anything other than the cars lined up in the pit lane.

'What's going on?' he asked Jamie who was closest to him.

'Bad crash,' he said, his eyes still glued to the screen as they waited for news. 'Someone crashed at the top of Eau Rouge, spun out, and hit the barrier.' He ran his hands through his hair, his eyes wide.

'Who?'

'Lorenzo Nunez,' Jamie breathed out like he didn't want to be saying it. Luke's stomach dropped and he felt sick.

He didn't hang around and retreated to his driver's room where he found Johan watching the same thing on his laptop.

'It doesn't look good,' he said as Luke sat on the bench. He ran his fingers through his sweaty hair as images of the driver, the one who was about to retire, flashed through his mind. He thought of his family, his two young kids, and bile rolled around his stomach.

They remained there, in silence, watching as the commentators filled the time for what felt like hours. Nothing in his mind except for the hope that it would be good news at the end of it.

There was a knock on the door and Emma poked her head round.

'Just to let you know, they've cancelled the fan forum this afternoon.'

Luke nodded.

'Any news?' he said, his voice a little hoarse from not having spoken for a while.

'Nothing yet, but I'll let you know as soon as I know something.' He nodded again and she shut the door behind her, leaving him and Johan to resume their silence.

It felt like forever until there was another knock, it was Emma again and she had tears in her eyes.

She shook her head when Luke gazed up at her.

'We've had word that Lorenzo didn't make it.' She held in a sob and hurried away. Luke's head fell forwards as he closed his eyes.

Twenty-two

Belgian Grand Prix – Circuit de Spa-Francorchamps – Stavelot
August 31st

It was the risk they all took.

Every single time they climbed into that car they knew that they may not make it out alive. But letting the fear hold them back would stop them from competing.

They were fearless, they had to be. Even one seed of doubt would stop them from striving for that extra hundredth or thousandth of a second that would make them the best. And that's what they all wanted.

To be the best.

Luke stared at the blank wall of his motorhome, reliving some of his worst crashes and thanking the stars that he had made it out of every one of them alive. Bruised and battered maybe but alive. Which was more than could be said for Lorenzo Nunez.

His name echoed around Luke's head and Emma's words that he hadn't made it. It had been a few years since they'd last had a loss in the motorsport family and it never failed to sober everyone up on the realities of what their career involved.

The FIA decided that the race on Sunday would go ahead, with the blessing of his wife, who said it was what Lorenzo would have wanted.

Racing was his whole life and it was Luke's too.

He sighed, trying to rid his body of the unsettled feeling he'd been harbouring since the news earlier in the afternoon. He, like everyone else in the paddock, was shaken. The news rippled out of the medical centre like a capillary wave, touching each and every person, both at the track and all over the world.

Johan had gone to bed to call his parents. It was moments like these that made you want to hold the people you loved close. Luke's parents had called him straight away and he'd assured them he was fine, putting on a brave face so they didn't worry. They weren't there this weekend and Luke knew it was his mother's worst nightmare. It was every mother's worst nightmare. Even Nick had called, remembering a time she had sat with Lorenzo and his kids to watch a race last year in the Wilson motorhome. Luke heard her tears and did his best to be strong for her.

He stood to turn the light off and head to bed for the night when a soft knock on the motorhome door made him jump.

He swung it open to find Tyler, looking the same as Luke felt, standing at the bottom of the steps. He glanced around the empty paddock before stepping over the threshold into Luke's space.

Tyler reached the top of the stairs and pulled Luke into his arms, hugging him tight. Luke let himself be held and breathed in the heady scent of Tyler's skin. It was comforting and he hadn't realised quite how much he'd missed it until he was there.

'Bad day?' Luke half laughed and then he felt the water on his cheeks. He sniffed, trying to put them back in but Tyler pulled away and wiped his thumb over Luke's skin, collecting the stray tear with it.

'You could say that,' he said with a small smile before drawing Luke back into him. 'You make out you're this emotionless bastard and look at you, you're a softy inside eh?'

Luke laughed, his body shaking with the mix of emotions. He didn't think he pretended to be emotionless, but he was careful who got to see that side of him.

'Grab the snacks,' Tyler said letting go of him but holding onto his hand, their fingers intertwined. He pulled him towards the door to the left, behind which Luke's small bedroom lay.

The bed was barely big enough for Luke but Tyler squeezed himself up against the wall and made space for Luke to curl into him.

'Tomorrow's going to suck. I don't know how I'm going to do it,' Tyler said as he stroked Luke's hair.

'You just do. Once that visor goes down and those lights come on, you have to forget about it.'

'Were you there last time?'

Luke nodded. It had been his rookie year, the whole day was engraved in his memory but he didn't revisit it very often. It was compartmentalised somewhere deep inside, behind lots of locked doors.

'How did you do it? How did you keep going?' Tyler asked and his voice cracked.

Luke draped his arm over Tyler's waist and fisted his t-shirt, his thumb finding hot skin. He knew how it felt, he'd been Tyler back then, with no experience and no idea how he was supposed to continue but he had.

'You have to. It comes from here...' He hit himself square in the chest. 'It's automatic. I promise you'll be fine. And if you're not, then you stop. You get out of the car and you walk away. But you were born for this. Racing runs in your blood, if you're like me, you're nothing without it, so you'll find a way to get through this because you have to.'

Tyler propped himself up onto his elbow and looked at Luke, searching his face with wide eyes. Then, he tilted his head down and put his lips on Luke's. Soft at first, like he was holding back, trying to not overstep but when Luke responded curling his fingers into Tyler's hair, he gave in and gave all of himself to Luke again.

They lay in the quiet, intertwined and tangled in each other, skin on skin. Their hands laced together like a lifeline.

'Do you ever wonder what you'd be doing if you weren't racing?' Tyler asked.

'I'd be running an alpaca farm,' Luke said, his face deadpan.

'What?' Luke could see Tyler's expression out of the corner of his eye and laughed. 'Dude, I thought you were serious.'

'I can't keep a plant alive, let alone a herd of alpacas.' Luke chuckled, pulling Tyler closer so he could snuggle into his chest. 'What about you?'

'I wouldn't have a clue. What do you think I'd be good at?'

'A male model? Is that cliché?' Luke mused. 'You looked so good on that runway in Monaco.'

'Me? Did you see yourself? I don't know how I managed to not kiss you then to be honest. My whole body was screaming at me to lay one on you but I thought you might have punched me. A black eye was the one thing stopping me.'

'How vain.' Luke laughed, feeling that warmth inside his chest again. 'I probably would've to be honest.'

'When did you realise you didn't hate me?'

'I never hated you.'

'Okay let's not lie to each other.' Tyler laughed, kissing him as he waited for an answer.

'After I kissed you in the lift,' Luke concluded.

'After? What about before? Was that a hate kiss, oh my god. Really?' Tyler flung himself back onto the bed in mock despair. 'And here I was thinking you'd been pining after me for months. I'm glad I didn't try anything earlier then. God.'

Luke smirked. It felt nice to know Tyler had been thinking about him in that way long before Luke had even realised.

'When did you realise then? Because you were very good at pretending like you didn't like me.' Luke quirked an eyebrow, rolling onto his side so they were face to face on the pillow. The tip of his fingers played with the hair above Tyler's neck, soft, almost baby-like, and of the darkest black.

'I never disliked you. I envied you, I admired you, way before I made it into F1. The world adores you, I'm no different. I never thought that the great Luke Anderson might swing the same way I did, but god I knew I fancied you the minute I laid eyes on you. Who wouldn't, look at you?' He gestured up and down Luke's naked body.

'Okay stop it,' Luke said smiling despite how the compliments made him squirm.

'You asked.' Tyler kissed him again and they held onto each other in silence for a moment longer.

'You should probably go,' Luke said, wanting nothing more than for him to stay. 'It's getting late and I don't want to fall asleep at the wheel tomorrow. And the paddock will get busy in the morning, it's safer if you go back to your motorhome now.'

Tyler's body tensed up as he looked to Luke with a

probing stare.

'Fine.'

He pushed himself over Luke's body with difficulty to retrieve his clothes from the small patch of floor beside the mattress. He bundled them up and walked out of the room. Luke felt the familiar sensation of having screwed up run through him but his mind reeled as he tried to figure out how. He sighed, then got up to follow Tyler when he heard Johan's voice.

'Oh for fuck's sake. Put it away.'

Luke came out into the communal area to find Johan hiding a still naked Tyler from view with his hand, his eyes squeezed shut in case.

'Sorry,' Tyler muttered, rushing to pull his clothes on.

'I feel like I've seen your dick as many times as Luke has now,' Johan grumbled, turning back to his room. 'Let me know when he's gone,' he shouted over his shoulder before shutting the door.

'Is everything okay? Did I say something?' Luke said holding his bed cover over his lower half.

'I'm fine. It's fine.' Tyler waved him off but the tone of his voice told Luke it wasn't fine and he was anything but.

'Tell me,' Luke pressed, taking a few steps towards him, putting his hand out to touch him. Tyler withdrew, like Luke had on their run that last morning. With one backwards glance, Tyler walked down the steps, and before he opened the door to disappear into the night he said: 'I don't want to be an easy shag to you.'

With that, the door swung shut behind him and left Luke staring at the grey plastic handle, where Tyler's hand had been a second before.

Luke didn't sleep. The next day he felt tired and drained, far from the refreshed he should have felt before a race.

The atmosphere in the paddock was solemn. People walked slower, there was less rushing around than normal and less chatter. Whenever he walked past someone from the team, they grasped his arm for a moment, a silent promise, a whisper of hope, of determination. They were a family, the entire paddock, all the categories of motorsport, they all came together and held each other close in the hard times.

Between that and Tyler's parting words of the night before, Luke's mind was all over the place. Johan had pep-talked him over breakfast and again a moment ago before he headed out of his driver's room but he still felt heavy. The weight of it all pressed down on his shoulders, not relenting for a moment.

'One has to understand that braveness is not the absence of fear but rather the strength to keep on going forward despite the fear,' Johan said as they walked through the sliding doors of the Wilson motorhome.

'Who?'

'Paulo Coelho.' Luke nodded as Emma fell into step with him.

'There's going to be a minute's silence after the national anthem. I'll walk with you.'

Luke hiked his fire suit up as it threatened to fall past his narrow hips and dived into the back of the garage in time to avoid Petra who was making a beeline for him. He wasn't in the mood and he didn't want to say something to her, either professionally or personally that he would regret.

Vicki waited for him by the car, her face set and a little weary from the last few days.

'Ready?' she asked.

'I guess so.'

'We've been here before. You're better than before,' she said and he was grateful that he had her on his side. 'Do your best.'

'Thanks Vick. I'll see you on the other side.'

After he'd parked the car on the grid ready for the start, Emma walked him down to the front for the national anthem. They stood in a line under the lights on the temporary red carpet as usual, and a local singer prepared blast out the national anthem in front of them.

Some of the drivers were already there, waiting in silence. Luke took his spot next to Tyler and tried to latch on to his energy despite the metre or so that separated them. Tyler looked straight ahead and Luke saw the twitch in his jaw, like he was trying to hold it together. He wanted to reach out and touch him, pull him close and reassure him but he knew he couldn't.

The drivers moved in closer, so they were shoulder to shoulder as the singer began. Luke could feel Tyler next to him, he leaned in and pressed his shoulder into his to let him know he was there.

After the last note, the crowd went silent, a hush falling over the track and the trees, the air heavy with grief and sadness. Luke's eyes stung as he kept them down, focusing on his feet as the silence dragged on. He knew now wasn't the time to grieve, that would be for tomorrow. He blocked out his memories of Lorenzo, concentrating on the spot where Tyler's arm rested against his.

All too soon, the minute was over and Luke was walking back to his car and away from Tyler.

He climbed into it and as he had promised Tyler the night before, he clamped his lid shut and blocked out the world, blocking out all thoughts and fears. It was him and the car.

LUKE ANDERSON: ONE HIT WONDER?
What's happened to the dependable World Champion?

By Sara Holdsworth

Date published: September 8th

After an incredible season from Luke Anderson and Wilson Racing last year, the world expected great things from the championship-winning team and driver. After a string of less than impressive results, the question begs, what's happened to Luke Anderson?

The Ferraris have come back swinging after the summer break with two consecutive wins and seem to have left Wilson Racing trailing in the development race, but Anderson hasn't always been in the fastest car.

Arguably, last year, the Ferrari was much faster than the Wilson but Anderson still managed to wrap up the championship before the season finale. We've seen immense determination and resilience from Anderson over the years, notably Suzuka 2017 when he came back from a huge crash in qualifying to win the race. Or Silverstone 2018, when despite the rain, Anderson managed to put his Wilson on the top spot when most of his nearest rivals couldn't keep the car on the track.

What's changed?

The WR19 isn't great in the wet, it's harder to drive than the Ferrari, it understeers and at Spa, it slid all over the place. Qualifying in eighth, Anderson managed to get up to fifth however his performance could hardly be classed as epic.

Understandably, the conditions at the weekend were hard, with the major crash in the Porsche Supercup race that led to the death of Lorenzo Nunez, most were feeling the strain of the race.

They then moved on to Monza, Italy, home of Ferrari, and again the scarlet machine shone as Lewandowski took another win ahead of Brambilla the Italian Lotus driver, much to the joy of the crowd. Anderson trailed in third, only just beating his teammate and Schulz.

Is it the Tyler Finley effect? Is having a teammate on the same level destabilising him? He had an easy ride with Vasquez last year, with the Brazilian already planning his retirement, he didn't push Anderson like Finley did this year.

'Luke's performing admirably,' Team Principal Martin Clark said. 'We're happy with both our drivers and we're all working hard as a team to make sure the car is the best it can be. Ferrari has brought some upgrades to Belgium which seem to be working well for them so we will knuckle down and make sure our guys have the best machine underneath them to challenge that.'

'He's a grafter, he works hard both on and off the track. It's been great being able to learn from him so far this year,' Finley said, despite the rumoured feud that is still ongoing between the pair behind closed doors.

'He's overrated. He always has been, I don't get the appeal. The press has made him into a superstar but he only won last year because no one had the car underneath them to beat him. I wouldn't hire him,' said Monster's team principal. The most outspoken and controversial person in the paddock seemed to be the only one who didn't rate Luke Anderson as a driver.

Still holding onto the lead of the championship with 245 points to Lewandowski's 234, there are seven more races before we find out who will be the Formula One World Champion in 2019.

Twenty-three

Singapore Grand Prix – Marina Bay Street Circuit – Singapore
September 22nd

The last few weeks had been rough.

Although Luke had wanted to pretend like what had happened in Belgium hadn't affected him, he was struggling to keep it together.

Back at home, in the middle of the night, he'd woken from a dream where he'd seen Tyler crash. The rising panic had pulled him back into the world of the living where cold sweat ran down his body like rivulets down a mountainside. It felt like something heavy sat on his chest and he struggled to breathe. The familiar feeling coiled itself around him and he was but a passenger as his body tensed up and refused to work for what felt like hours.

He found himself, more often than not, worrying about Tyler as he hurtled around the track and he'd fought his thoughts through the entire Italian Grand Prix at Monza a few weeks ago.

He'd seen Tyler's car spin out ahead of him, clipped by De Leon who tumbled down the order and although Luke's whole body screamed for him to stop to check if he was okay, he couldn't. He had to keep going, so that's what he did. He was straight on the radio, asking if Tyler was okay, and after two turns and no answer, he felt the walls of his mind closing in. He had tunnel vision for three more corners as he gasped for air inside his helmet and then Dash's calm voice came over the radio.

'Yeah, fine. He's lost a few places.' His tone noted the surprise of the question but Luke could breathe again and that's what mattered. Tyler was fine and so was Luke.

Luke finished in third, another disappointing result for the team.

He sat rather than stood on the podium, exhausted from the effort, exhausted from the extra stress his mind had put his body through. Brambilla and Lewandowski were beside him, with the latter taking another win. Brambilla gave him a quick thumbs up to check he was okay, which Luke returned with a small smile.

He was so distracted, he wasn't giving it his all and it was showing in his results. Tyler consumed his thoughts and after Belgium, it was constant worry.

He left straight after the race in Italy, no press, no interviews. Emma gate keeping him from the onslaught of questions, sensing and seeing in his eyes that he wasn't well.

He'd hopped in the car with Johan who drove them the two hundred miles back to Monaco and as the car devoured the roads along the Italian coastline, Luke had time to think. His head was all over the place, in a constant tug of war with his heart.

After sneaking around in Monza, stealing a few kisses whilst Johan kept guard, Luke had ignored all of Tyler's messages. Tyler wanted more, he'd been clear about it and Luke knew he couldn't give him that.

The Singapore air was heavy, humid, and hot, despite the sun having set a while ago. The paddock heaved with people, lit up by the giant lanterns outside each motorhome and the floodlights from the pit building opposite. The potted plants, which had been shipped in to make the place look good, wilted in the heat.

Luke walked from the motorhome to the back of the garage, dodging reporters, fans, and mechanics. The European season was over with only fly-aways left for the rest of the year. Luke tried not to think too far ahead, wanting to take it one race at a time. He still led the championship, the margin decreasing with every race and he felt it slipping through his fingers.

He never let his personal life interfere with his professional one, except for that one season way back when, but this year he could trace the ups and downs of his life in his results on track and he hated it.

'Are you ready?' Johan asked with a small smile and a concerned look on his face, his eyebrows pulled together.

'As I'll ever be.'

'Serena Williams. Overpower. Overtake. Overcome.'

Luke nodded then put his earplugs in and pulled on his balaclava.

After driving to the grid, he returned to the shaded, air-conditioned pits and hid in a meeting room until it was time to race.

It wasn't a spectacular race by any means. It was hot and sweaty, speeding around the track under the floodlights, the sky above inky black and starless from the light pollution.

The fireworks exploded as Tyler took the win in front of Lewandowski, keeping the three-way fight alive. Luke took the finish line in fourth, the McLaren of Tanaka managing to sneak into third place after the safety car, decreasing his championship lead to five points.

Five points wasn't a lot when a win was worth twenty-five but coupled with his current form, Luke wasn't hopeful. He was frustrated and he struggled to be happy for Tyler and the team. There was no explanation for his lack of pace, he should have won the race, like Tyler had but he hadn't even made the podium.

His mood flooded over him, dark and stifling. He struggled to lift it as he did his post-race interviews, all questions leading back to the championship, to Tyler's win, and to what happens now. He didn't know where to go from here, he didn't know how to change course.

The winner's photo was next on his schedule and he managed to put on a smile for the press and congratulate Tyler, the cameras flashing around them, glinting off the trophy. He felt Tyler's eyes searching him as they knelt a metre apart on the tarmac outside the Wilson garages but he couldn't bring himself to give him a reassuring smile.

Luke felt uneasy, unaligned, like something was out of place. A splinter on a sanded piece of wood, jarring, stabbing at the hand that ran across the otherwise smooth surface. He walked back to the Wilson Racing motorhome to collect his things, to catch a flight, and move on to the next one. Johan was there, laptop packed up, team kit bagged, ready to go. Luke rubbed his face with the palm of his hand, digging the heel of it into his eye sockets, as Johan stared at him, trying to figure out what was going on. Johan opened his mouth to say something but a knock on the door made them jump.

Luke pulled it open and found Tyler standing there, the trophy dumped on the bench in his room visible through the open doors. The rest of the team were a few metres away in the café and Luke glanced around to see if anyone was looking their way.

'I'll see you outside,' Johan said, squeezing past the two men and obscuring the view of the corridor. Luke stood aside to let Tyler in and the door swung shut behind him.

'Congratulations...again' Luke said not moving from where he had opened the door. The room was small but it felt claustrophobic with Tyler taking up the space Johan usually occupied. Shorter and not as broad as the Scandinavian, the space still felt tight around them.

'What's going on?' Tyler said, putting his hands on his hips. His forehead creased, blue eyes narrowed and flashing.

Luke couldn't formulate what he wanted to say. He knew what he had to do but looking at Tyler standing there made it hard.

Releasing his hands and letting go of the anger on his face, Tyler sensed that that wasn't the way to get what he needed.

'Please talk to me,' he pleaded, reaching his hands out towards Luke.

'I...I don't think I can do this anymore,' Luke choked out then turned his back on Tyler. He didn't want to see the look on his face, he didn't want to be swayed into changing his mind. He knew it was the right thing to do, everything had pointed at that, before it went too far, before they were found out but it didn't stop it from hurting like hell.

There was no place for them in this world and racing was his whole life. He wanted to win and having one foot in a world where he and Tyler were together meant he didn't have two feet in the championship, fighting for that title like he had set out to do.

'You can't do what?' Luke could hear the tension in Tyler's voice.

'This, us,' he replied waggling a finger between them

behind his back. 'It was never going to work, we were stupid to even entertain the idea.'

'Are you kidding right now?' Tyler asked, incredulity laced in every word. This snapped Luke out of his funk and into an angry place. He swung round to face Tyler, his thunderous glare made Tyler lean back.

'No I'm not kidding. You've made it very clear you want more from me, but we both know that can never happen.'

'Why not?' Tyler asked, surprised.

'Because even if I wasn't distracted and terrified of you having a crash, this is a scandal too far for Clark. Look around, we're teammates in one of the most competitive sports in the world. A sport that has never supported us and who we are,' Luke exploded, frustration pouring out of him like sweat.

'That's not true, the sport has made so much progress towards acceptance,' Tyler countered.

'Not nearly enough for us to be anything more than teammates.' Luke ran his hands through his hair, grabbing fistfuls of it and pulling hard.

'I don't believe that. You're scared.'

'If they supported who we were like they said they did, we wouldn't be racing in countries that criminalise the way we love. They wouldn't put money into governments pockets who disagree with who we are. Can you even imagine? What they would say? It doesn't even bear thinking about. That's why I never, never mix my life outside of the track with the job. That's why I've left that part of myself on the back burner for so long. It's distracting, it doesn't fit.'

'Who gives a shit what they say? You started this by kissing me in that lift, you can't back out now. It won't be easy but god I'm sure it'll be worth it.'

Luke tensed, it was his fault but he'd never thought it would turn into this. He hadn't thought before he'd done it and he'd let it go too far.

'Luke,' Tyler said, taking a step towards him but Luke backed away. He knew that if Tyler so much as touched him he would change his mind.

'I can't do it. I can't. I can't be a racing driver and be with you.' He knew his words stung Tyler and he felt his heart contract, the sick feeling returning to his stomach.

'Yes, you can, we can do this. Please Luke...' The sadness in Tyler's eyes was too much. Luke turned his back on him again not letting himself consider the other options, his mind was made up. 'Don't do this.'

Luke blew out a sigh, picked up his bag from the floor, paused for a second, and without a backwards glance opened the door.

'I'll see you in Russia,' he said before walking out of the motorhome.

He held it together until he climbed into the car beside Johan. Ten minutes after they left the paddock, Luke's phone pinged in the silent car.

At the top of his unread messages was a new one from Tyler. Their conversations from a month of getting to know each other plain to see above Tyler's latest message which read:

I don't care what anyone else has to say about this. I want you and only you. Don't do this xx

Luke didn't reply, the cracks in his heart far deeper than he thought possible for a short-lived fling. He didn't understand what was happening but he knew that from now on, Tyler had to be the furthest thing from his mind. There was no escaping the fact that Luke had struggled to concentrate on his job for most of the year and now it was serious.

He was on the brink of losing the lead in the championship and he wanted to be double World Champion more than anything. That had to be the sole thing to occupy his thoughts going forward. Training, driving, winning.

No more distractions.

He wiped his eyes as they neared the airport and Johan parked ready to return the rental car. Johan put a heavy hand on the gear stick, sighing.

'When you're standing on that top step, holding the World Champion title in your hands, Tyler Finley will feel like a distant memory,' he said and Luke could only hope that he was right.

Twenty-four

**Russian Grand Prix – Sochi Autodrom – Sochi
September 25th**

'It's the worst idea he's ever had,' Emma said as she took two steps for every one of Luke's. They walked through the paddock on their way to the official Thursday FIA press conference. It was a clear, cool day and the weekend was promising weather-wise. Luke felt good and was looking forward to driving around the Olympic Park again.

'It's not his best,' Luke acknowledged.

'Can you imagine you and Tyler posing for the Aldi magazine? The worst.'

'I didn't think we were that poor.'

'We're not! That's why I think it's stupid,' Emma muttered as they entered.

Journalists were setting up, the officials getting the table and chairs ready and the driver's microphones were laid out to the side.

Emma and Luke hovered by the door as Mikolaj Lewandowski came in with his press officer. Emma struck up a conversation with him, leaving Lewandowski and Luke to make small talk.

'How's it going?' Luke said. They had raced against each other for years, they weren't friends but they were friendly, despite fighting for the same championship for the last two years.

'Good,' the Pole replied. 'I don't like….this,' he said gesturing to the press that waited for them. 'It like putting needle in eye.'

Luke laughed, despite being one of the best drivers, Lewandowski's English was the worst on the grid.

'I get ya man,' Luke said as Tyler walked into the room, Jessie following behind. Luke tried to ignore the squirm in his stomach and Tyler looked deadpan, almost straight through him. Luke could understand why he was upset.

All of Tyler's messages to him over the last five days, and there had been a lot, had been left unanswered but Luke didn't want that tension to transpire here. He wanted to pretend that everything was fine.

Luke tried to meet his eye but instead, Tyler gazed down at the floor. He nodded towards something and Luke followed his gaze. He hadn't noticed until Tyler had pointed it out but Lewandowski was wearing a pair of white trainers with a distinct rainbow flag running down the side and as he walked off towards his seat, Luke saw the sole of the shoe which was unmistakably the LGBTQ+ rainbow flag.

Tyler shrugged and cocked his head before following Mikolaj to the seats. It took Luke a moment before he followed suit. Moreau, the French Mercedes driver, and Kelly the Australian Lotus driver completed the line-up.

It wasn't until they sat down that Luke noticed the rainbow flag pin on Moreau's team shirt, larger than the one Kelly had worn in Hungary. At first, Luke couldn't help but think he had been exposed but when the press started the questions it all made sense.

'Mikolaj, I see you're sporting some fantastic trainers today,' a young man with a notepad and glasses asked from the middle of the pack. 'Can you tell us a little more about them?'

'Sure, my sister make them. She is nine.'

The press laughed and the FIA officials relaxed.

'She make them because she say, "love is love". She not wrong.' Lewandowski chuckled but there was something about his attitude that stopped anyone from disagreeing with him.

'Raphaël, you also seem to be showing your support for the LGBTQ+ community today?' said another journalist, a blonde female that didn't look too unlike Petra but wasn't her.

'I am. It would be wrong for us to come to places like these and not use our platform to show our support. Formula One has initiated the We Race as One campaign and under that, I think it is important for us to highlight the discriminations that are happening in the countries we race in, including Russia.'

'Do you believe it will make a difference?' she continued.

'Can I, one man, change the ways of an entire country? Absolutely not.' The journalists chucked and Luke's body shook with laughter too. 'But if I can make one person feel less alone, then I'll have achieved something good.'

Luke was uncomfortable having this conversation, more so today. It wasn't the first time some of the drivers had come out in support of the LGBTQ+ community but today it felt targeted. He couldn't help but wonder if Tyler had had a hand in this or if it was because they were in Russia.

'Luke…'

Luke's head snapped up and his muscles tensed in his shoulders and neck. He felt Tyler shuffle beside him. They were all squashed up like sardines in a can. It was impossible to ignore the touch of Tyler's skin when their arms brushed against each other.

He stayed frozen, his eyes moving trying to pinpoint in the crowd in front of him who had spoken.

'You've had a difficult run lately, your lead in the championship reduced to five points, with some fourth and third places. How're you feeling about this weekend?' Luke breathed a sigh of relief when he spotted the lady from Sky's lips moving.

'It's not been easy, no but each race we come back and we try harder. The team has been working very hard to keep improving so we can get the best results.'

'The car seems good, your teammate managed a win last time out, how come you're struggling more?'

Luke leant back into the plastic seat, the sides narrow and curled up, digging into his thighs.

'I'm not sure, to be honest,' he lied and hoped no one noticed. He put on his media smile and grinned before adding, 'Maybe he's better than me.'

The rest of the drivers laughed, all except Tyler. No one said their teammate was faster than them, so they knew he was teasing.

'Another for Luke, do you still think you can come back and win the championship, even with the Ferrari's current form?'

'I do. If I didn't, I wouldn't be here,' he said.

'I think it's so cool that the drivers are speaking up about some of these things,' Emma said on the way back to the motorhome after the press conference. 'I mean professionally it's kind of a nightmare having to deal with outspoken drivers but personally, I'm pretty proud that people are making waves.'

Luke sipped on his drink and tried not to say what was on his mind. He wanted to focus on the race and yet again there was extra chatter, noise in the background distracting him.

He left Emma by the main door and headed for his driver's room. A figure silhouetted against the light stood down the corridor and he knew it was Tyler by the shape of the shadow. After finding him outside his flat back in August, he would recognise him anywhere. His heart pinched at the memory.

Luke slowed down hoping Tyler would go into his room before he got there but he was on the phone, oblivious to Luke's presence.

'Friday the 4th? Yep. Basil Street, Knightsbridge. Sure. Can you e-mail me the details please? Okay, I'll let my stylist know and he can check out the location to make sure it's all cohesive,' he paused, his back still to Luke who couldn't fit past him without making himself known. 'I can ask the team, they keep them at the factory. Oh, that's an option. I'll talk to Martin and see if we can shoot there too. Okay, great, thanks, Dylan. Yep, speak soon, bye.' As he hung up he turned, nose still in his phone but his peripheral vision picked up Luke's presence. He studied Luke for a moment, then opened the door to his room and disappeared behind it.

Luke felt the pull in his chest, the sadness gripping him even though he'd boxed it up and shoved it away.

'How was it?' Johan asked when Luke walked through the door.

'Grand.' Luke flopped down on the sofa, his knees splayed out, his back slouched.

'Did you see Tyler?'

'I did. I think it would be fair to assume that he and I will be in all the press conferences until the end of the season, with Miko.'

'How long have I known you?'

'Mate, I can't even remember.'

'Exactly. Longer than either of us can remember. I have seen you at your best and I have seen you at your worst. I don't think you're at either right now. You get to choose where you take it from now. Forget the world outside, forget what you're feeling, and concentrate on what you want. Because if you put your energy into what you want, then you'll get it. If your energy is all over the place then nothing will come to you.' He paused to take a breath but Luke knew better than to interrupt him. 'You have to decide what's most important right now and focus on that with everything you have. I know you can do it, I have seen you do it before and I will no doubt see you do it again.'

Luke nodded his eyes unfocused, Johan's words bouncing around his mind. What did he want more than anything? He couldn't say for sure but for today and this weekend, it would be that race win.

Nothing else mattered.

Saturday afternoon, Luke Anderson climbed into his purple Wilson Racing car two minutes before qualifying was about to start and told himself in no uncertain terms that he would put that car on the front row of the grid, whatever it took.

He refused to let his eyes wander to the other side of the garage or even consider what Tyler might or might not be doing. Everything faded away, melting into the background for the next hour.

Luke topped each of the first two sessions and he had forgotten how amazing it felt to be flying, to be at the top, to be beating everyone else. There was no feeling like it, a shot of dopamine straight to the heart.

He kept his head down as he went out for his final run, unlike Spa he made sure he was ahead of the queue and launched himself over the line, ready for his flying lap. Dash was silent on the radio, trusting his driver to do what he had to for both himself and the team.

The whole way around, Luke knew it was a good lap, he could feel it in his bones that he had nailed it. He rounded the last corner, the line coming fast and then he waited.

He waited for the rest of the top ten to cross the line and try and beat his time. First came Tanaka, Kelly, and Nabiyev, none of them even close. Then Schulz, De Leon, and Moreau, Schulz popping up into second right behind Luke, the other two further down.

Dash continued to update him over the radio as Luke guided the car back to the pit lane.

Tyler slotted in behind Schulz, leaving Lewandowski to finish his lap.

Luke held his breath. He was halfway down the back straight, just past turn eleven when the radio crackled in his ear.

'It's pole mate, it's pole,' Dash was euphoric and so was Luke.

'YEEEEEES!' he shouted down the radio, pumping his fist with adrenaline.

'Well done Luke, epic lap,' Martin came over the radio.

When he got out of the car, having parked it on the track right outside the pit wall, he had to sit for a minute and soak it in. He tried to revel in it because he didn't know what the next day would hold.

Once he'd taken his helmet off, he was accosted by the presenter doing the interviews.

'Fantastic day today Luke, how does it feel to be back on

top?' Luke waved at the crowds, who cheered, waving the purple fag with his number on it.

'Ah, it's amazing. It's been a little while eh?' He laughed, his beautiful smile back on his face as he wiped the sweat up and into his hairline. 'The car felt so good and the team has worked so hard. We'll enjoy this, then tomorrow it's head down.'

'What's the plan for tomorrow?' The presenter asked.

'Stay in front, don't let anyone past, and keep it clean,' Luke said but despite the positivity he was putting out there, the adrenaline faded and there was something hollow and empty inside of him. It was like being starved after knowing what having a full stomach felt like.

He waved once more before heading back into the garage where his mechanics greeted him with back slaps and fist pumps.

The next day, Luke stayed on the winning wagon, darting off the line much faster than anyone else, and keeping his head down, lap after lap. An impeccable pit stop by the team got him back out in front and after an easy fifty-three laps, Luke took the chequered flag in first place.

Tasting the bitter tang of the champagne on the podium above the pit lane should have been the sweetest feeling. He sprayed it over his mechanics and glugged it like he'd never taste it again with Lewandowski and Brambilla by his side.

But despite the elation, there was a nagging feeling deep down that something was missing. A piece of him, that he had found over the last few months was gone again, and where he hadn't known it was missing before, now he felt its loss like rain in a drought.

TYLER FINLEY REVEALS ALL

The Formula One Rookie tells all in a sit-down interview with ModernLondon Weekly.

By Dylan James

Date published: October 11th

Very few people have achieved what Tyler Finley has in their first year of racing. The rookie met us at The Beaumont Hotel in Mayfair to talk through his first year competing in the highest rank of motorsport, what it feels like to become a household name, and the rumours that have surrounded him since he started.

The newest member of the Formula One grid debuted his career this year at Albert Park in Melbourne. With a successful junior career behind him, it still shocked the paddock when he secured one of the most coveted seats in Formula One, at reigning World Champions Wilson Racing.

'They'd shown interest in my career previously, [former team boss] David Crosby came to watch me race a few times. I knew I was on their radar but it wasn't until Martin Clark was appointed that they contacted my manager about the possibility of having me race this season with them.'

Martin Clark has a close personal relationship with Finley's billionaire father, Joseph Finley, (CEO of Finley Fair), which was instrumental in starting the rumours about how Tyler had secured his seat at the team.

'I've known Martin most of my life, he's fair and passionate about motor racing. I guess it may have helped that he knew me, but Martin's sole goal is to win. If he didn't think I could help them achieve that, he would have gone with someone else. No doubt about it. He's no more forgiving of my mistakes than he is of my teammates.'

And mistakes he has made. At the season opener in Australia, a crash between him and his teammate ended poorly for him and an explosive exchange between the two drivers in the paddock afterwards cast him as the villain to Luke Anderson's Prince Charming character.

'It's not easy, coming into a sport as a rookie and being expected to perform at the same level as your World Champion teammate. I put a lot of pressure on myself and it got the better of me. I've definitely grown over the year, learnt a lot, and calmed down a smidge.'

Since, Finley has produced some impressive results for his team, coming first in no fewer than five races, a slew of second place finishes and always competing at the front. But Tyler wants to achieve so much more in the sport than breaking racing records.

'As the first openly gay driver on the grid, I want to make sure that the We Race as One initiative isn't performative. We need to lead from the front, especially in such a male-dominated sport. It's important to show the world that we can be who we are without shame.'

Finley, who was born into a conservative family struggled to own up to who he was as a teenager at a private boy's school during the week and racing at weekends.

'I told my mum first, I think I must have been thirteen or something. She didn't care, she told me to be proud of who I was and not to let anyone else tell me otherwise. When she died I thought my secret would die with her but it was the kick I needed to be myself. I didn't feel the need to come out to anyone, I owned it and one day I came home and introduced my dad to my boyfriend. It was tough, he wasn't sure how to take it but over time he got used to the idea and we've been fine ever since.'

We asked Tyler if he felt Formula One needed a gay icon to become more progressive, despite its efforts to become more inclusive in the press, more work needs to be done behind the scenes.

'I'm not sure I'm a gay icon in any way or will ever be. But being there and being happy with who I am, shows everyone else that they can be too. It's subtle. It's part of who I am but it's not all that I am.'

There has been a lot of support for the LGBTQ+ community from other drivers, notably from Kyle Kelly, Raphaël Moreau, and Mikolaj Lewandowski, but with Formula One still visiting controversial countries, that have a long way to go with gay rights, it seems contradictory to their messaging.

'I can't comment, I don't know. It's hard to not see how the money talks but equally, could we help make a change in those countries? Time will tell.'

There are a few races left in the season, having wrapped up round sixteen of the championship at the Russian Grand Prix. Finley aims to end the season strong even though his hopes of the championship are dwindling, as he is seventy points adrift of his teammate who leads it.

'I came into F1 wanting to be World Champion, and that hasn't changed but this year I've achieved so much more than I ever thought I could. I will help Luke as much as I can in the coming races. My goal is always to get the best result for the team, and if supporting my teammate to the championship is in its best interest then that's what I will do.'

Finley and Anderson have been embroiled in a very public feud since the beginning of the season, with the fans splitting themselves down the middle. TeamLuke on one side TeamTyler on the other.

'It's funny how that happens, there isn't a feud between us. I know I came on a little strong at the beginning of the season and made some questionable choices but I have the utmost respect for him as a driver and a person. He's very focused and very passionate about his work and it's admirable. Will we be best friends? Who knows eh.'

Twenty-five

Monaco
October 20th

The shiny marble floor of the Monaco train station gleamed under the lights. Luke scuffed his trainer across it, his baseball cap pulled down, hands deep in his pockets. He checked his watch again as he heard the rumble of the train coming down the tunnel to the underground platform.

The silver machine pulled up and slowed to a stop beyond the barriers and Luke waited with bated breath until he laid eyes on her.

His sister's long blonde hair flew all over the place with the wind as she stepped out onto the platform. Luke lifted his hand to get her attention and the biggest smile broke out on her face. They hadn't seen each other since the summer and he was so glad she was there. He needed some normality, some stability in his life and there was no one better than Nick to provide that.

She pulled her suitcase across the concourse and through the turnstile, reaching him within minutes.

'Ah my big brother,' she said pulling him into a tight squeeze. He had to bend down to rest his chin on her head. Luke grabbed the handle of her bag and walked out into the dazzling sunlight.

'How was the flight?' he said guiding her down the road towards his apartment building.

'It was fine. I won't be too mad you didn't send a helicopter to pick me up from the airport.'

'It's a twenty-minute train ride, I thought you'd cope,' he said nudging her.

She flipped her sunglasses down onto her nose, looking more like a celebrity than he ever could. He was wearing black shorts, a grey t-shirt, and an unassuming cap. His sunglasses covered his eyes, no one would know who he was.

'You better, at least, have some cocktails waiting for me, especially if you're now making me walk to your flat.' She huffed as the road veered uphill. Luke felt a million times better already, his heart rate slowing, his breathing losing its raggedy edge.

'I have, you'll be pleased to know,' he said slowing down so he didn't leave her behind.

They reached the apartment block and headed for the lift. Johan was in London for the day, working, so they had the whole afternoon together before he got back. Johan and Nick had always snipped and sniped at each other and Luke could do without their bickering today. They were like siblings, but the ones that pushed each other's buttons for fun. He was glad his relationship with his sister wasn't like that.

'Oh it's nice to see you've made an effort to tidy up,' Nick teased after dropping her stuff in the lounge where Johan's exercise gear was over the floor, the blanket on the sofa in a messy pile with some books and magazines lying around.

'I did make the bed for you,' Luke said from the kitchen where he'd opened the fridge and pulled out the pitcher of strawberry mojito.

'Oooh,' she said when she spotted the jug. 'You do treat me well.' Luke rolled his eyes. 'Have you got any snacks? I'm starving.'

Luke opened the cupboards and was reminded of the time he was looking for food to feed Tyler. It felt like such a long time ago and not the two months it had been. A dull ache stirred in his chest but he pushed it away. He offered her some dry crackers but Nick screwed her nose up.

'You're gross. Thankfully I know you well enough to pack my own.' She pulled a melted Snickers out of her bag.

'Yeah, chocolate doesn't last long down here.'

'But it's October,' she huffed putting it in the fridge.

'In the fridge? Are we from the same family?' Everything with Nick was easy, a rhythm he was used to and a calming balm to the rough seas of his life lately. The scrutiny of the press and the paddock was a distant memory for now.

Back in the lounge, his sister picked up the magazine he'd been reading for the hundredth time before he'd gone to get her.

'Oh I saw this, can you believe it?' she said flicking the cover shut to reveal a gorgeous photo of Tyler posing on a brown leather sofa that exuded masculinity. The rest of the set was a sleek modern house, in shades of white with the odd plant dotted around. It was very him and it made him look more handsome than ever. His blue eyes and his dark hair were the first thing you saw when you glanced at the cover.

Nick took the magazine out onto the balcony where she pulled her trouser legs up, reclining on the seat to soak in the afternoon sun before it disappeared behind the mountains and the palace hill. Luke stayed silent as he joined her, hoping she would move on from the topic but she didn't.

'I was so surprised, I didn't have him pegged as being gay,' she mused leafing through the magazine pages, photos of Tyler staring up at them. Him leant up against a door frame in a dark blue sweater and light chinos, or by his Lamborghini outside the most picturesque London townhouse. There was one of him at the factory holding his latest winner's trophy, sitting on the wheel of his WR19 and the Wilson trophy wall behind him. And one of him as a kid, beside his kart, holding a little trophy that was barely bigger than Luke's hand.

Luke had looked at them over and over again since the article had come out over a week ago. Sadness but also pride rushed through him as he read the words and scrutinised the photos. Tyler looked incredible in each and every one of them and it hurt to see that on a page rather than in person.

'How would you know if he was gay?' Luke said, looking out over the view and anywhere but at his sister.

'You're right, I don't have a gaydar. Did you know?' Her eyes narrowed as she scrutinised his face.

Luke clenched his jaw. He didn't want to lie to her but he didn't want to tell her the truth either. Because to admit it would be to admit that he missed him, and he wasn't allowed to feel that way because he was the one who had ended it. He was the one who put his career above what they had, and he hated the niggling thought that maybe he had gotten it wrong.

He didn't need to say a word because she saw it written all over his face.

'Oh my god. Tell me everything,' she said snapping the magazine shut and slamming it down on the table.

'I'm going to need something stronger than this for that,'

he said pointing to the jug of mojito. He poured himself a neat vodka and sat back down with a big sigh. Where to start?

'I'm equally jealous as hell, angry as fuck, and over the moon for you. Who else knows?'

'Johan, he walked in on us. As far as I know, no one else knows, but Tyler may have told someone.' He shrugged. 'It doesn't matter, it's over.'

'What?' she said, her mouth ajar and her eyebrows almost disappearing off into her hairline. 'If this,' she pointed to the magazine, 'isn't a declaration of something more than casual sex then I don't know what is. This is the most romantic thing that anyone has ever done for anybody. I promise you.'

'That's not about me,' he said confused.

'How is it not about you? He's showing you, proving to you, that you can be you in this world. What happened in Japan when it came out?'

'I mean, not much?' he said, still trying to understand where his sister was going with this. 'There were some pride flags at the race I suppose when I've never seen any before. There was a lot of press attention for him, I don't know. What do you want me to say?'

'Did anyone chuck a shoe at him? Did his mechanics shun him? Did he get fired from the team? Did the FIA sanction him?'

'No of course not, why would they?'

'You tell me, Luke. You're the one who's so terrified that your career will be over if you admit that you like someone.'

'But he's not just someone,' Luke said feeling frustrated now. 'He's my teammate, we work together, we're competitors, rivals.'

'And? Is it not worth it?'

Luke didn't answer, he hadn't expected her to take this stance. She knew how hard he had worked to get where he was. He thought she would have the same opinion as Johan.

'What's the worst that can happen? You lose some fans, some sponsors. Their loss. But look at what you set to gain,' she said.

'But I want this championship. I've tried doing both and it didn't work. I couldn't concentrate. I sucked,' he said with emphasis, his excuses sounding weaker even to him.

'You're already World Champion, no one can take that away from you. I know you want to win again and you will but don't turn your back on something amazing because you're scared.'

Luke stared out beyond the balcony but his eyes were unfocused, glazed over as he wondered if his sister could be right.

'Is that what Russia was about?' Nick said pulling him out of his trance.

'Russia?'

'Miko and Moreau in the press conference and then Brambilla on the podium with the "love is love" shirt?'

'No, I don't know what that was about,' he said with no trace of humour in his voice. 'If it's anything like the We Race as One initiative, then it's nothing real. It's there so they look like they're doing something but they weren't doing anything real.'

'You think Miko, Moreau, and Brambilla don't believe in gay rights, they wanted to be seen to believe? That makes no sense.'

'I don't know Nick, we don't talk about it. I have no idea what they believe,' he said, rubbing his face in frustration.

'I think that what those guys did in Russia was call out a nation who discriminates. It was showing support to all those people in Russia who are like you. Don't you think?'

'Yes, I suppose so,' he conceded.

'Maybe the sport itself has a long way to go, but you could

help that. Tyler's already doing it and this,' she pointed to the closed magazine on the table between them, 'is him asking you to do it with him.'

Luke paused, and then a smile spread across his face.

'When are you leaving again?' Nick's shoulders shook as her whole body succumbed to the laughter.

'I love you, Luke, you know that, right? I want the best for you. Don't let what happened when you were younger stop you from living your best life now. Think about it yeah?'

Luke poured some strawberry mojito into his empty glass and considered her words.

'So where are we going dancing tonight?' she grinned, swinging her legs up onto the table, hiding Tyler's face from view for now.

'Nowhere, I have an early flight to Mexico tomorrow.'

'Spoil sport,' she huffed. 'In that case, we're going day drinking.'

'We're already day drinking.'

'You know what I mean.' She waved him away. 'And you're calling a cab this time. I'm not walking anywhere.'

Luke did just that and before long they were in the back of a car, headed for the rooftop bar of the Fairmont Monte Carlo. They sat on the balcony, looking over the Mediterranean, the breeze in their hair and the sun on their faces.

'I can't believe this is your life,' she said closing her eyes and tilting her face up to the sun. 'The scrawny teenager who spent his days tucked away in a garage fiddling with car parts or hidden under a helmet most weekends, and now you're an international heartthrob who lives this life of luxury. It's mental.'

Luke was inclined to agree. Although he had always hoped and worked towards the success he had, he'd never imagined as a kid that he would get here. Last season felt a world away but Nick was right. He was the World Champion and his name would forever be in the history books as that. Nothing could take that away from him. What if he didn't win this second one? Would that diminish what he had achieved?

As he sat there looking out over the sparkling sea and the yachts, he should have felt whole and complete but he didn't. Something was missing and he knew what it was. He just didn't know if he could bring himself to let go enough to let himself have it.

Twenty-six

Mexico Grand Prix – Autódromo Hermanos Rodriguez – Mexico City
October 28th

The small plane sat on the runway of the Mexico City Airport, not moving. Luke looked over to see what the hold-up was, Johan was absorbed in his laptop as always. He checked his watch to confirm that they should have left ten minutes ago.

'What's going on?' he huffed, the door wide open and letting in the stifling Mexico air. They were due to land in Austin by four so Luke could get a workout in before attending a sponsor event at the Hilton later that evening.

As he watched his running time dwindle, his irritation grew. His first-place trophy sat on the seat opposite Johan on the other side of the aisle of the private jet.

Martin Clark hadn't wanted to hear it when Luke refused the plane after his win.

'Only the best for my star driver,' Martin had boomed after the race, his cheeks red from the champagne. Luke had managed to extend his lead in the championship but only by fifteen points, it was going down to the wire. With Tyler backing him up on track, being his rear gunner, Lewandowski had come in third.

Luke jiggled his foot in the aisle, his leg crossed over the other, ankle on knee. The plane wasn't huge, the cream leather seats were comfortable and Johan had a table which was all they needed.

The attendant kept glancing over, dragging her eyes over his body whenever she walked through the cabin. She'd offered him three drinks, all of which he had declined.

Focused on the weekend ahead, he was more determined than he had ever been, keeping his head down in Mexico, ignoring the noise and Tyler who seemed to have given up trying to talk to him, both in person and by text he'd brought it home. Luke's heart pinched but he'd decided to think about it after the season had ended. Once he had a clear head and could think logically.

'Here we go,' the flight attendant said coming back through the door. It took Luke a moment to realise that she wasn't alone. With the biggest smile on her face, she squished herself up against the wall of the plane to let the person following her on board.

Clad in jeans and a white t-shirt, black shaggy hair covering his blue eyes, Tyler pushed his bag onto the plane. When he looked up, his eyes landed on Luke, who felt the instantaneous pull of their souls trying to bond together again.

Luke cleared his throat and turned to stare at the dull grey tarmac below, the heat waves rising from it like too much vodka and not enough lemonade in a glass.

'Oh,' he heard Johan say as the air attendant took Tyler's bag to the back of the plane, and out of the corner of his eye, Luke saw Tyler sit down opposite him. Their knees were inches apart and he could feel his presence and every tiny movement Tyler made.

The air attendant shut the doors as they prepared for departure.

'Nice trophy,' Tyler said, the silence too oppressive for him. Luke looked at it and then back to Tyler, his face deadpan but his brain going at a hundred miles per hour. It didn't need a car to speed through everything that had happened between them in the last few months and his sister's words echoed around his head.

'Hey,' Tyler said as the plane started its journey to the runway. He went to reach out and touch Luke's leg but the look on Luke's face made him pull back.

Johan caught his eye.

'Don't worry about me,' he said pulling something out of his bag. 'Noise cancelling headphones.' He waved them around and then wedged them over his ears.

Tyler leant forward onto his elbows, bringing his head closer to Luke's. Close enough that Luke could smell his aftershave. It sent him straight back to them tangled up in his bed sheets and his stomach jolted.

'I know you want space but…' Tyler held his hand out flat between them, palm up. 'I've missed you.'

Luke looked at the outstretched hand and wanted with every fibre of his body to reach out and grab it but he didn't. He turned back to the window, eyes wide to dry them out.

Tyler sighed and pulled his hand back. Luke knew that if he didn't say something he would lose him. Tyler would walk away from this and if he was being honest with himself, he didn't want him to.

'I'm...' he started, his voice higher than he'd expected. He cleared his throat, thick with emotion, and tried to gather his thoughts.

Tyler sat patiently, relieved that Luke was talking.

'I don't...' Luke struggled. He was stuck in the tug of war again, his resolve melting the longer Tyler sat in front of him. Tyler's hand found Luke's knee and the warmth of it seeped through him like a shot of whisky.

Mexico City disappeared beneath the clouds and Luke put his hand on top of Tyler's. He felt Tyler relax and grab his, not wanting to let it go.

'I spoke with your sister,' Tyler said.

'You did what?' Their intertwined fingers jerked apart as Luke pulled his hand away.

'She said not to say anything but I clearly can't keep my mouth shut. I legged it to the airport when Jessie said Martin had chartered you a plane and I talked my way onboard. I'm sorry, I...I need to understand.' When Luke didn't say anything, he continued. 'Your sister was very complimentary about my article in ModernLondon.'

'I bet she was,' Luke said rolling his eyes.

'What happened to you? Who made you so jaded? Please tell me,' Tyler asked, his hand finding Luke's knee again.

Luke sighed and wiped his hand across his lips and chin, trying to find a way to explain.

'I'm not jaded,' he said, wondering if maybe he was. 'It's just that I've learnt over the years that I can't let what happens out there, affect what I do on track. I was told in no uncertain terms that if I wanted to be World Champion, I would have to pretend to be "normal".' Tyler laughed hollowly, like he'd heard the same thing before but didn't care for that narrative.

'There's nothing wrong with you,' Tyler said, leaning back into his chair now that Luke was opening up.

'I know that. I'm not ashamed of who I am, I didn't want it to affect my dreams. I'd always known I was different, even before I realised I was into racing. But there was this one guy when I was fifteen, he was from Sweden, came over to race and stayed for the whole season. We got close and I knew I'd never like girls the way the world wanted me to. It didn't bother me, he made me happy and that's what I'd always thought life was about. But the team manager caught us kissing and that was it. He pulled me into his office and told me that I would never make it if I was gay. That I had to pretend to like women because we weren't just drivers, we were marketing tools, we were the brand. Racing was a business and if I wanted to make it, I had to be the most marketable person I could be. That meant being the perfect poster boy. It was a lot of pressure for me at fifteen, I wasn't sure I could be both, so I took a break from racing.'

Tyler listened, his face neutral as he took it all in, not giving anything away. It was unnerving.

He was telling Tyler something he had never told anyone, not even his parents. He'd come out to them about six months after the incident when he couldn't hide the anxiety that plagued him. He took the year off but realised he couldn't live without racing. He itched to get back into the car every week so he buried that conversation at the bottom of his soul. He returned to racing with the decision that he would never mix his personal and professional life. He wouldn't settle down until he had achieved everything he had wanted in the sport. He wouldn't reveal his secret to anyone until he was World Champion.

'Then you came along.' Luke laughed, and the weight lifted off him.

'And I turned your world around,' Tyler said and his smile faded. 'I'm so sorry you've had to go through that. No one should ever tell you who you can and can't be and what that guy said was his personal opinion, his own internalised homophobia. It had nothing to do with you.'

'I know that, I...it's been a long time. I've been living like this for a long time.' Tyler reached over and took his hand again, this time Luke let him. The feel of Tyler's skin against his soothed him. 'I know you want me to be like you, but even if I did come out to the world, we still couldn't be together.'

'I don't want you to be like me, I just want you. Come out to the world if you want or don't, I don't care. Don't shut me out. It won't be the easiest relationship I've ever been in but I think it's worth it.' Luke glowed from the inside and he leant forward to meet Tyler, their fingers tangled between them. 'Let's not worry about the future. What you decide to do is up to you, I will never pressure you into anything but Luke...'

Luke lifted his head, his eyes meeting Tyler's who were less than half a metre away.

'Nothing bad has happened since that article. No one has pulled me into a room and told me to not be who I am. I've not been fired and if anything, everyone has been very supportive. We could be role models in a different way. We could pave the way for a better future. I promise you, everything is dandy on this side of the fence.' He laughed, his thumb stroking the back of Luke's hand.

'I'm not there yet,' Luke replied, his face a picture of apology. 'I want this championship. I want it so bad, I can't let anything distract me.'

'Am I a distraction?' Tyler asked raising an eyebrow, a smirk playing on his lips.

'You know damn well you are.' Luke laughed, a glint in his eye and Tyler pounced. He moved the tiny distance between them and planted his lips square on Luke's mouth.

Luke leant into the kiss, relishing what he had missed out

on. He pulled Tyler close by winding his hand behind his neck and tugging at his hair as Tyler's hands found Luke's waist.

'I know I can't hear you but I can still see you. PG thirteen please,' Johan said, forcing them to pull away from each other, to catch a breath and laugh.

'Sorry,' Luke said, his forehead resting against Tyler's, until the attendant poked her head around the corner and they pulled apart.

'Can I get you gentlemen a drink?' she asked and a cold shiver ran down Luke's spine. How much had she heard?

Tyler must have seen the look of fear on Luke's face because he leant forwards as she walked away and whispered: 'Don't panic, they have to sign NDAs before they can work on private jets.'

Luke nodded but his jaw was tense. How on earth was he going to manage this secret until the end of the season? It seemed an impossible task, pretending like his heart didn't beat at double time whenever Tyler was nearby, not stealing glances, hand grazes, and secret kisses.

'I'm not sure I know how I'm going to stay away from you now,' Luke said, his fingers gripping Tyler's.

'You won't have to, you'll win every race and I'll be right there pushing you along and keeping everyone else behind me.' Tyler grinned.

'That's not what I meant and you know it.'

'I've got no chance of winning it this year anyway, so I'll do everything I can to help you. I promise.'

'Don't make promises you can't keep.' Luke raised an eyebrow. What Tyler was suggesting posed a whole host of other issues for their personal and professional relationship but he didn't want to think about it. That could be next season's problem.

Tyler leant over and kissed him again.

'I take it you two have kissed and made up?' Johan said pulling his headphones off. He sat back in his seat and closed his laptop lid with a snap. The air attendant came back with three drinks, a beer for Johan, sparkling water for Luke, and some kind of cocktail for Tyler.

'We have,' Tyler said sipping the orange liquid. 'Is that okay with you?' he quirked an eyebrow and Johan put his hands up in surrender. Luke looked between the two and shook his head, had Johan been that transparent?

'It's none of my business,' Johan said and Tyler nodded once.

'Three left then,' Tyler said turning back to Luke. 'How're we going to beat Lewandowski?'

'I literally don't have a plan, apart from drive fast and hope for the best.'

'Yeah, solid plan. I thought the World Champion would have more up his sleeve than that.'

'Oh and no distractions,' Luke said staring at Tyler but with an intentional glint in his eye that meant right now he wanted the complete opposite. Tyler got his message loud and clear.

'Okay, we'll be right back,' Tyler said standing up and dragging Luke behind him to the back of the plane.

'Oh God, no. Please don't,' Johan said grimacing, picking up his headphones and putting them back over his ears.

Twenty-seven

United States Grand Prix – Circuit of the Americas – Austin, Texas
November 3rd

On the outskirts of Austin, Texas, the Circuit of the Americas emptied at a steady pace with yellow buses full of people being ferried back to the capital city. Luke was waiting for the crowd to die down before he left the circuit, sitting alone with his second-place trophy on the narrow bench inside his driver's room.

It hadn't been the worst race, but first place was what he had targeted, falling short by half a second because he couldn't get past Lewandowski. With two races left, Luke couldn't afford to lose any extra points if he wanted to secure the title again.

The good thing was that after his flight with Tyler, he felt good. He'd half expected the anxiety to return but it hadn't, not this weekend anyway. He'd been fastest through all practice sessions and missed out on pole by one thousandth of a second.

He heard the soft knock on the door, glancing up as it cracked open and Tyler's blue eyes peered through the gap. With one last glance behind him, Tyler slipped into the room and closed the door with a soft click.

'Good job today,' he said nodding to the trophy and Luke gave him a small smile. Tyler sat down on the bench beside him and squeezed up close, his leg pressing against Luke's.

'Not what I wanted, but it'll do,' Luke said finding Tyler's hand. He pulled it close and kissed the back of it.

'So, um…' Tyler started shifting in his seat, his eyes glancing around the small room. 'I've got a couple of friends with me this weekend, you may have seen them.'

Luke had seen them. Two posh boys, in pastel shirts and chinos, who'd been hitting up the bar like they'd never seen free booze before. Luke had watched one of them shamelessly flirting with Petra and the other bowing down to Jessie, neither of them getting anywhere fast.

'Anyway, we're heading out downtown tonight and I wondered if maybe you wanted to join us?' Tyler said, his fingers tensing under Luke's touch.

Luke was both elated and terrified. It wasn't the smartest idea but he wanted to go.

'You want me to come with you?' Luke asked.

'Absolutely,' Tyler said, his nerves disappearing. 'It would look like a bunch of lads out having fun and I reckon most of the fans will have left, so you know…'

He didn't need to finish his sentence, Luke knew what he was saying. They would be less at risk of being noticed on a Sunday night after everyone had left the city.

'Then, yeah, I'd love to come.' Luke dropped another kiss

on Tyler's hand and Tyler's mouth found Luke's. 'Do your friends know? About...this?' Luke asked as he pulled away.

'They know some of the story, but they don't know it's you,' he said, running his fingers through his hair. 'Although they're smart guys, I don't think it'll take them long to figure it out if you do come.' Tyler shrugged, leaving the metaphorical door open. The ball was in Luke's court.

'I want to come,' he said with determination and Tyler's face broke into a huge smile.

'I'll see you later then.' As he leant forwards to kiss him again the door flew open, and they jumped apart like they'd been burnt.

'Only me,' Johan said from the door.

Tyler slipped off the bench and past Johan into the corridor.

'You guys need to be more careful,' Johan said his face deadpan. It wasn't the best time to mention something but Luke couldn't help himself.

'Will you come out with me tonight? Downtown?'

Johan eyed him, his white eyebrows pulled together.

Three hours later, Luke paced his hotel room, stopping to check his reflection in the mirror every once in a while, running his hands through his hair, to rearrange a strand or two. He was nervous to meet Tyler's friends and for them to figure out what was going on but he was more excited to spend some time with Tyler that didn't involve stealing moments and sneaking kisses with always one eye looking over their shoulder.

Luke checked his watch, he was early but he couldn't stay cooped up in his room, so he headed down to the hotel bar. He fired off a text to Johan saying he'd meet him there.

The hotel was modern and designed in shades of blues and muddy greys. Comfy brown leather sofas and armchairs were scattered around and the lampshades were old trumpet bells that reflected the light. The foyer was empty compared to the last few days and no one blinked as Luke walked through the cavernous space, past reception to the bar.

He grabbed a stool and ordered a beer. The bartender was a young man whose eyes grew wide as he recognised Luke but he didn't say anything, he simply pulled the tap and handed him the glass full of amber liquid.

Luke took a sip, his leg jiggling on the footrest as he waited. He couldn't decide if going out with Tyler in public was the worst idea ever or if it was all worth it to be around him. Tyler had said in the plane that it wouldn't be easy but he knew it'd be worth it. Luke wanted to be as sure as him. He wanted a road map telling him exactly how it would all pan out, preferably with the happy ending, but like most things in life, there was no guarantee.

It wasn't long before Luke felt a hand on his shoulder and turned to see his trainer, not in his usual sportswear but dressed up in jeans, a black polo neck, and trainers so white they didn't look like they'd ever been used. He eyed up Luke's beer.

'D'you want one?'

'Oh, go on then,' Johan said, perching on the seat next to him. Luke ordered him one, his eyes flitting to the doorway, keeping an eye out for Tyler and his friends. They'd said they'd meet at reception at nine and it was already half past. Luke was nervous again and wondered if they'd changed their mind.

'Why do you keep looking at the door?' Johan asked downing half of his beer in one gulp.

Luke wondered how to explain to him who they were meeting when he saw Tyler emerge from the lift, flanked by his two friends.

They looked like overgrown private school boys, wearing

pressed shirts in white, blue, and pale pink, and black trousers. Luke and Johan looked underdressed compared to them. Tyler though, had paired his white shirt with dark jeans and he looked so good Luke had to hold back from going straight over to him. Instead, he lifted his hand to catch their eye.

Johan spun to see who he'd waved to and his face pulled into a scowl.

'Really?' he asked and when Luke didn't answer he sighed heavily. 'This is not a good idea.'

Luke ignored him and stood up when the three men approached, he stuffed his hands in his pockets so he didn't reach out to Tyler who was grinning like a kid in a candy shop.

'Hi guys,' Tyler said, 'this is Ben,' he pointed to the guy in the pink t-shirt who had been flirting with Petra, 'and George.'

'The suit designer, right?' Luke said holding out his hand.

'That's me, if you ever need a suit, I'm your man,' he said with a warm smile. 'An Anderson suit in my portfolio would do wonders for my brand.'

'I'd be delighted,' Luke said returning his smile.

Dragging their eyes away from Luke, the two men looked at each other with a knowing smirk. Luke felt himself blush under their scrutiny.

'This is Johan,' Luke introduced his friend, who nodded at the group.

'Shall we go?' Tyler said. Johan picked up his beer and finished it in another gulp, wiping the back of his hand over his mouth with a sigh of happiness. Luke left his half-drunk one on the bar top and threw down a twenty-dollar bill tip for the bartender before he followed Tyler and his friends out the front doors.

The night was balmy, not chilly like a November night

back in England, but a soft heat lingered after the warm day. Luke and Johan followed a few paces behind as they headed towards Sixth Street. It was quiet out, most people had left the city after the Grand Prix or were back home ready for the new week.

'Are you sure about this?' Johan said in no more than a whisper so that the guys in front couldn't hear. 'If you guys get caught.'

'We won't get caught,' Luke said a little frustrated. 'We're a group of friends hanging out.' He shrugged and pushed back the little voice in his head that agreed with Johan. Nothing was going to ruin tonight.

They walked past empty and dark construction sites, multi-storey car parks, and abandoned vehicles at the side of the road until they made it to Sixth Street. It was far busier here and they blended into the crowd of partygoers going hard for a Sunday night. Festoon lighting hung over the street along with the traffic lights and electricity cables. The mix of buildings, brick, render and stone were alight with flashing signs, and warm chatter and music escaped each time someone opened the door.

Tyler fell back from his friends to walk in step with Luke and Johan.

'Are you okay?' he asked, his body jittery.

'I'm fine,' Luke said, leaning his arm against Tyler's to reassure him.

'Have you been here before?' Tyler asked as they walked up to Pete's Duelling Piano bar.

'I have, we came here last year with the team before the race. It was good fun.' Luke noticed Johan absorbed in his phone, pretending to not be interested in their conversation. Ben and George hung around outside for a minute waiting for them to catch up.

The place was long and narrow, a bar spanning the length

of the room opposite two pianos face to face on a stage. The lights were low and the crowd was dense, their eyes on the performers. The perfect place to hide in plain sight. The plinking of piano keys and the cheers of the crowd were like a smoke screen as Luke followed Tyler through the throng, no one taking a second look at them.

They found a space at the back to hang out, Ben and George at the bar. The song finished in a flourish and the crowd cheered louder before one of the performers pulled a slip of paper out of the bowl on the piano between them.

'Oh good lord, who put this in there?' The pianist closest to them asked the crowd, his nose pressed up against the microphone. 'I refuse to sing that,' he said with a grin handing the slip of paper to the other player.

'You won't play it because it's about you,' the second pianist said with a cackle. He placed his fingers on the key and played a chord. The song was instantly recognisable and the crowd erupted in cheers as they both launched into *Like a Virgin* by Madonna.

'I hate this song,' Johan shouted, handing Luke a beer. 'Madonna's overrated.'

'I'm wounded by your comment,' Tyler replied, his hand on his chest in indignation. 'Madonna is the Queen of Pop.'

'Isn't that Cher?' Luke said with a smile.

'No, she's the Goddess of Pop or something,' Johan said.

'I'm appalled you don't know that,' Tyler said with a laugh.

After his second beer Luke relaxed and chatted to Ben and George until they were accosted by a bachelorette party. The gaggle of girls, head to toe in pink, screamed and danced and when they found out the boys were British they lost it. They didn't seem to have a clue who Tyler and Luke were which meant that when a bench at the back came free they sloped off together, leaving Ben, George, and Johan with the girls.

It wasn't long before George was up on stage singing *Never Gonna Give You Up* at the top of his voice, the bachelorette party screaming at his feet. It was comical and cringey in equal measures.

'I'm glad you came,' Tyler shouted over the music, his fingers pressing on Luke's leg in the darkness of the back corner. No one was looking their way, no one cared that they were there. 'Austin is wild.'

'Is this your first time here?' Luke asked, still shouting.

'Yeah, I've been to a lot of new places this year.'

'How do you know them?' Luke nodded towards Ben and George who were back chatting to the girls.

'Our mums were friends, I've known them forever. They're more like brothers to be honest.'

Their heads were close together as they spoke, their hair touching as Tyler leant in closer so he could be heard above the music.

'I saw Petra hanging around outside the motorhome on my way out, was she waiting for you?' Tyler looked down at his glass as he spoke. Luke scrubbed his face with his free hand.

'She was.' He sighed.

'She seems very taken with you,' Tyler said looking up from under his lashes. Luke laughed, his eyebrows raised and a slight nod of his head. She *was* taken with him, she'd made that much clear.

'I feel awful about it,' he admitted. 'I don't know how to tell her, you know, without *telling* her.'

Tyler nodded, cradling his beer as he mulled it over. He put a hand on Luke's knee.

'Try not to feel too bad about it, she'll find her person one day, I'm sure. She's a catch if you're straight.' That made Luke feel better, even if he wished she would find that person sooner rather than later.

'Two more races,' Tyler said leaning in close again. 'Then

it's the end of the season.' Luke nodded, wondering how the year had gone so fast but had also felt like the longest year of his life.

'Your first of many years in racing,' Luke said, nudging him.

'I hope so.'

'Where are you headed tomorrow, straight to Abu Dhabi?' Luke asked.

'I'm going to New York for a few days with the lads,' Tyler said, nodding to his friends. 'You should come,' he said suddenly animated. Luke wished it was that easy, changing the flight wouldn't be an issue but he didn't trust himself. Spending time outside of racing with Tyler was a risk, one he wasn't willing to take with two races left.

'I shouldn't,' he said, bending his head down so his eyes found the foamy residue of his beer clinging to the sides of his glass. Tyler's hand found his back as he leant even further in, speaking into his ear.

'I know this is hard for you,' he said. 'I don't want to pressure you into coming out when you aren't ready but keeping my hands off you is torture.' Warmth pooled in Luke's stomach; the feeling mutual. 'We don't have to have the future all figured out right now, but I want to spend time with you, and I need to know that you want the same. I want to wake up next to you in your crummy flat. I want to run down the seafront with you and kiss you when I want to. I want to meet your family and see you at Christmas, take you skiing.'

In his mind's eye, Luke could see it all unfurling in front of him, their lives melting together like wax. It sounded perfect, the life he'd dreamt of having, but for now he couldn't see how he could get from where he was, to where Tyler was describing.

'I want the same thing,' Luke said because it wasn't a lie.

'But right now…'

'The championship,' Tyler said with a resigned nod. 'I understand.'

The future hung between them, the complications of their relationship an elephant in the room. What if it worked out? Could they still be teammates? Would the competition tear them apart? And what if it didn't…Luke couldn't bear the thought of never speaking to him again, of watching him from afar and knowing he couldn't be near him. There wasn't a simple answer. Nothing about them being together would be simple. It posed so many questions that Luke didn't have the answers to.

They stayed for a few more songs and then they bar-hopped for a while. Johan left to go back to the hotel after the third one and he encouraged Luke to go with him but Luke was buzzed. He'd had a few drinks, more than he usually would, and he felt warm and fuzzy inside. The high after a race, being so close to Tyler for so long, enjoying the music, and relaxing.

At around two a.m., they stumbled out of the last bar, a chill in the air. Ben and George had found a few more women to chat up and it was clear they weren't heading back to their hotel alone. Luke yawned ready for bed but Tyler grabbed his hand and pulled him off in the opposite direction.

'See you in the morning,' he shouted over his shoulder to his friends, but they were lip-locked with the girls.

'Where are we going?' Luke said, amused but following him, not letting go of his hand.

'You'll see.' They dived down a side street, the pavements were wide and lit by streetlamps. Cables hung down overhead and the traffic lights turned despite there being no cars. They ran down the road, high on life.

'You don't even know do you.' Luke laughed, trying to catch his breath. He was too tired to be running but he felt like he was floating with Tyler's hand in his. It was so late, he was sleep-deprived and a little drunk, he didn't care.

'A taste of our future,' Tyler said, and when Luke looked up again he saw the giant dome of the Texas Capitol lit up ahead of them, surrounded by the trees from the capitol park. He followed Tyler into the darkness and beneath the trees Tyler spun him around, pulling Luke close to him and kissing him like he'd been dying to do it all evening. Their hands explored each other's bodies as the blanket of the night engulfed them.

Luke was hungry for it and pushed Tyler up against a tree, the bark harsh and dry on his hands as he left them on Tyler's back to protect him. It was intoxicating, the air, the freedom to be themselves.

They pulled apart and Luke chuckled.

'Oh god that sound,' Tyler said, his knees buckling. He leant against Luke for support. 'Do you know how sexy you are?'

His blue eyes sparkled as he stared up at Luke and under his gaze Luke wasn't hard-pushed to believe it.

'Not in the way you think either,' Tyler said as Luke stood back. They held hands as they walked through the park together, taking their time, no more running. 'The media make you out to be this sex god, which you are of course, but they don't know the real you. That's even more special.'

'You can stop now, I already like you. Flattery won't get you anywhere you haven't already been.' His eyes darkened with desire and he pulled him in for another kiss.

They stood with the lit-up capitol as their backdrop, foreheads together and Luke's hands on Tyler's arms.

'I wish we could do this forever,' Luke said with a sigh.

FRIEND, FOE OR LOVER?
Are Tyler Finley and Luke Anderson more than friends?

By Sara Holdsworth

Date published: November 13th

The Formula One circus wrapped up the nineteenth leg of the World Championship in Austin Texas, for the United States Grand Prix over the weekend. But it wasn't the spectacular battle between championship rivals Luke Anderson and Mikolaj Lewandowski or the pile-up on the first lap with three of the back markers that stole headlines.

Images have emerged which seem to show World Champion and championship leader Luke Anderson and his teammate Tyler Finley locked in an embrace that appears to be more than the "friends" Wilson Racing press team would have us believe.

The question begs, are Luke Anderson and Tyler Finley in a secret relationship?

At the beginning of the Formula One season, the two teammates were embroiled in a very public feud which Wilson Racing has been denying ever since. However, it would now appear that the feud was completely fabricated to cover up the budding relationship between the two drivers.

Finley recently came out in an interview with ModernLondon magazine, however, there has been no confirmation from Anderson's team as to his sexual orientation or relationship status. It has been noted over the years, the distinct lack of female (or other) company in Luke Anderson's camp. His private life always remained as such until now.

The deeper question behind these images is the deceit from the Wilson Racing press team, who have been insistent over the past year that their drivers are cordial and respect one another, despite the obvious feud that has been ongoing. Was the feud a made-up story and the subsequent friend's narrative a cover-up for what's been happening?

Have they been insistent on their drivers hiding their relationship to protect their image as the clean-cut, conservative racing team that they are? Not wanting to compromise sponsorship deals, appearances, and dragging unwanted attention onto them as they fight for their next world title?

Since Martin Clark's was appointed as Team Principal at the end of last year, the team has been embroiled in a series of rumours and scandals, none of them favourable. Will Clark be the demise of the great Wilson name? Its legacy, which spans over thirty years, is at stake, despite the team finally seeing the glory and reward for all of the work they have put in over those three decades.

CultRacing has reached out for comment from both drivers and the team but has had no response thus far.

Twenty-eight

**Abu Dhabi Grand Prix – Yas Marina Circuit – Abu Dhabi
November 14th**

It was stifling hot as Luke walked through the turnstiles into the Yas Marina Paddock. The pointed tent tops of the pit building were visible above the tall garages. It was late morning, but with it being a night race everything was pushed back during the day too, so it was first thing in the morning to him.

He made it two steps into the paddock before he spotted Petra in her usual skinny jeans and high heels hanging around, her eyes roving, searching every face that came through the turnstiles. A number of other journalists circled too and Luke had a bad feeling in the pit of his stomach. The minute Petra laid eyes on him, she rushed over and he wasn't used to the sympathetic look in her eyes. She spread her hands out like she was trying to protect him as the other journalists spotted him, descending like hawks on a field mouse.

Startled by the sudden attack, Luke froze on the spot and then they started talking, thrusting microphones at him.

'Luke,' she said, desperation in her voice and then he spotted Sara Holdsworth who looked like she knew that what she was doing was wrong but she didn't care.

'Do you have any comments on the article that broke this morning?' she said as Petra pleaded with her eyes.

Bewildered, Luke stared at Sara.

'What article?' he asked, still taken aback by the sudden questioning.

'No comment,' Emma's voice cut straight across whatever Sara was about to say. She pouted, irritated that Emma had foiled her plan.

Emma grabbed hold of Luke's arm, he could tell she was not in a good mood and dragged him towards the huge purple motorhome.

'Where are we going?' He asked trying to free his arm but she was surprisingly strong.

'Meeting room,' she replied as her little legs walked as fast as they could. 'Keep your head down and don't say a word.'

'What the hell's going on? Can I at least drop my stuff off?' He asked as they walked into the air-conditioned temporary building.

'Nope,' she said finally letting go of his arm. He stopped for a moment and noticed most of the mechanics in the café staring, glancing, or pretending not to look at him.

'What's going on?' he asked again but his feet moved and followed her to the stairs under the scrutiny of his team.

'Do you ever check the internet?' Luke shook his head. 'Then you'll find out soon enough.'

He wracked his brain, skimming through the last week and

a half to try and find something that might have happened to cause this kind of reaction.

After the night out in Austin, Luke and Tyler had gone their separate ways, Luke back to Monaco and Tyler off to New York for a few days then back to London. They hadn't seen each other, they'd spent a lot of time texting and video calling but unless someone had access to their phone records then no one would know. It couldn't be that.

He tried to remember what else he had done but aside from training, one sponsor event, and an afternoon at the kart track, there was nothing that stood out.

They reached the top floor, the meeting room door ajar. Emma went through first and Luke saw the room was full.

Jessie was at the head of the table, papers strewn out in front of her. Her head in her hands as she jotted down notes on a pad.

Across the room, Martin Clark sat talking to none other than Albert Wilson, the CEO and owner of Wilson Racing. And Tyler, his back to Luke, reclined in his chair, relaxed as always.

Emma sat down beside Jessie, leaving Luke to take the free seat beside Tyler, who didn't look around when Luke pulled the chair out.

Luke scanned the faces around the table who had fallen silent now he had arrived.

'Hi Luke, thanks for coming,' Jessie said. She looked tired and stressed.

'I mean, I'm not sure I had a choice,' Luke tried to laugh but it fell flat, everyone looked so serious. He started to worry, the knot in his stomach growing with every second.

'I take it everyone has seen the article?' she continued, holding a sheet of paper between her hands.

'No,' Luke said as everyone else nodded. They stared at him, eyes wide with surprise.

'Luke doesn't like the internet,' Emma said with a tut and Jessie pushed the piece of paper across the table. He picked it up and his eyes were drawn to the grainy picture in the middle.

He recognised it straight away. It was him and Tyler, face to face in front of the Texas State Capitol in the middle of the night, his hands on Tyler's arms.

His heart pumped faster, his blood turned cold beneath his skin. He felt the walls of his mind appear as they closed in. He skim-read the article by Sara Holdsworth then swallowed hard as he laid the piece of paper back down on the table.

His palms were sweaty, his stomach so twisted he didn't know if it would untwist itself again. He stared straight ahead, over Martin's head as all eyes were on him. They waited for him to say something, for a reaction but he had left the room. He was back in that park, he was searching his memory for something he had missed. Who else had been there? Who had seen them? What more had they said to the press?

His secret was out and he wasn't ready. The world wasn't ready. He swallowed again, a lump forming in his throat so big it was restricting his airways.

He hadn't expected this, he'd wanted to wait until the season was over to do it, if he decided to, on his terms. These were not his terms.

'Luke?' Emma's voice was distant, not strong enough to anchor him.

'Luke.' This time it was Tyler. He turned his head towards him and their eyes met. He didn't understand what he was seeing in them. He could get lost in that shade of blue and right now he wanted that more than ever.

To dive into them to another world, to disappear, and to not have to deal with any of this.

'Guys, what's going on?' Martin said, bringing Luke back

into the room. His breathing slowed, and his heart stopped trying to escape his chest. He looked back to Tyler who watched him, everyone waiting for him to say something.

His tongue felt heavy and large in his mouth and even if his brain had known what to say, he didn't think he'd be able to get the words out to explain what that photo was about.

He could lie and say it was nothing because aside from the fact that it wasn't clear that it was them, they weren't doing anything apart from standing face to face. The fact that they had been kissing minutes before was redundant because this was the snapshot that was taken. But he didn't want to lie, he didn't want to pretend that what was happening with Tyler was nothing.

So, he just stared back at them, words failing, as they waited. The seconds ticked by into minutes and still no one said anything.

'I love him.'

An audible gasp filled the room and Luke snapped his head round to settle his eyes on Tyler, on the mouth where those words had come from. Tyler shrugged unapologetically, his face impassive, but his eyes wide.

'Really?' Luke managed to say, his mouth dry but his heart soaring. Tyler nodded and it was like no one else was in the room. Luke knew he did too, it was so very obvious and he couldn't believe he hadn't been able to admit it to himself until then.

'I love you too.' Luke reached out and grabbed hold of Tyler's hand, not breaking eye contact even when Emma said 'Oh my god' in the sweetest way.

Luke cleared his throat but didn't let go of Tyler's hand as he turned back to the room.

'Sorry, yeah, erm...' He rubbed the back of his neck with his free hand and waited for the comments to come, for Martin to tell them that it couldn't happen, that if they wanted to stay at the team they'd have to stay away from each other or one of them would get fired.

'It's certainly an unusual situation but not unmanageable,' Martin said with a huge grin on his face. Albert Wilson nodded next to him, his finger up to his mouth, his eyes damp.

Luke turned to Emma who had both hands over her heart and a soppy look on her face and Jessie, scribbling away on her notepad.

'We need to contain the situation, from a team perspective,' she said, looking at the article again. 'It's the constant attack on Martin, on the team management, and this whole narrative that we need to figure out. But ultimately, what do you want to do?'

She looked to Tyler and Luke, who turned to each other, all trying to gauge where they went from here.

'I don't know,' Luke said because he knew it was up to him. Tyler was out, Tyler had wanted to shout about it from the moment it had happened, Luke was the one holding back. Luke was the one who had to choose what he wanted to do now.

'We can deny it all,' she started.

'No. I'm not lying about it.'

'Okay,' she said scanning down her list. 'I mean, we don't need to address the situation directly. We can address the rumour side of things and how things are managed, with a blanket line of "management doesn't dictate how their team and colleagues interact in or outside of work", and something along the lines of "whatever drivers choose to do in their private time is up to them". And you guys,' she pointed to Luke and Tyler, 'need to keep talking about the racing, there's enough action happening in the championship that what happens outside of it shouldn't matter.' Her suggestion lay in the air as everyone contemplated the options. 'Or we could release a statement confirming the rumours…'

Luke's heart sped up again, he didn't know if he was ready for that. It must have been clear what he was thinking because Tyler grabbed his other hand and said: 'You don't have to do anything you don't want to.'

'I need more time,' he said. 'I want to finish the season, I want to win this championship and then we can go down that route.'

'That's fine Luke,' Jessie said, crossing a line out on her pad.

'I like the sound of that,' Martin said and Albert nodded again, his face still thoughtful.

'There's a lot of press duties slated for today, are we all happy to go with the first suggestion, not denying, not confirming?' she asked looking around the table at those who would be in the line of media fire.

'I don't think I can do that,' Luke said, his hands shaking.

'I'll do it,' Tyler said.

'Okay, I'll get you out of as much as I can, we may need to white lie and say you're not feeling well?' Jessie questioned and Luke nodded, his mind spinning.

They sat in silence whilst Jessie scribbled some more notes.

'I'll have to do some sort of press release but I'll send it round for confirmation before it goes out. In the meantime, stay in the motorhome,' she instructed.

'All done?' Martin asked as he went to stand up.

'I want to tell the team,' Luke said in a whisper. Martin sat back down. 'They deserve to know, and I want them one hundred per cent focused on the weekend ahead, which they won't be if they're all whispering and wondering.'

'Some may not like it…' Tyler said.

'Then they can leave,' Albert interjected. 'Those who don't like it, have no place in the Wilson family.'

'Agreed,' Martin said. 'We still have time to replace them.

We're a team and we're united no matter what.' He nodded his head once, the matter closed.

'Team meeting in twenty, Jessie is that enough time to get something drafted?' Martin said, standing now. She shrugged, it would have to be.

They filed out of the meeting room leaving Tyler and Luke alone.

Luke let out a long, slow exhale as he let go of Tyler's hand, running both of them through his hair.

'That was not what I had planned for today,' Luke said with a sigh.

'It's definitely not how I was planning on telling you that I loved you.' Tyler chuckled, standing up and stretching his legs out.

'Me neither.' Luke said. They stood face to face and Luke put his hands on Tyler's cheeks, stroking them with his thumbs. 'But I mean it. I love you.'

'I love you too,' Tyler replied before kissing him.

When they pulled away, Luke chuckled. It was the happiest he had ever felt, despite the uncertainty of what would happen now. The one thing he did know, and he was certain about, was that Tyler loved him, and in that moment that was all that mattered.

'Are you sure about telling the team?' Tyler asked before they left the room.

'I am, I don't want any of them thinking about anything other than winning this weekend. As long as you're happy with that?'

'I would shout it from the rooftops if I could, you say the word,' Tyler said and with one last kiss, they headed downstairs.

The atrium had never been fuller, team members all in purple polos mingling around having been told about the emergency team meeting. Tyler peeled off to speak to his race engineer who was chatting to the chief strategist and Luke found Vicki with Dash and Johan.

'Any idea what this meeting is about?' Vicki asked as Luke approached. Luke shrugged and grabbed the coffee Johan had got for him. Johan eyed him and jerked his head towards Luke's driver's room.

'Are you okay?' Johan asked.

'I know you don't approve,' Luke said putting the drink down and pacing.

'I never said that,' Johan countered.

'Right, but you don't.'

Johan sighed, a rare show of emotion on his face but it wasn't what Luke was expecting.

'I want the best for you, I want you to have everything you've worked so hard for. I've watched you grind every single day since you were sixteen to get here and I want you to be sure of what you want before you jump in with both feet.'

'Do you think I can't have both?' Luke stopped pacing to look at Johan's face as he answered because he knew he would be able to read what he thought in his eyes.

'I think you can if you let yourself,' Johan said. 'Your mind is your own worst enemy and I could see how that has affected you this year.' He shrugged and Luke pulled him into a hug.

'Thank you,' he said letting him go. 'I knew there was a reason I kept you around.'

Twenty-nine

Brazilian Grand Prix – Autódromo José Carlos Pace – São Paulo
December 1st

There was nothing more exciting than the season closer in Brazil. The track was iconic, steeped in history, it never failed to put on a great show, and was home to historic wins like Senna's victory in 1991. Many a championship had been decided on the tarmac of Interlagos.

This year was no different.

Luke walked into the paddock on Sunday morning with a one-point lead over Lewandowski. Another close championship battle for the records.

The atmosphere was electric, the fans out in force despite the early hour. The seas of purple and red lined the grandstands, flags flying, flares bursting smoke across the track.

The paddock wasn't as glamorous as some of the newer tracks, with fewer celebrities, and less showbiz. It was the heart of Brazilian racing and Luke couldn't have been happier than to finish his season here.

Interlagos had always been good to him, he had a string of great results over the years, some he hoped to replicate today. All he had to do was finish ahead of Lewandowski. One better, it didn't matter where in the order, just one better.

With Johan in his wake, they walked the short distance from the garage to the Wilson motorhome entrance, and as the doors slid open a loud squeal erupted from inside.

Nick, hair flailing behind her came rushing over and wrapped him in a hug.

'How did you get here first?' he asked surprised. 'I thought you were asleep back at the hotel with Mum and Dad.'

'I couldn't sleep.' She waved his comment away, slipped her hand through his arm, and walked with him to his driver's room. 'Tyler brought me in earlier.'

'He what?'

'He saw me in the hotel reception and I think he took pity on me.' She laughed. 'I came in with him and his trainer.'

'Of course, you did,' Luke said. 'Where's Dan?'

'Asleep probably, he'll come with Mum and Dad later.'

The three of them squeezed into his little room, Johan taking his usual spot by the desk as Luke unpacked his bag.

'How're you feeling?' she asked.

'I'm fine. I feel good. I want to get going.'

And it was true, it had been an agonising wait to get here from Abu Dhabi two weeks ago. After finishing second again behind Lewandowski, Luke's previous lead in the championship dwindled to one singular point, he was itching to get back in the car and get one final win this season.

He'd played the long game and it had come down to this.

A whole year with its ups and downs, the rumours, the chatter, none of it mattered now.

The crowd outside wasn't here to see if Tyler and Luke were in a relationship, they were here to see some hard racing and that's what he was going to give them.

The media had dropped the questions around the photo over time, every single team member changing the subject, giving blanket statements drafted by Jessie, and closing ranks around their drivers. It was like getting blood from a stone and the Wilson team had come out shining despite Sara Holdsworth's best efforts.

There were still some tabloids in the UK digging around, wanting to know more about their two heartthrob drivers but they found nothing.

Luke and Tyler hadn't seen each other since the last race, being very careful to stay away from one another, with a promise to talk about it at the end of the season. Luke had made that promise and he intended on keeping it. For now, though, he had a job to do.

'Right well, you guys are boring so I'm going to go and find some fun,' Nick announced before flouncing out of the room, leaving Luke chuckling.

They watched some TV, played cards and Luke did his best to relax until Emma came knocking. It was time for the final driver's parade of the season.

Luke pulled his Wilson cap on and headed into the pits. Tyler fell into step with him, a huge smile plastered on his face.

'Hello,' he said with a grin and for only Luke to hear, 'I've hired a jet, we're flying home together.' He winked before peeling off and joining Brambilla in the other queue.

Luke's heart fluttered.

Sometimes they got vintage cars to drive around the circuit for the parade but today, like most other races, it was the flatbed lorry with the F1 branded skirt below the crowd barriers.

Luke climbed the back steps with Kyle Kelly and Raphaël Moreau and stood with them as the limited press were allowed on board. Luke sipped his water, waving as the truck drove out onto the track.

'Nervous?' Raphaël smiled, leaning on the barriers. Luke shrugged.

'You know how it feels,' he said.

'Maybe one day I'll be fighting for championships too.' Raphaël laughed.

'You will, your time will come,' Luke said, lifting his hand again to wave at the crowd. Raph looked thoughtful for a moment.

'I'm rooting for you,' he said, 'both of you.'

Luke didn't respond, he didn't know what to say or what Raphaël thought he knew but before Luke could ask, an overzealous Brazilian presenter shouted into a microphone, broadcast round the track, right next to Luke's ear.

'And then we have current World Champion Luke Anderson. Luke, how are you feeling?' he shouted and Luke had to take a step back.

'Hi everyone,' he said into the microphone. 'Thanks for coming out today. I'm loving all the purple flags.' He waved again with a wide, genuine smile as the fans erupted into loud cheers and whistles.

'You've had a controversial year off track, has that affected how you're going to attack the race today?' The presenter shouted again, not understanding the principle of a microphone.

'I approach every race the same.' Luke smiled. 'With the intention of winning.'

The presenter clapped him on the back after a hardy "good luck" and then moved on to talk to Raphaël.

Once off the lorry, Luke was pulled into team meetings about race strategy and meet and greets with the VIPs on the rooftop of the motorhome and inside the pits. It was a never-ending slog until he was back in his room alone with Johan, getting dressed into his race suit for the final time this season.

His Mum and Dad arrived at the track and popped in to wish him good luck before heading to their spot at the back of his garage where they would be watching the race.

'Are you ready?' Johan asked, Luke's water bottle, helmet, and gloves in his hands. 'Would you like an inspirational quote?'

'You're going to give me one anyway so you may as well,' Luke said with a grin.

'Winning doesn't always mean being first. Winning means you're doing better than you've ever done before,' Johan said.

'That's shit. Who said that?' His face pulled into a smile, relishing these last moments before he got into the zone.

'Bonnie somebody or other, speed skater.'

'I want a do-over, hit me with another one.'

'Winning takes precedence over all. There's no grey area. No almosts.'

'Better, who said that?'

'Kobe Bryant.'

'Okay, one more, please. Make it good.' They walked across the faded grey tarmac into the back of the pits as Johan thought.

'To win, you must leave it all out there. Everything you have, everything you have learnt, and everything you have lost.'

'Deep. Who said that?'

'Me,' Johan said, his face breaking into a smile. 'I'll see you on the other side.' He pulled him into a hug and back clap, leaving Luke's helmet on his seat.

It was time.

He tugged on his balaclava with one last smile at his family, his mother looked tense and unhappy as she always did at races, her fingernails finding her teeth before the race had even started.

Across the garage, he saw Tyler mirroring his actions, pulling his own balaclava on, Tyler's dad stood behind the half wall of the VIP box, his face set despite his son not being in the running for the win anymore.

The two teammates locked eyes and Luke could see all he needed to know in them. He pulled his helmet on and snapped the lid shut.

The five lights went on, one at a time, Luke's hand steady on the steering wheel as he lined up in second on the grid. Tyler beside him, Lewandowski in his mirrors.

The plan was to follow Tyler, pull away from Lewandowski, find a groove, save the tyres, and at the right moment, Tyler would move over and let Luke take the win. A one-two wrapping up the driver's and constructor's World Championships for Wilson Racing. That was the plan.

The lights turned off, he released the clutch and they shot off the line, heading for the first corner, the famous Senna S. Checking his mirrors and aiming his car for the racing line, Tyler stayed ahead of him as they turned the first corner but going into the second one Luke felt a tap on his rear end, his car jerked and spun. He watched the grid flash past him, including the two red blurs of the Ferraris before he got going in the right direction again.

'What was that?' Luke shouted through the radio at Dash. Was that his race over? 'What's the damage?'

'We're checking. You were tagged by Schulz.'

'Are you fucking kidding me?' Dash didn't reply for a moment as Luke chased after the tail end of the pack. This was not part of the plan.

He was in the fastest car, it wasn't over until the chequered flag fell, he knew that but he needed to convince himself of that too.

'The car looks good on the data. How does it feel?'

'Fine. It feels fine. Man, what're we going to do?'

'Head down, get over taking,' Dash replied and Luke did just that.

On the next lap, he overtook two of the back markers and the lap after that another one. He sweated buckets inside his race suit, the sun dipping in and out of the clouds but the heat rising. Humidity was high and some of the clouds looked greyer than others. Despite the Wilson being terrible in the rain, they'd made great progress with that and Luke was so confident in his driving that he almost wanted it to chuck it down.

By lap twenty, Luke was back up into the points, but that wasn't enough, he needed to beat Lewandowski no matter where they finished, he needed to be in front of that scarlet Ferrari.

'What's the order?' Luke came over the radio again.

'Finley is first, five seconds ahead of Lewandowski and ten seconds ahead of Moreau and Brambilla, who are fighting over third. You have Schulz and Nabiyev ahead of you. They're next on your list.'

Luke nodded to himself as he curved around Ferradura. His mindset, he kept pushing, pumping in the times, each of them like a qualifying lap. The crowd cheered each time he drove past a grandstand and he took it as personal encouragement.

He managed to jump Nabiyev in the first round of pit stops and then stagnated in sixth for a long stint. He was losing momentum, the championship and the win slipping through his fingers as he pushed on but couldn't seem to catch up to Schulz ahead of him.

'Finley and Lewandowski have pitted for the second time, they're now behind you.' Dash confirmed as Luke jetted down the pit straight once more. He rounded the Senna S, up past Curva do Sol, and down the back straight of Reta Oposta. As he made his way down the tight and twisty second section, he heard the crowd before he saw the screen, where a white Haas flew off into the barriers.

It looked like a nasty crash but it was behind him so he kept pushing until he saw the safety car signs flash on.

'Box, box,' Dash shouted, and Luke, rounding the final turn, plunged his car into the pit lane, slamming on the pit limiter and trundling down to his pit box.

The team was supreme and within seconds he was back out, heading for the track. He caught up to the train behind the safety car but it wasn't as long as he'd expected, he tried to count how many were in front of him but it was difficult as they weaved in and out trying to keep their tyres warm.

'Where's everyone?' he asked, breathless with the effort.

'Finley's still first, then Lewandowski, then Moreau. You're in fourth,' Dash kept his voice even and flat but Luke couldn't believe it. He was up to fourth with a third of the race left to go. It was harder to overtake the faster cars so it wouldn't be easy but he was giving it all he had.

Another four laps and the safety car turned its lights off, leaving them free to race again. Tyler bunched up the pack, giving Luke the best chance to jump someone if he could but it didn't pay off.

Luke watched ahead as the Ferrari of Lewandowski glided past Tyler into the first turn and his heart sank. His one chance of holding up Lewandowski had failed and he was in fourth without a backup plan.

'It's not over yet,' Dash said, his words reassuring but Luke's brain could not come up with a way to make this work. He explored all ideas as he hurtled around the track at one hundred and seventy miles per hour.

As the laps ticked down, stuck behind Moreau, Luke watched his title disappear off into the distance and into the hands of his rival. Tyler struggled after the restart and after five laps, ten still to go, Moreau overtook him down the main straight.

At the next corner, Tyler slowed down to let Luke pass, as he chased after Moreau but there was nothing he could do. The Mercedes became the widest car on the track and it didn't matter which way he tried he couldn't get past him.

As they fought, they lost time to Lewandowski who they couldn't see anymore. The fight was leaving him, it was over. There was no way he was going to catch Lewandowski. He was too far up the track, too much time between them let alone the Mercedes.

'Signs of rain on the radar,' Dash said and Luke's heart leapt into his throat.

Maybe it wasn't over. He redoubled his effort and concentration even though he was exhausted, that tiny shred of hope was all he had to cling on to. His whole body screamed for him to stop. His neck was killing him on the anti-clockwise circuit, not used to the left-hand heavy turns but he had to keep going.

There was no stopping, no pause, no break.

'Five laps left to go, five.'

'What about the rain?' Luke shouted and he knew his voice betrayed the desperation he felt.

'Possibly in the next few minutes.' Dash didn't sound hopeful. There was no certainty. The clouds looked ominous but that was no guarantee.

Luke kept pumping in the times, sticking to the back of Moreau and praying for the best.

He wasn't a religious man but he'd pray to every God there was for a miracle.

'Two laps left,' Dash said, and when Luke was about to give up hope, he saw it.

The tiny little spot of rain on his visor.

'Is it raining?' he asked, unable to believe it.

'A-firm, reports of it down the back end of the circuit.'

Luke followed Moreau around the first sector of the track, waiting for the rain to hit his visor, and as it did, getting heavier, he felt the car slide beneath him.

The track got slicker, the old tyres losing grip on the surface. They turned into the last corner and Moreau went wide, leaving the door open for Luke as long as his car stuck enough to the track to get a good exit.

Luke tested the accelerator and to his amazement, the car found some grip, enough for him to pass Moreau and leave him behind.

He needed to keep it on the track for the final lap and hope that Lewandowski didn't. The rain got heavier and heavier, the black tarmac turning shiny as the spray from the tyres made it impossible to see.

He tiptoed around the back end of the circuit, cars around him skidding off the track left, right and centre, and then he saw the Ferrari. Up the road.

With four corners left to go, the rain came down in sheets, and it was almost impossible to keep the car on the track. Luke ran wide with two corners to go but as he regained the tarmac, up ahead he saw Lewandowski lose the back end into the last corner.

The Ferrari spun twice before stopping and Luke pushed the accelerator more than he wanted to but he could see victory. He pulled his car up alongside the Ferrari as it regained the track pointing the right way and it was down to balls.

Who had the bigger balls? Who trusted their car more?

Luke squeezed the accelerator and pushed his Wilson over

the line as the chequered flag fell.

Bewildered, he looked around for Lewandowski but he had no idea who had crossed the line first.

'What happened?' he shouted over the radio. Then, a cheer erupted in his ears as the usually calm and collected Dash screamed.

'It's yours, it's fucking yours!'

'What?' Luke said but he could feel the tears leaking from his eyes as he realised.

'You are the Champion of the World for the second time, Luke Anderson. You fucking beauty!' Dash was crying.

'Luke, my boy. What a drive. What a win!' Martin sounded emotional too but Luke was too busy trying to staunch the stream of his own tears to reply. He brought his gloved hands up to his helmet and held them there for a moment in disbelief.

He'd done it.

He'd only gone and done it.

And it was so much better than the first time. The battle was harder so the victory was sweeter.

Adrenaline ran through his body, chasing away the exhaustion. He waved to the fans and cracked his helmet so he could hear them. They were going nuts, cheering and screaming until they lost their voices.

Luke guided his car back down the pit lane and pulled up next to the Ferrari and the Mercedes. He lifted himself out of the car, replacing his steering wheel, intending to enjoy the moment.

He hopped out and ran over to his team gathered behind the barrier, screaming at him as he screamed back behind his visor. They all grabbed for him, touching any part of him that they could, tapping his helmet, his back, his arm, his chest. They thumped him, as ecstatic as he was.

With one last holler, he pulled away and took his helmet

off, grinning, his hair drenched in sweat sticking up in all directions. Mikolaj, understandably disappointed, tapped him on the back and congratulated him, as did Moreau and a few others.

He was on cloud nine. He was flying. He was at the pinnacle of his sport for the second year running. He was the World Champion.

When he turned around to head inside to the winner's room, he came face to face with Tyler, the most beautiful smile on his lips.

Luke didn't think twice, fuelled by adrenaline and dopamine, he grabbed hold of him and pulled him close. He snaked his arm around Tyler's back and planted his lips on his in a passionate kiss.

Tyler was surprised for under a second before he returned it, pulling at Luke's hair.

The crowd around them hushed in shock and surprise.

The eerie silence that wrapped around them pulled them apart, as Luke looked into Tyler's eyes. What had he done?

Then he realised, he didn't care.

Epilogue

The internet – Twitter
December 6th

Petra Vogel ✓ @petraRTL · Dec 6
F1 World Champion Luke Anderson arrives at the FIA prize givin with third place man and boyfriend Tyler Finley

💬 7.6K   🔁 1.8K   ♡ 67.8K

Luke's Girl @lukesgirl · Dec 6
OMG look how cute they are 🖤

💬 1   🔁   ♡ 35

Mrs Finley @f1girl1245673 · Dec 6
I can't even handle. A couple this beautiful should be illegal.

💬   🔁   ♡ 1

Baz @bazracingfan · Dec 6
Eurgh unnecessary We don't care what they do behind closed doors but we don't need to see it

💬   🔁   ♡ 1

Aaron Zoooom @Brambifan · Dec 6
Seems like you need to change your name to @bazhomophobiafan

💬   🔁   ♡ 13

Man of ur dreamz @britboyf1 · Dec 6
Daddies.

💬   🔁   ♡ 3

Love in the Fast Lane

San
@andersan48062

Cannot believe our boy is world champion again #sohappy #andersonarmy

9:14 PM · Dec 6, 2019

1 Retweet **7** Likes

San @andersan48062 · Dec 6
Cannot believe our boy is world champion again #sohappy #andersonarmy

💬 4   🔁 1   ♡ 9

Mrs Finley @f1girl1245673 · Dec 6
#teamtylerandluke

💬 1   🔁   ♡

Lydia @lydia3649 · Dec 6
You mean #teamlukeandtyler right?

💬 1   🔁   ♡

Mrs Finley @f1girl1245673 · Dec 6
Can we just agree we love them both?

💬 1   🔁   ♡ 1

Lydia @lydia3649 · Dec 6
YES! ICONS!

💬   🔁   ♡ 1

Tyler's Number 1 @Finleyfaaaan1456 · Dec 6

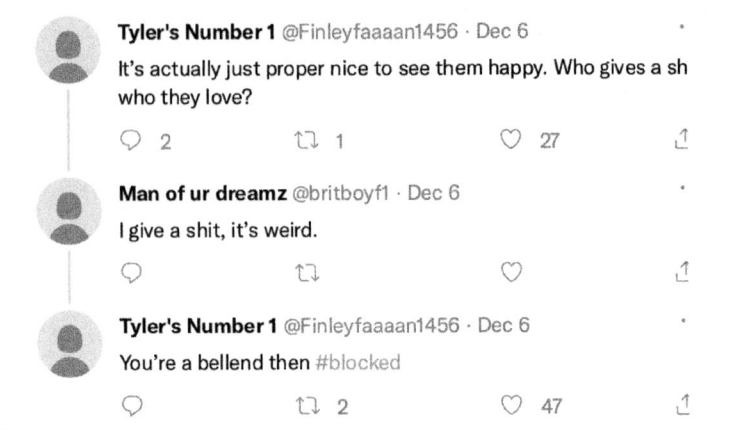

It's actually just proper nice to see them happy. Who gives a sh who they love?

💬 2 🔁 1 ♡ 27

Man of ur dreamz @britboyf1 · Dec 6

I give a shit, it's weird.

💬 🔁 ♡

Tyler's Number 1 @Finleyfaaaan1456 · Dec 6

You're a bellend then #blocked

💬 🔁 2 ♡ 47

Note from the Author

I've been watching Formula 1 since the French Grand Prix 2002, where a grumpy Kimi Raikkonen in second place caught my eye. My dad used to put it on on Sunday afternoons before falling asleep in front of it but from that moment, I was hooked.

I've always wanted to read about F1 in a fictional way, *Chasing Daisy* by Paige Toon being the first one I found. Since then I've wanted to write about it. Over the years I've drafted some that have never seen the light of day (and never will) but Luke and Tyler's story deserved to be shared. I've got a few more ideas up my sleeve for some of the characters we meet on their journey and I can't wait to share those with you too.

Some of you super fans will have noticed that in this story the season ends in Brazil, which hasn't happened since the 2008 season (a shame if you ask me!). Abu Dhabi took over as the closing event from 2009 but according to Sharia Law all non-heterosexual relationships are illegal. I chose to finish the season in Brazil instead, so that Luke and Tyler could have their final kiss the way they did.

I hope you enjoy Luke and Tyler's story and it brings you as much happiness reading it as it did me writing it.

TOP THREE CHAMPIONSHIP RESULTS

Driver	AUS	BHR	CHN	AZE	ESP	MON	CAN	FRA	AUT	GBR	GER	HUN	BEL	ITA	SIN	RUS	JPN	MEX	USA	ABU	BRA
L. Anderson	2	2	1	2	1	3	2	1	1	7	1	DNF	4	3	4	1	2	1	2	2	1
M. Lewandowski	1	5	3	DNF	2	2	DNF	2	3	1	2	1	1	1	2	2	1	3	1	1	2
T. Finley	DNF	1	2	1	3	1	1	3	5	10	3	DNF	3	5	1	5	DNF	2	4	8	4

CHARACTER LIST

Luke Anderson – Formula One Driver for Wilson Racing (Number 1)
Johan Salonen – Trainer and best friend of Luke Anderson
Emma Bacon – Luke's Press Officer
Vicki – Chief Mechanic
Jamie Wake - Mechanic
Petra Vogel – RTL Germany Reporter
Sara Holdsworth– CultRacing Reporter
Pedro Vásquez – Former team mate
Tyler Finley – Current team mate (Number 24)
Joseph Finley – Tyler's billionaire father
David Crosby – Previous Team Principle of Wilson Racing
Martin Clark – Team Principle of Wilson Racing
Toby Wright – Tyler Finley's Race Engineer
Dave "Dash" Marx – Luke's Race Engineer
Jessie Portland – Wilson Head of Communications
Nicola Anderson – Luke's sister
John Anderson – Luke's Dad
Lynn Anderson – Luke's mum
Ben Dawson– Tyler's Friend
George – Tyler's Friend
Lorenzo Nunez – Porsche Supercup Driver

Mikolaj Lewandowski – Ferrari Driver (Polish)
Jan Schulz – Ferrari Driver (German)

Manuel De Leon - Mercedes Driver (Spanish)
Raphaël Moreau – Mercedes Driver (French)

Matteo Brambilla - Lotus Driver (Italian)
Kyle Kelly – Lotus Driver (Australian)

Asahi Tanaka - McLaren Driver (Japanese)
Firas Nabiyev - McLaren Driver (Azerbaijan)

Twitter Characters:

Team Luke	Team Tyler	Team other/troll	Press
@lukesgirl	@f1girl1245673	@bazracingfan	@petraRTL
@lydia3649	@Finleyfaaaan1456	@brambifan	@saracultracing
@badboyf1bants	@F1dramallama	@britboyf1	@fia
@andersan48062	@iceman17	@LulunNabi	@ferrari
@joshlovesf1	@brunof1		

ACKNOWLEDGEMENTS

My biggest THANK YOU goes to all of you who have purchased this book. Without you this dream of mine wouldn't be a reality and I'm eternally grateful for your support.

To Chris, my rock and sounding board. You've been there from the first spark of an idea, listening, contributing and understanding what I needed from you. To listening to me read it out loud and sense checking some of the things I wrote.

To my best friends, Jamie, Gillian and Caroline for always believing in me and my dream, for convincing me that I could do this even when the imposter syndrome was loud.

Thank you to the online community of writers and readers who supported this project, provided feedback and encouragement. To Dani in particular for listening to my ramblings, sharing your wisdom and creative intuition with me.

Thank you to my Beta readers, whose feedback and suggestions were invaluable to the finished book and was made so much better by your input.

To my writer group friends for proofreading this one and for always encouraging me to reach for my dreams, in particular Helen and Melissa.

And finally, to the boys and girls of the Kimi

Raikkonen online forum in 2005, thanks for talking about F1 all the time with me when my real life friends and family were sick to death of it.

Sophie's passion has always been for creating stories and exploring relationships through words.

Brought up in the French countryside, she spent hours writing short stories, poems and songs throughout her childhood, culminating in a BA(hons) in English Literature, Creative Writing and Spanish.

After university, she finally wrote her first novel, and self published another in 2022, *One French Summer.*

Sophie lives in Bedfordshire with her husband Chris, her daughter and her son and can often be found out walking, baking or listening to country music.

Follow Sophie on Instagram
@sophiemillswrites

One French Summer

By Sophie E. Mills

ONE

There is something about the way the morning sun shines off the kitchen tap as I wait for the toast to pop, that's a sure sign that summer is on its way. The golden hue holds a promise of lighter evenings and sunny days, a hope that maybe this year will be a little better than the last.

With my hands on the unit, my eyes glaze over as I stare at the street outside where the cars move at a snail's pace, honking and willing each other to keep going.

'Babe,' Liam shouts from the bedroom, barely a few feet away from where I stand. 'Can you bring me a coffee please?'

Dutifully, I flick the kettle on and retrieve a mug from the cupboard as my toast pops out. I slather it in butter and leave it to melt as I finish getting Liam his coffee.

'Is that toast I can smell?' he shouts again. I don't answer as I put two more slices into the toaster. I need to leave soon so I take a bite of my breakfast as I get my lunch and Liam's breakfast together.

Our kitchen is small, just enough space for one person, two if you're very comfortable around each other. The cupboard doors are dark and the counter tops black, not what I would have chosen for such a small space, it makes it look dingy and cramped, a stark contrast to the endless white of the rest of the flat.

The kettle boils, steam pouring out the spout and the toast pops up, the slight smell of burnt bread filling the air. I scrape off the black bits, cover it in butter and grab another bite of my own before I take it to the bedroom.

We've lived here for three years now, but our bedroom, like the rest of the flat, is untouched since we moved in. The only personal touch is the photo on my bedside table from our first holiday together in Spain. A selfie taken at the top of the mountain by the Temple of the Sacred Heart of Jesus that looks over the city of Barcelona. We look so young, squinting up into the bright sunlight but I can see the traces of sadness still living in the shadows of my eyes. Mum had insisted we take a break, even for the weekend, to try and relax. The whole trip's a blur now.

'Ah cheers,' Liam says as he pulls himself up to sitting and grabs the coffee mug from me. 'You're the best.'

Even though I'm running out of time, I hop onto the bed and snuggle into his naked chest.

'I don't want to go,' I mutter into his skin, breathing in his scent one more time.

'Aw, it will be okay,' he says, his free hand rubbing my arm gently. 'Last day before the weekend.' He tries to inject some enthusiasm into his voice but I can tell he is as tired as I am.

He munches on the toast as I get up, my limbs heavy in protest. I'll have to finish my toast on the way to work because I'm going to be late.

'By the way,' he says through a mouthful of food. 'My parents want us to go over to theirs on Sunday for lunch, I didn't think we had any plans so I agreed.'

With my hand on the door frame, I stare at him blankly for a minute, working through my feelings until I reach the right answer.

'Great,' I say keeping my voice flat. 'That'll be nice.'

I spin on my heels, not wanting him to see how much I don't want to go and sit at his parents dining room table and pretend to be interested in what golf score his dad got, or the new project his mum has taken on with the WI. We get very little time together as it is, with us both working all hours under the sun, the last thing I want to do is sacrifice one rare weekend together to spend it being reminded of everything I have lost. And with the constant digs about kids or if I'm going to get a "proper" job, it's all a little too much these days.

In the hallway, I sling my bag over my shoulder, toast clamped between my teeth and head out the door. It swings shut with a loud bang as I stomp down the stairs and out into the morning breeze.

I walk past the Thames, the distant sound of a siren cutting through the noise of cars, horns and people's chatter and across the glassy surface, the ripples of the water move in perfect unison as boats glide past.

The trees sway gently in the breeze, as they always do, just like the old man who sits on the same bench every single day, feeding the birds from a packet of seeds. Everything around me familiar, comforting and exactly as it should be.

Morning commuters rush past me, hot footing it to work like I should be but I take my time breathing in the fresh air, filling my lungs, finishing my toast before the slog of working the shop floor all day and lunch with Liam's parents hanging over me.

'But I want a refund,' says the forty-year-old woman on the other side of my counter.

'Yes Madam, I completely understand but policy dictates that I can't give a refund when the product has been used,' I reply, pleading with the "Karen" in front of me. Some people love their jobs, I am not one of those people. I can feel my shoulders rising towards my earlobes as she glares at me through her dark rimmed glasses. Her dyed brown bob perfectly coiffed, sleek and glossy, moves as one sheet.

'The mug is broken, surely you can see that too. It was broken when I got it home,' she looks over the top of her glasses condescendingly.

'But I can see tea stains on the bottom,' I explain, trying to show her the watery brown marks that clearly weren't there when she bought it. She doesn't look at the mug, she just stares at me, shrinking me into the floor.

'I don't appreciate your tone young lady. I want to speak to the manager.'

'Sure,' I sigh, all too happy to walk away from her and try to find Dawn, who's no doubt shouting at one of my colleagues somewhere on the shop floor.

I landed here after university, turning my part time student job into a full time one. Seven years later and I'm still here, still working for Dawn. The stability of coming to the same place every day, to the same people, the same tills, the same stockroom, makes me feel safe.

I take my time looking for her, although it will infuriate the customer, I can't bear to be shouted at any more today. Dragging it out as long as possible as the clock hand ticks closer to the end of the day, putting off the inevitable a little longer.

I find Dawn snooping behind a rail, tailing Tasha the new girl. With her greying hair pulled into a tight bun, bobby pins invisible, she's bent over trying to hide her bulky frame behind the bright clothes on the clothing rack.

My phone buzzes in my back pocket as we walk back to the check out, where I keep out the way as Dawn listens to the customer's ridiculous complaint. As the customer starts to shout at my manager, I tug at my long-sleeved black top, picking off the loose strands of my hair one by one.

'Evelyn, could you come over here a moment please?' Dawn pulls my attention back to the room. 'Could you issue a refund for this lady please?' I nod, irritated at being undermined again.

'See, you have a lot to learn young lady, the customer is always right.' I force a polite smile even though I know it doesn't reach my eyes and I feel a streak of anger and resentment towards the awful woman.

Dead on five I escape to the staff room to collect my bag. Tasha and Ruby, who has been here as long as I have, are changing out of their black uniform. Tasha, who looks barely eighteen, slips into a crop top and baggy jeans.

'Evie,' Ruby sing songs, 'girl, that woman was a cow.' She nods knowingly.

'She really was.' I open my locker and pull out my shoulder bag.

'We're heading to Weatherspoon's for a drink, wanna join us?' Ruby says pulling her curly brown hair out of her ponytail, letting it bob down to her shoulders.

'Maybe another day,' I say avoiding eye contact.

'Ah come on, how long have I known you? Seven? Eight years? And not once have you joined us for after work drinks.'

I shrug, not sure what she wants me to say.

'Live a little,' she laughs but it's not unkind. 'Is Liam home tonight?'

'Not tonight, he's on a late shift,' I say as a couple of guys from the menswear department come through the door, my mind flicking back to our conversation this morning.

'Then what's your excuse?' she laughs again. 'Come on babes, just one,' she pleads.

'Honestly, I'm just really tired,' I say with what I hope is an apologetic look on my face. I rush to shove my jacket over my black uniform and scuttle out the door. 'See you on Monday.'

'Are you not working this weekend?' Ruby says eyeballing me. I shake my head again. 'Lucky cow,' she laughs as I leave the room.

I grab my book from behind the counter before I dash out the sliding doors.

It's not a particularly warm day for mid-June but I'm glad the evenings are lighter as I walk home. My feet protest, wishing I'd taken the bus, but the fresh air fills my lungs happily after a day stuck inside. Liam won't be home till late, so I take my time as I stroll through the streets of Richmond, the comfortable familiarity of the route like a soft blanket around me. The buildings soak in the last rays as I walk down the high street towards the river.

Like metal to a magnet, I'm drawn to the little book shop on the corner, the one I can't seem to stay away from. I push through the door, the walls covered floor to ceiling in towering bookshelves. It smells of wood polish and untouched book pages, my favourite smell in the entire world. I love how bookshops are ordered, everything exactly where it should be, where I can find it. All the fiction in one place, the classics with the classics, and the non-fiction as far away from me as possible.

There's a display table in the middle with new releases and I pick up a few to take home. I think of the shelves in our small flat already overflowing but I pay for them anyway. Mum used to laugh at me, nose always lost in the pages of someone else's story, distracting me from the things I couldn't understand in my own. If I close my eyes, I can still feel the touch of her hand stroking my hair as I read.

I hold the books close to my heart and, despite the coolness in the air, decide to take the long way home, round by the riverside to watch the boats gliding past. With its stone arches, Richmond Bridge glows orange in the evening sun, tourists milling around as the summer holidays loom closer. I sit on one of the benches to look out at the water. A moment of calmness to destress from the day, trying to erase that vile woman from my mind before I get home.

The old couple in front of me are replaced by a younger one, maybe in their mid-twenties. They cuddle up, his arm over her shoulders as she chats. I smile at the tender gesture, not able to remember the last time Liam and I shared such a moment of utter complicity.

She rests her head on his shoulder as they watch the tourist boat cruise past. He shifts nervously and I can't help but watch them as he slides off the bench, down onto one knee.

I shudder knowing what's about to happen, but she looks completely elated, her cheeks flushing and her eyes brimming with tears. He produces a little box from his pocket, fumbling as he tries to open it. I'm not the only one staring, people around us have stopped too, watching as the proposal unfolds.

'Fools,' I mutter to myself, collecting up my books and bag, unable to keep the cynicism off my face as unpleasant memories resurface.

Back on safe ground, pavement replacing the grass beneath my feet, I hear the faint sound of cheering and assume she gave the right answer.

My phone interrupts my thoughts as Liam's face flashes on my screen, with his deep brown eyes and dark black hair.

'Hey you,' His voice is light and comforting.

'How's it going?' I ask, slowing down as I walk towards our home.

'So far so good, it's quiet at the moment but it won't stay like this,' he says but I can tell he's a little distracted.

'Friday nights in London rarely do.'

'You're not wrong. How was work?'

'The usual. Miserable, entitled customers who demand rather than ask.' He doesn't seem to be listening as the line goes quiet for a moment. 'I'm just debating what to watch tonight, maybe Casablanca or Gone with The Wind.' I ramble on, chuckling a little as I imagine his expression at my suggestions. It takes him a moment to reply and all I get is a quick, hollow laugh before he says:

'Hey Evie?'

'Yeah?'

'Don't make any plans in the morning yeah?'

'The only plans I have for tomorrow morning involve me staying in bed.' I joke to cover the unease I feel at his caginess. I dismiss it, it must just be work getting to him tonight. The anticipation of trying to deal with a bunch of drunk scumbags is probably not something he's looking forward to.

'I'll see you in the morning. Love you,' he signs off, as I reach our building.

The key slips easily into the door and as I close it behind me it only dulls the sound of the street outside slightly, the hustle and bustle of the city the permanent soundtrack of my life.

I plod up the stairs and once inside, I exhale, safe and hidden from the world, the comfort of my life with Liam surrounding me.

Our flat is sparsely decorated and still has the same white walls as when we bought it. The old, tattered sofa, we got for cheap when we moved in has seen better days with the bars pushing up through the squashed foam.

I drop my bag by the door and add my books to the stack on the shelves. It wobbles for a moment but decides to stay put. Below it, the old record player, the only thing I have left of my dad, sits with a few vinyl records I managed to save from my mum.

I flick the kettle on and change into my pyjamas, the stripy ones my mum bought for my twenty first birthday. I'm pretending there isn't a hole in the back where the pocket has come unstitched because I can't bear to throw them out.

With the opening credits scrolling the screen, snuggled up in a blanket and the oven pizza on a tray beside me, I settle in for the night.

To read more visit www.sophie-mills.com